MERCHANT

MERCHANT
TRAVELING MERCHANT BOOK ONE

William J. Seymour

MERCHANT: TRAVELING MERCHANT BOOK ONE is a work of fiction. Names, places, and incidents either are a product of the author's imagination or are used fictitiously.

A Book Furnace Publications Book

ISBN 978-1-943266-07-4

Cover Design: Book Furnace Publications

Cover Image: ©Grandfailure | Dreamstime.com

Skull Header: ©Chadlonius/Adobe Stock

To Those Who Will Always Believe In Me. Even Through All The Darkness

Chapter 1

**Year: 2027
Location: Middle of Nebraska**

Empty.

Alone.

The world is silent and dead. Only Old Man Winter calls your name, and then even he forgets who you are.

White tornadoes cross the road, and then disappear into the dark shadows of night. Cyclones of ice and sand skirt across a field of white snow and the cracked asphalt of Interstate 80. The tiny storms bounce between the rusted skeletons of cars and trucks that line the ditches and fill the fields like gravestones burned beneath mounds of white and shadow. Road signs sag and droop in misery and pain. Snow piles on their rusted edges, claiming them like it does everything else.

A golden beam of light sways with booted steps. Brittle snow crunches with each step but quickly reforms and fills deep impressions.

Crunch.

Crunch.

Crunch.

Merchant continues forward, head tilted to the

ground. Stinging particles of ice pelt his bald scalp and weather-worn face. Jacket pulled tight to ward off the worst of the storm.

"You're going to die out here, demon," the ghost who trails him taunts.

Thick canvas Army bag shifts higher onto his shoulder. Heavy jacket ballooning open and steam rising from dark, exposed skin beneath a thin cotton T-shirt. Merchant does not bother to respond.

"The infected are going to find you and tear you to pieces," the specter whispers, his lifeless breath tickling the back of Merchant's ear.

A grunt escapes sealed lips. The steps of worn leather boots beat a rhythm over snowy pavement.

"I can hear them coming. Their hunger pulls them to you. Don't expect me to help. I'll be laughing as I watch you scream for mercy."

Laughter like a cackling bird echoes into the night.

Glancing over his shoulder, Merchant watches the hazy figure of the dead man ripple in the wind. Dark hair and empty eyes, a void against the pale skin and snake head tattoo that blinks upon his neck where the empty sockets of his skull no longer work.

Nothing follows him but the cursed dead.

A solitary figure pulled across the abandoned bread basket of a county gone to Hell.

"You can feel them, can't you?" the bastard ghost continues.

Like an itch he can't scratch, Merchant grits his teeth and continues to ignore the annoying asshole.

A small flicker of light, yellow, but still only a speck against a veil of black, dances with the shadows.

Merchant stops. Cold fingers of ice and water run down his spine. His eyes search the light ahead. Still too far away to be noticed, he could avoid them if he wanted to.

North or south of the I-80 interstate is nothing but empty plains. Skirting whatever that light is by at least a mile would be easy. The worst he would find is isolated pockets of the infected. Those are avoidable. They will slow him down if they get the chance. Some will fight him every step of the way. If there are enough of them, he'll be forced to backtrack a few times but, eventually, he will find his way back to the highway and be one step closer to his destination.

The other option is to continue forward. Boots to the frozen asphalt, he will find the source of the light, and to it be drawn like a moth to a flame.

"Another victim awaits us, demon," the ghost's voice sings within his head.

Puffs of breath escape his lips, a white cloud in the beam of his flash light. Merchant continues on his way.

* * *

Golden flames in the world of the dead.

Long shadows dance in an alcove formed beneath a toppled billboard pitched at a hard angle against skeletal oak trees. Branches stripped bare by weather and war. A hundred yards away from the highway, Merchant can feel the pull of his path trying to drag him back and on his way. He ignores it, as he often has to.

Merchant stands silent in the darkness, and the wind begins to sing a sorrowful song. Starting low, it reaches a high pitch and the temperature puckers the skin as it continues to drop. He does not move, the shadows and storm hiding his presence.

Watching.

Waiting.

A solitary figure moves behind the thin flames. A body only a tenth the height of the shadow that stretches across the torn advertisement.

Repent for he is the Lord

Words painted in golden letters that peel away like cheese beneath the teeth of a grater.

Canvas strap digging into his skin, Merchant steps away from the deep shadow and approaches calmly.

His footprints fall deep in the shin-high snow. He does not bother to call out for welcome or warning.

Crunch.

Crunch.

The individual gives no notice to his approach, or they hide it well. Slumped shoulders cradle a head hung low above the fire with an old trucker's cap pulled tight against brown greasy hair. Long strands break loose around ear and neck. Winter coat, light-brown but stained with road grime, stretches over knees pulled close against chest.

"Find your own hole to die in. This is mine, and I will blast you from here to Hell and back if you think you are going to take it from me," the woman says.

Merchant, ten feet away, stops with his toes in the light and his back still to the darkness.

Slender shoulders, now noticeable, move under the heavy jacket. Her arms crusted beneath ash and the fabric frayed to fibers around gloves with missing slots where the thumb and middle finger now burn red and threaten frostbite on her right hand.

"Hell I've seen," Merchant says before taking a step forward. "I don't plan on going back."

She cocks her head to the side, one eye the color of steel peering out beneath a brim shredded to the board.

Tap.

Tap.

The double-barreled end of a sawed-off shotgun stares at him from beneath her jacket, ready to bark violence. Her lack of fear tells him whether it is loaded or not.

"We don't always get what we plan want, stranger."

Merchant nods his agreement before putting one hand up, palm out and shifting his canvas bag across his shoulder.

"Do you mind if I sit down?"

"Not much for listening, are you?"

"I've done my fair share of it. Never ended well," Merchant says as he scuffs at the ground with a boot in much better shape than the ones she wears. Clearing a last bit of snow that has not melted, he turns back the way he came. "Why start now?"

He sits down beside her, placing his bag between them. The barrel shifts on her knees but is not pulled away.

Ashes swirl around him, the smoke pungent in his nose, but welcomed.

"What do you want?" she asks, head tilted back to the ground and eyes on the fire.

"Fire is an easy thing to see out here. Will draw the attention of everyone and everything for miles,"

Merchant says, his hands spread inches from the hungry flames.

"For miles?" She chuckles. "Only the infected can see out there in that mess, and if they even get a sniff of me, I'll fuck their night up really good."

The shotgun slides from her knees and finds its resting place by her side, inches from the hand she flexes for warmth.

"Infected aren't the only monsters out there tonight. Still, the warmth is nice to have, even if it's only for a little while."

"And who the fuck are you? Preaching to me like some god-damn know-it-all."

"Traveler, that's all. Making my way west."

"Fuck the west. Nothing but disease and death." She spits into the fire. Sizzling phlegm mixes with the crackle of the burning fuel. "Why the fuck would you want to go out there?"

"It's where I have to go."

"Thought you said you don't take orders from anyone."

"Not an order. I'm going to get something that was taken from me."

The woman shifts her seat on the hard ground before tossing another piece of dried board on the fire. A pile of wood, more sticks and bits of furniture than lumber, sits in chaos behind her. Another hour of flames, maybe two before they are left with embers and the rapid embrace of the storm.

"That is all there is left in this life. Take what you can and forget about anything you lose. Must be damn important if you are going to risk your life trying to cross this hell. Remember these words or you'll be dead before you get the chance to regret them." She blows snot from her nose and wipes the bit still stuck to her face with the back of her hand. "What's your name or should I just forget you?"

"Does it matter?"

Her head tilts again and those eyes of hers, almost silver beneath narrowed lids.

"No, it doesn't."

She grunts and wraps her arms around her chest.

"You got any food?" Merchant asks.

He pulls his coat open enough to get his hand deep inside.

"No. You have any?"

Merchant glances around their tiny shelter. There appears to be nothing but her and her shotgun.

"Isn't much, but you can have a piece if you want it," he answers.

Hand length piece of jerky in hand, he watches her eyes glance at the meat, and then turn back to him. Not as hungry as she should be.

"What do you want for that? I've got nothing you don't see in front of you, and if you have even the simplest thought of trying something…"

Her hand slides back to the shotgun.

"No price. I have enough for myself to get where I'm going. If you want some, you can have what you need."

She eyes the bag that sits between them. With a huff, she reaches for the dried meat.

"I've told you a little about myself. What brings you out to the middle of nowhere? Something you want out here by yourself that you can't find in the cities?" Merchant asks before placing a small piece into his mouth.

Dry and salty, the jerky is getting harder to soften as the weeks go by.

"Ha, there isn't anything I want from anyone or anything," she scoffs.

Shifting her seat, she turns until she faces ever so slightly away, the back of her shoulder to Merchant but still keeping him within her sites, she pulls herself into a tighter ball.

"Everyone wants something. Deep inside they know it's there."

"Fuck off, Preacher. You can take that shit somewhere else tonight."

"Can't do that. Storm is growing stronger and you have the only fire for miles. You can call me Merchant, if it is all the same to you."

He adjusts his seating until he is marginally comfortable beneath the rotting boards and lets his legs straighten. Putting his hands behind his head, he lays back to stretch what he can around the fire. Boots sticking outside of the alcove, he can feel the falling embers landing on the worn leather.

"It isn't, and I don't need anything or anyone. That's what I want. Everyone can fucking leave me alone."

Merchant can hear a sob between the subtle shivering of the woman's shoulders.

She won't say anything more tonight, that he is sure of. Watching with the corner of his eye, he can see her pull out a small bundle from her pocket and shuffle the contents in her hands.

Closing his eyes, he lets the voices of the dead echo in his mind.

Yes, everyone wants something. Even a lonely survivor in the middle of the end of the world.

Chapter 2

Five Years Ago

Rain pings off the tin roof.

Rat-tat-tat.

Rat-tat-tat.

The heavens above open, and all the rain in the world drops down in a single storm. Puddles boil, and the air is heavy on the tongue and wet in the lungs.

Merchant tastes the iron and salt of blood between his teeth and pooling within his throat. His mind is clouded, and his skull feels cracked from crown to base, his neck feels broken and swollen stiff. Legs weak, he wants to fall to the ground and sleep, but they won't let him.

Angry men. Squeezing his arms, they pinch, and he grows numb, the beating of his heart throbbing beneath his skin.

Numbness.

He wishes his entire body was numb, but he feels like he has been run over by a transport truck. Heavy tires pulverizing his bones into fresh paste, but the torture doesn't seem to want to end that quickly.

A dark figure approaches from beneath the metal canopy. His captors stiffen with attention, but he does not have the strength to imitate.

The shadow dissolves and starched shoulders remain flat as the officer approaches. Green uniform goes dark instantly as he steps into the weather, no hesitation, all determination.

Water drips from Merchant's nose. Focusing his blurry eyes, a dark drop falls from the tip and splashes in the mud. The water is ice-cold on his knees, but he doesn't have the strength to move. Ripples make their way through the puddle at his feet. One, two, a thousand. Tiny waves that carry with them all of life's choices and the mistakes we must pay for.

"There is our man. Thought you could just walk out of here, didn't you?" the general asks.

Merchant can't lift his head. He can barely move his lips. The ripples continue to spread.

Dirty, wet fingers dig nails into the skin of his forehead and pull his face up.

"Answer your commanding officer!" The soldier holding him by the right arm screams.

Spittle and blood leaks from Merchant's lips, and he forces a smile.

Lightning cracks across the night sky. Thunder, the canons of the gods, rattles the branches above their heads. Dark leaves flipping in the storm, shiny in the single light bulb that burns above the tin roof. Steam lifts into the night sky off the vintage green guard that sways in the wind. A moving sun in the dead of night.

"Never been a man of many words, have you, boy?" the general asks, squatting until his face is inches from Merchant's.

Four stars blink on stiff collar with the next flash

of light that turns the darkness above into a colorless gray. Twenty men with rifles and dark heavy rain coats shift uncomfortably beneath the monsoon.

"Loose lips sink ships," Merchant mumbles, his voice tearing at the flesh inside his throat.

"What was that, boy?" The officer puts a cupped hand to his ear. "I couldn't understand anything between all the bullshit coming out of your mouth."

Light flashes before Merchant's eyes, but not from the storm. Fire lances through his skin, and blood rushes over his tongue as the slap rocks his face to the side. Strength drained, Merchant slumps in the men's arms.

They struggle to keep him from drowning in the mud.

"Pick that piece of shit up. I'm not done with him."

A boot crunches the vertebrae in Merchant's back, and he is forced to arch until his face stares at the rain that pelts his swollen skin. Blood and water mix on his face and his heart threatens to beat itself from his chest.

"Who did you tell? Who is your contact?"

General Gordon Steele reaches and wraps his hand around Merchant's throat. Tiny storms lance through nerves, and blood pounds beneath the pressure.

"Tell me, you little piece of shit, and we'll end this quickly. No one knows you are here. As far as anyone is concerned, you went AWOL and ran home to your family."

Adrenaline surges through Merchant's body, and he finds the strength to push his head forward.

"Ah, I finally have your attention. It was so shocking to hear what you did to them when you returned home to find your wife with another man. A real tragedy."

Merchant snaps his teeth, ignoring the pain that racks his jaw and cheekbones. Both men struggle to hold him up. He reaches, stretching his muscles as far as they will go to let him fall on the officer and chew his throat out.

The general smiles, his lips stretching and his bushy white mustache straightening across red cheeks.

"You wouldn't dare," Merchant says between inhuman growls.

"The dog can speak after all," the officer says before slapping him across the face again. "There is no saying what I would do if you force me. Tell me who you talked to and where to find them."

"My family. Leave them out of this!"

A fist as hard as a stone crunches into the sweet spot between Merchant's stomach and chest. Air, blood, and life forces its way from his lungs, and the men let him drop face first into the dark puddles.

Gasping at breath he can't find, thick liquid fills his body, and he struggles to breathe as he drowns in three-inch water.

Arms wrench his shoulders, and they pull him back to his knees.

Coughs send a black spew across a perfect uniform.

"Leave them out of this!" Merchant screams, though the words ring hollow in his own ears.

The general wipes at his chest, drips of vomit and mud running rivers down his legs.

Merchant sucks in the humid air. His lungs scream as he struggles to bring in enough to stay awake.

"You are the one who brought them in when you refused your orders."

Fingers pinch his cheeks and crack a tooth. More blood floods his mouth, and he coughs droplets all over the senior soldier's face.

"We knew where they were so we knew where you would go. Tell us now, and we'll spare you the nightmare."

Pain sears its way across Merchant's face. He tries to mouth the words, but his jaw will not connect and his tongue is swollen.

"Fuck'en A, boy. Spit it out already."

"My family."

A shadow runs in from behind the soldiers who stand watch. Water drips from his dark poncho, and his face is obscured by thick cloth.

"General!" The stranger salutes.

"For fuck's sake, can't you see that I am busy here?"

The soldier doesn't answer. His hand remains stiff against the cowl of his coat.

"Get on with it then," the officer barks.

The general turns away, and Merchant's head slumps. He watches as his blood mixes with the temporary river they are all standing in.

"They are coming, sir," the messenger says with a voice that is not his own.

Merchant recognizes that tone. Familiar and far too cocky to be from a soldier.

"Who is coming?"

"The infected are coming for you, demon. I can smell their hunger."

Merchant lifts his head and Snake-Eyes stares with his dead eyes from the heavy cowl. The tattoo on his neck continues to blink, and the general turns back around.

"The infected are coming, demon," Snake-Eyes says again.

Light flashes across Merchant's vision, and everything goes dark.

* * *

Merchant snaps awake, the echoes of the memory still screaming in his ears. He pushes himself up until he is seated, bones aching, cracking and stiff. The sky is a lighter shade of blue in the east, the first warnings of the new day that will soon arrive.

Cold ash swirls in the morning wind, its bitter bite scratching the skin of his bald head. Next to him, the women snores. Her breathing is shallow and even. The oily barrel of her weapon remains silent, the stock and trigger inches from her resting hand.

"They are here, demon. I'm going to laugh when they tear you apart," the ghost brags, and the snake eyes on his throat blink.

He sits beside the woman, knees pulled to chest, he claps with excitement.

The air is silent. Merchant can feel his nerves on edge, razor sharp and ready to pounce. Nothing approaches. Rough canvas soothes his burning skin and various collected belongings rattle as he pushes himself to his knees. His hand grips his bag tight. Such a burden it has become, but only he can carry it.

Like a tidal wave, they attack from both sides of the shelter. He is on his feet in a flash and driving into the first wall of bodies as they turn the corner.

Crazed men and women scream.

Frantic wails of hunger and rage.

The first dies, head spun until his chin rests between his shoulder blades. A second wraps Merchant in a bear hug, muscles squeezing tight and bones cracking.

Merchant's skull crunches cartilage and infected blood sprays across the frozen ground. More monsters barrel in. Dirty hands grabbing for limbs and clothes. Merchant kicks and one falls, knee twisted and bone ripping through skin.

Pressure builds, and it becomes harder to breath. A woman screams and attackers rage. Teeth, rotted into points and bleeding gums, are bared, and a man snarls.

Boom!

Red mist floats in the air and the body staggers. Shoulders shake before the headless form falls with a thud. Merchant bends forward and tumbles into a roll. The iron embrace that has him breaks his descent. Arms loosen. Head cracks against jaw, and he is free.

Back on his feet. Dodging arms and punching for throats, he moves without exhaustion. Another bark of the shotgun. Blood and tissue fly, and more bodies drop.

Angry words threaten. Snarls and screams answer. Space begins to fill. Merchant can't push them back. One falls and two fill in. Jacket is pulled until it hangs from one shoulder and shirt is ripped. The taste of blood fills his mouth, and he can feel it running down his arms.

Heads, shaven or going bald, sway as the bodies push forward. The entire world has come for them. Merchant's fist cracks against jaw. A tooth goes flying, and the man smiles, blood streaming between the new gap.

"Let me go!" the woman screams.

Merchant turns. They have her lifted into the air. Arms and legs kicking, she bites a finger. Blood flies with the falling digit.

Pain floods through Merchant's body. Fist to stomach, he topples to his knees.

They are dragging her away.

He deflects the next arm and spins the body away. Light erupts across his face. Wood *cracks*, and Merchant falls. The strength drains from his body, but her screams continue. He tries to push the ground away.

The branch snaps against his back. Arms will not move. Blood and dirt fill his mouth. Her voice is only an echo.

She is gone.

Merchant turns his head.

They look down at him. He snarls.

The world goes dark.

Chapter 3

Five Years Ago

Light breaks in like a thief in the night. A tiny hole beneath a steel door. His personal little secret. Unnoticed and forgotten.

Merchant watches the little stream of life flicker as booted feet march past. Pain has finally turned to numbness. Everything in his body is torn. All his bones are broken and the taste of blood is in the air.

In his mouth.

On his tongue.

Part of him wonders if there is still any left in his body, or is he a ghost living his hellish punishment until the end of time? But that can't be correct. The explosions and gunshots, men screaming and dying, ended hours ago. Or was it minutes? He can't tell.

The enemy was coming. It's all he knew before they threw him into this cell.

He can't stretch his legs. Seated, his knees press up against his chest, making it hard to breathe. Laying down on the cold, hard earth relieves the pressure, but the moisture trapped within his tiny room chokes him anyway.

Why don't they kill him and be done with it?

He deserves death. He needs death. He wants it more than he did the first time he was with a woman. Every fiber that still works within his body is on fire and begs for its final release.

Men talk on the other side of the steel. Unimportant bullshit about duties they are forced to do and whose ass is being kissed to get a better seat at the table. Merchant wishes they would just be quiet. Let him die in peace, but then he'd be alone. In the darkness with nothing but his thoughts and memories that call to him from the shadows.

His wife and children running from the front porch of their home. Down the cobblestone path he took a summer to build. Bright eyes and happy squeals. His wife in that flower sun dress she always wore even in the dead of winter. Whenever he would arrive home from deployment, there she would be, cloth swirling in the air. His very own Marilyn Monroe. Deep red with purple lilac flowers printed along the side up to where the fabric gave way to her bare shoulders. He could still smell her perfume. The way it enveloped him whenever he wrapped his arms around her petite frame, burying his face into that spot on her neck that made her purr and hold him tight. The warmth of her red hair falling over his smooth scalp and across his face.

All of this was gone. They were dead, and it was because of him.

Merchant wants to kick, lash out, but he is on the ground like a child. He hasn't the strength to move nor the tears to cry.

When would they come for him? Would they come for him or was this his sentence? To die a slow agonizing death behind reinforced walls where no one will find him for years if he is lucky?

He takes a deep breath, and his mouth fills with the taste of dirt and iron.

No, they will not leave him here. The general is not done with him. He smiles at the thought. If he has anything left, he will use it against that man. They know the strength of his body is gone. All of them are certain they have broken his will and wait for him to be putty in their hands.

Pain and torture, he has endured. God knows he has done enough of it in his own time. Now, he will watch them burst with frustration. Things he can barely imagine will be done to him, but he will resist. He must. It is all that he has left.

Men go silent.

Hard tack boots snap together.

The light, his tiny secret, burns bright until the darkness approaches. A slight graying that quickly becomes a daunting darkness as the pace quickens.

How many are coming?

Merchant tries to roll so that he is seated when they come for him. His muscles cramp and tear. He cannot move.

Metal locks turn and dust falls onto his head. Hinges scream, and the scorching rays of the sun blind Merchant. Dried blood and dirt cake the hand that shields his eyes. All of a sudden, he is reminded how thirsty he is.

"Get this piece of shit off the ground."

The orders are barked. Men hustle from both sides of the door. Shadows lost in the searing light as hands tear at his shirt and pull him from his cage.

"Didn't think we were done with you, did you?" the voice asks.

Merchant doesn't have the strength to stand. His bare feet drag across rock and hardened dirt.

"The general has a few last things to ask you." The voice is inches behind his ear. He can feel the breath, wet and sticky against his neck. "Play nice and we can end all of this. Keep up this silent bullshit and you can't imagine what he is going to let me do."

The man chuckles.

Merchant spits fresh blood at the dirt trail that passes slowly under him.

"Fuck you," he mutters as spit drips from broken teeth.

"That's it, boy. Keep fighting. They don't call me the Dog Breaker for nothing," the stranger says.

Laughter fades as Merchant is carried away. Buildings pass, and the sound of soldiers marching and preparing begins to blow away with the wind. Lifting his head, he musters what strength he can to see where they are going.

A clearing on top of a hill. A solitary tree sits atop the ridge. Peaceful in its simplicity.

Why hasn't he noticed this before?

Seated in a simple chair beside the tall tree with its full, perfect crown is a shadow that waits. He knows who is up there, and he hasn't the will to fight back.

* * *

Blood melts snow. Bright red at first, but then dark and black as it pools below his face. Pain wrecks his body. Cuts and bruises swelling as Merchant pushes the ground away, lifting himself until he is seated.

"Thought they were really going to finish you off there," the ghost says.

Merchant turns to look at the annoyingly dead man. With his wild sneer stretching across his face and that damn tattoo on his neck.

Always blinking.

Always watching.

The ghost is seated where the woman had sat that evening. His translucent body flickers as he picks at dirt beneath his nails. Flicking, he sends the grime flying to disappear in the space between his world and the living.

The sound of snow tumbling and falling breaks the silence of the day.

Morning light burns its way across the sea of snow and ice. Like golden fire, the east is a flame across the entire horizon, and the temperature refuses to play her part. Merchant can feel the brisk frost biting at his skin and irritating his newly acquired wounds that decorate him like tattoos.

Bodies lay scattered around him. Men, women, and some he cannot tell the difference. All of them no longer move. Torn parts lay scattered in the slushy red snow that surrounds the long-extinguished fire.

"These bastards don't usually get such an upper hand on you," Snake-Eyes says. He gazes at the corpse he sits on. His attention draws Merchant's to the figure lying face down, back blown apart. "If only I was still alive. I would have joined in on the fun. Kicked that sorry ass of yours."

A sigh like a disappointed child escapes translucent lips.

A growl rolls from Merchant.

Reluctant to accept a dead man's opinion, Merchant moves to where the ghost sits and rolls the dead weight onto its back.

Flesh, guts, and blood pull out as the lifeless sack of meat lifts from the icy turf. The bullet hit bone, exploding the man's chest like a watermelon of tissue and gore.

"Well, isn't that interesting," Snake-Eyes says.

His face hovers over Merchant's shoulder, and the eyes of his tattoo continue to blink.

Infected skin stretches over the man's body. Scales as tough as leather ripple the man's left arm and up the side of his neck. The hole in his chest peels back with infection, muscle as hard as granite flexed taut even in death.

Merchant searches the body. Not that the infected carry identification with them, but it is a start. Pockets are empty, but some of the clothes are still in moderate shape.

Infection attacks the brain and molds the skin into a tough living shell while the body starves on the inside. Whoever this was, he is still a big man, and a heavy corpse as Merchant works the denim along muscle and bone beginning to stiffen beyond help.

"Our little mystery here keeps getting better," Snake-Eyes says.

He pops up, his body forming by the dead man's head. He begins to pick at the same nail on his hand that he is always cleaning.

On the left thigh, six inches from the knee, Merchant notices a bullseye of scarred flesh. Red, puffy, and oozing, the brand has never healed. Merchant lifts each leg, but there are no other marks.

"Now who would go around branding the infected. Back when you hadn't killed me, we couldn't rid ourselves of them fast enough."

Snake-Eyes flicks another piece of dirt from his nails and watches it disappear.

Merchant takes a deep breath. Regardless of the cold, the smell of rot and death is beginning to build and fill the area. He hates to admit it, but the asshole is correct. These infected are not the same. Looking down at the body, and then at the others scattered below the billboard, he can't help but wonder how this is different.

"Funny thing is, how they didn't finish you off," Snake-Eyes says.

He's walking now. Chewing on the tip of his finger and gingerly stepping over the stiff corpses and avoiding the pools of blood.

"Why didn't they eat you or something. I mean, I'm not gay or anything, but there seems to be plenty of you to go around. If I was hungry enough, well…"

The ghost lets the thought hang, forcing Merchant to peer over at him.

"What? I'm telling you I fucked more women than you can count back when my pecker still worked, but when a man needs to eat, he is going to find the biggest meal he can find," Snake-Eyes continues, his arm sweeping over the horizon. "Out here, you are as big as they get. Unlike that girl they took, all skin and bones. You know, I wouldn't have even spared her a glance before you threw me out that window. Now, I tell you, even some of these monsters look enticing."

The asshole taps at this crotch like he's checking to see if there is anyone home.

"The girl," Merchant whispers and begins to look out across the horizon.

Snow stares back at him with eyes bright enough to burn. An endless world of white.

Flat.

Boring.

Dead.

"Oh, don't you go worrying that ugly cue ball head of yours, Mr. Clean. Wherever they took her, she is long dead," Snake-Eyes says, and then picks at the space between his front two teeth. "What little meat there is on her is probably already rotting inside the belly of one of those half-breeds. Going to be nothing but a stinking pile of shit in a few hours."

Merchant spins around, his eyes hard and full of fire. Snake-Eyes sticks his tongue out like a child.

"Too bad, though. She wasn't much to look at, plus with that shotgun of hers, she had one hell of a kick, but I'd do her if I was still alive," he continues. "Probably kill her, though."

"Shut the fuck up and go away for a while," Merchant demands.

"Can't do that, demon. You know the rules. You killed me, and you carry that damn rabbit of my bastard son in that bag of yours. So, here I am to torment you until the end of time."

"I should have cut your damn head off," Merchant says.

"Hindsight is 20/20, and it's a bitch isn't it."

The smile on Snake-Eyes face grows longer, even the empty sockets of his eyes smile. Those tattoos on his neck do what they always do, blink.

"By the way, where is that bag of yours? Wouldn't want that gift from that little bastard of mine to go missing, now would we?" Snake-Eyes asks.

His body fades away as a stiff breeze swirls through the alcove, picking up a tornado of ash and the iron stench of cooled blood. Merchant searches the ground around him.

What would the infected want with a single woman and his bag? He knows they could not have gotten far with it. The burden is his alone to carry. No man, living, dead, or otherwise, can bear it for more than a short distance.

He finds no trace of the Army canvas, but something else catches his eye. Beneath the stripped corpse, with its pale white flesh, untouched by infection, he sees a corner of paper. It's not simple trash, nor did he pull it from the infected.

The ridged body rolls over like a log, all stiffness and bulk.

"What do we have here?" Snake-Eyes asks, peering over Merchant's shoulders.

The Queen of Swords and Death.

Merchant rolls the blood-stained cards through his fingers. The Queen's eyes bore into him as she turns to face him, and then back again. He does not see any other cards scattered through the carnage.

"Let me guess, we now have to go get her."

Snake-Eyes sighs.

The morning is bright when Merchant turns away from the death and the blood. Around them, the world is silent beneath a crystal-clear sky. He puts the cards gently into his pocket.

"Where do we start?" Snake-Eyes asks.

Picking at his teeth, he stands beside Merchant, who tilts his head toward the ghost.

"What?" Snake-Eyes shrugs. "It's not like I have much say in the matter."

Merchant says nothing as he begins to pick his way back toward Interstate 80.

"Are you going to at least fill me in?"

"First, I'm going to get what belongs to me back," Merchant replies.

He does not turn to see if the ghost follows.

"Then what?"

Merchant does not answer.

Chapter 4

Five Years Ago

The sky is a deep shade of red. It darkens at first, and then grows lighter as his eyes open and his vision clears, returning to the bright blue of late summer.

Crack.

Another strike of the hammer drives the nail deeper. Iron scratches bone, Merchant screams, and he can feel his throat bleed. The rod cracks the insides of his arms. His shoulders are stretched, limbs pulled tight, and they force him to hug the trunk of the tree in reverse. Railroad spikes pin his limbs to the oak. Both arms split, dark blood running rivers down the sharp bark to the saturated soil.

He tries to fall, but gravity has lost its control.

Crack.

The tree shudders, and he vomits blood and bile over his chest. Bright rivulets bead on his brown skin. Red jewels that glisten in the sun, sparkling as they chase rivers over his cramped muscles.

His vision goes red and the darkness closes in.

"Now, don't you start dying, yet. We can't have that until we are done with you," the general says.

Adrenaline is injected into Merchant's shoulder by the man they call the Dog Breaker. His heart beats like a drum at a rock concert. A car engine revving in his chest, he can feel the bone stretching against the pounding.

Crack.

Wood chips fly, and Merchant screams. Strength is gone and all the muscle in his legs give away. Fire erupts through the skin of his abdomen. Razor wire cuts deeper, holding him tight. Blood and other fluids drip from his shirtless torso down over his belt.

He can't fall.

The binding pulls tighter. The blades dig beneath his skin. Merchant grinds his teeth, and blood drips from his lips.

"I'll tell you," he whispers.

Crack.

The tree fractures again and several leaves float lazily to the ground. Merchant's eyes roll back into his head. Sweat drips down his face. A slap rocks his head to the side, the pain lost to oblivion.

He's awake.

"You'll what?" the general asks.

A hand pinches Merchant's lower jaw. He can see the blood and spit pooling in the officer's palm.

"I'll tell." Merchant struggles to speak, and the wire pulls tighter. More blood spews. "You."

The general smiles. He pulls his hand away, and then wipes the gore across Merchant's face.

"We are past that, my boy."

He turns and walks back to his folding chair. One of those cheap ones you get at the army surplus tent.

With a smile from ear to ear, he sits down and crosses one knee over the other. Turning his hand, he wipes blood onto a white handkerchief.

"You lost your chance for a quick ending. We have other ways of find out. Now it is time for you to pay for your insolence."

The man nods.

Crack.

An explosion rips through Merchant's arm as the force drives the nail completely through and the hammer head cracks bone. Torture wins, and Merchant falls. Bark soaked with his life, tears through the bare skin of his back, and the razors sear through his midsection and into his chest.

He can see his guts. They pile on his legs that buckle beneath him. Death waits for him, but it won't stop the pain. Adrenaline keeps his eyes open. Men laugh as he tries to scream, but his blood-flooded throat chokes him.

Minutes feel like hours, which stretch into days.

Time seems to stop, and the world begins to darken. Slowly at first, the edges of the grass beneath his legs and the leaves above his head all lose focus. Merchant coughs but can't bring anything back in. He is suffocating in his own blood. More of him spills onto his lap. Bright pink, and then a deathly pale. All he can taste is blood, and his lungs burn.

Merchant cannot breathe.

Blood and spit drool from his lips.

He does not have the strength to lift his head. His eyes lock on the darkness that is pooled on his legs.

The end is here.

He does not fight it.

"Oh, by the way…" the Dog Breaker says.

Rough fingers lift Merchant's chin. The pinch of his skin is pressure lost to his exhausted senses. Blurry eyes roll around like marbles but settle on the soldier's face. A deep scar runs from corner of his left eye down into his bootstrap goatee. His overcompensating cologne is stronger than the stench of death.

"We'll send our condolences to your wife and kids. The news will devastate them. Especially that wife of yours. I'll personally make sure she has a strong supportive shoulder to cry on. Now don't you go dying with that weight on your shoulders. She'll be in good hands."

Breaker drops Merchant's chin, and it falls with no resistance.

Death has arrived.

There is no mercy.

* * *

Bloody boot prints in the snow. The sun high overhead with thin, wispy clouds following the trail of the storm that is now history. Three pairs. Two walk with regular steps, unhurried, and even-paced. The third lags behind. The first do not slow. They leave the other. To struggle, straining beneath the weight. They leave him to die.

Vehicle-sized hills litter the horizon. Smooth lifts beneath the white blanket, perfect and serene. Fresh drops of blood sprinkle the path that zigzags between them. Still red and diminishing. The man is healing, or almost dead.

Merchant follows. Each impression is drawing closer to the last. A weak leg drags behind, the weight becoming unbearable as now they can no longer lift the bag. The curse is pulled like treasure, creating a ditch that weaves left and right through the snow.

Where are they going?

There is nothing for miles. Dead towns, empty and forgotten, litter the open lands of Nebraska. He has seen enough to know only memories haunt the skeletal buildings and worn-down rock.

A brisk breeze whips across the field. The sting of sharp ice against his skin a refreshing bite as he continues pushing forward.

"Can you smell them, demon?" Snake-Eyes asks.

The ghost's nose turns up to the sky, his empty sockets dark, and his neck blinks.

"I don't need to smell them," Merchant answers.

"They smell like death walking. I can barely breathe their stench is so thick, and I don't even need to breath anymore."

Merchant looks over at the ghost, who smiles a tooth-filled grin. That spot he always picks at is back again.

"So, you are telling me you could find them if it wasn't so easy already."

Snake-Eyes disappears, and then materializes twenty yards ahead, hands on hips, jacket open, and chest puffed out.

"It's not like they haven't put a fucking sign out for you already, but yes, I can smell them. Can't you? The damn bastards probably haven't bathed in years."

"All I smell is the open air, and all I hear is you admitting something you should have told me back before we got into this mess."

Merchant walks through the ghost, his body nothing more than a momentary ripple of ice running through his veins. Snake-Eyes shutters and tries to wipe himself clean.

"I hate it when you do that."

There is no reply from Merchant.

"Who said I should have told you anything? You are damn lucky I even talk to you. The others do nothing but moan and bitch and complain. See, I'm different. You should feel damn proud to have me around.

Merchant stops.

"Come on, big man. Say something. I want to hear what you have to say," Snake-Eyes taunts from behind Merchant's ears.

"Shut up, won't you."

"God damn unpleasant is what you are."

The back of Merchant's hand passes through the ghost's head with a slap.

"Look," Merchant whispers.

The path they follow turns sharply back toward the east. Snow stretches for as far as they can see. Their world lives beneath a foot of snow but for a thin stream of dark smoke that lifts into the air.

"Where there is smoke," Snake-Eyes says.

"I'll find what belongs to me."

Merchant turns and picks up the pace.

Snake-Eyes mouths silent words that mock the big man, and with a shrug, he begins to follow.

Chapter 5

The smell of body odor, rot, filth, and blood chokes out all the air she can breathe. A stiff breeze bites at the exposed skin of her bruised cheek. Blood cakes on her scalp. She turns to try and take in as much clean air as she can.

A ripping on the cord pulls her forward. There is very little strength left in her legs, and her numb feet cannot keep up. She stumbles, and her knees crack against frozen earth. Her muscles cramp, and the bones feel broken and splintered. Ice and snow burns through the skin of her bound hands.

"Get up, beautiful," a man barks.

He yanks on her cord, and it does not have the effect he desires. Hands shift forward, and she topples until her face is buried in the snow. Her world goes dark and breathing fills her mouth with ice, and she begins to choke.

A rough hand grabs the back of her coat, thick meaty fingers wrapping around worn cloth and a significant amount of hair. Searing pain ignites fires behind her eyes as she is lifted. Coughing, she struggles for breath as her neck stretches back.

"You were ordered to get back onto your feet,"

another man says.

She can smell the rot in the man's flesh. His breath is like week old trash, sour and pungent.

Using what strength she can find, she shifts her leg until she has one frozen foot flat on the ground. The men do not help her stand. The tight grip on her coat and the rope that binds her to them forces her to struggle.

"Don't hurt the merchandise," the first man demands, his voice deeper with less infection-scratched vocal cords.

He gives the one who holds her from behind a strong shove. The smaller one stumbles and releases her without taking her with him.

The others back away from the man who holds her leash. Her height doesn't reach his wide shoulders, and the thick wolf hide he wears does little to take away from the bulging arms that stretch the thin fabric he calls a coat. Sun reflects off the dark skin of his shaven scalp, and his face is just as hairless.

Infection scales look like pock marks on the left side of his neck and face, more teenage skin than disease on a man with enough scars across the rest of his body to look like he lost a fight with a bear.

He gazes down at her, and she recoils. His grip on her binding strengthens, and she does not bother to pull against something she knows she can't defeat.

"You must keep up. We have been instructed to bring you unharmed, but we cannot afford to slow," he says before turning around.

The party begins to march, and another quick tug of her leash pulls her forward. This time, she is able to stay on her feet.

"Who instructed you to take me prisoner, and where are we going?" she asks.

Courage and anger boils deep within her. She yanks on the cords that bind her. Her weight and strength unnoticeable against the man's bulk.

"Hey! I'm talking to you."

Others look at her. Most of them with hungry eyes and infection that spreads further along their bodies. Twenty men and women keep pace around her. She cannot see any others tied up like she is. They are the largest infected she has ever seen, especially the monster who stomps one boulder of a boot after another in front of her. Besides the disease that mutates their skin, they look healthy, if only a little hungry.

A few of the men, and at least one woman, lick their lips as they keep an eye on every one of her movements. She wonders how much longer until they give into those urges and she is their next meal.

"I know you can hear me."

She yanks on the rope again, and this time the one who had picked her from the ground stumbles into her.

"Keep moving, bitch!" he yells.

A loud *slap* echoes across the open field, and she falls forward. Her eyes water as the world spins and the clear blue sky above her head rushes across her vision.

The ground is unforgiving as she hits the snow. Bones crack, and the world begins to grow dark. She tries to lift her head, but everyone around her swims through the air.

The lids of her eyes are rocks, and she doesn't have the strength to keep them open. She tries to scream, say anything, but her mouth tastes like blood. The giant one stalks forward, and the one who slapped her stands defiant. All the other infected back away, most of them making noises like wild animals excited for the kill.

Words escape the smaller man's lips, but she cannot understand them. A fist the size of a man's head cracks across jaw and temple. Blood erupts from a broken eye, and the victim falls to his knees. Her vision narrows on the sight of the mutilated man's face.

Destroyed, he looks up a moment before the fist of god hits him again. Skull fractures and crumbles inward. Lifeless, the body hits the ground beside her. She can see the steam rising from the snow before the others jump onto the fallen treasure.

The sound of chaos reigns over the day, and the darkness closes in. She can feel hands that could crush her between individual fingers pick her from the frozen earth, and she is carried away.

* * *

Dragged along like an animal, and now she is caged like one. Pain crackles through her skull, and the skin of her scalp is puffy and tender. She gently pokes at the wound at the base of her head and regrets it the moment the fire erupts beneath her touch.

Cold air sends chills through her body, the feeling of a shaved head something new to file away with the years of misery. Pulling her blanket tighter across her knees, which she has tucked against her chest, she breathes beneath the cover and lets the tiny warmth of her breath warm what it will. The skin of her legs is like ice, almost as cold as the air that bites at her cheeks, and she has lost all feeling in her ass, which she can barely keep within the material.

Snow continues to fall in large, fat flakes. Drifting from the darkness above, the pillow white softness lingers in the air before settling onto the ground. More than two inches has fallen since she was put into this cage, and she pushes herself as deep inside as she can. There isn't enough room for her to stretch her legs. Pulling her knees up tight to her chin, the cold of the bars at the rear of her confinement bite into her through the thin wool she has wrapped around herself. Small mounds of powder fall in between the rusted bars, the green paint chipping away to show the aged steel beneath its orange glory. The snow is not deterred by the barricade. It is a slow-moving enemy of white ice that inches toward her in torturous slow motion.

Shivers riddle her body beneath the material they provided her to cover her naked frame. It scratches at her skin. Old wool which is stale, stiff, and smells like it hasn't been washed in years. Bits of orange dye stick out between the dark blotches of blacks and browns. The material has seen better days.

The bones of her swollen joints ache beneath skin that is bruised and sore. Though she knows she is freezing, she can feel the warmth that begins to burn in her blood. If these monsters don't eat her soon, she'll die of exposure before they get the chance.

Her vision blurs beneath tears that freeze to her eyelashes. She can't decide if she would rather have them kill her quickly and serve her for dinner, leave her to freeze here alone like a discarded animal or simply let the fever that will soon take her do its duty. She can feel death approaching like a welcomed friend. The end lingers on the outskirts of her vision, waiting for her to discover it just as she tries to distinguish the origination of the piss and body odor that fills the space beneath her blanket.

Is it hers or the last bastard they had locked up behind these bars? She can't even remember the last time she relieved herself. It no longer matters.

Another spasm shakes her body, and she pushes aside the thought as she has a million others.

A single bonfire burns in the center of the camp, but the heat does not reach her. Part of her begs to feel the warmth against her skin, to sink inside of her and warm the cold fingers that have wrapped themselves around her bones. Inching forward, placing her arms through the openings of the bars has done little. What little warmth she can find is quickly lost by the pain of a baton or stick smashed into her fingers. She blows more breath into her closed fist at the memory. The moisture is thick as blood on her fingers.

The other part of her, the half that refuses to give up, is full of disgust and hatred. They want her weak, to beg and whimper. She will never give them that. She will fight until her last breath. If she could find her shotgun, her means of salvation, she would kill them all. That big one, the freak as big as a mountain took it from her. She can still see it tapping against his leg from where it was looped into his belt. One of these evenings, she is going to get it back. Even if she has to pry it from his dead hands, she will take back what is hers, and then she'll empty it on the bark-like face of his.

She smiles at the thought of his face imploding as

the shell rips through skin and bone. The taste of blood on her lips warms the fire inside of her that waits for its chance.

More than three dozen infected mill around the open flames that *crackle* and *snap* into the cold air and angry wind. She hates them all. Men and women, all of them young and with different levels of infection. Some of them are barely holding on to the sanity that fights the disease. She can see their uncontrolled movements, spasms and growls that escape lips they bite down on every time an outburst escapes. They remind her of new puppies. Fighting their urges to run and be free, but needing their masters to keep them in line. Those very masters bark orders, words which carry threats of death and pain, and they use blunted weapons to strike unguarded skin as they force their untrained beasts to fall back and whimper. Huddling together at the very edge of the light, they move as one from cage to cage. Dogs they are, the whole lot of them.

There are twelve other boxes like hers that she can see. All of them are spread in a wide circle around the bonfire. Those farthest, she can see only the tops through the six-foot flames, but they are all the same. The light of the fire dances with the shadows, but she cannot see if there is anyone inside even the closest. She has tried, and she continues from time to time. Staring, watching to see if any shadows move or any other captives make a sound, but the site is empty save for the angry voices of her captors.

Half-walking, half-crawling, the pack of the tameless moves closer. They are hungry. Their need is so rich that it permeates the very air that surrounds them. She is the furthest from the fire, and they can barely hide their stares as they move as silently as their cravings will allow. Their masters do not give notice. Some stay by the fire, hands and arms extended to keep themselves warm, their attention no longer on those that have finally followed their orders of silence and obedience.

She settles her eyes on the pack, her pupils, slivers over the edges of her blanket. There are four of them. Tender skin is swollen around joints that swell on knuckles and hands that are dragged through the snow. They crouch as their spines curl, and they draw closer. Lines of scars lace themselves around scales that cover entire limbs and render the left side of their face unmovable.

The smell of sweat and rotting meat is close enough now that it turns her stomach. No longer human, she can feel the difference before they reach her cage. Animals smell better, this is the plague that has wiped out entire cities. This band of infected, smarter and stronger than anything she has ever bared witness to before, has wolves within their flock.

Inching to the furthest corner of the cage without taking her eyes off them, she waits and they draw closer.

"Come…here, beautiful," the closest one croaks.

His voice is scratchy. Vocal cords torn, he sounds like he coughed the words through lungs full of cancer.

A face presses up against the bars. A tongue stretches out, saliva dripping and blood seeping between broken teeth.

She rears her head back and spits. A direct hit splatters across the monster's eyes. Four animals go wild, and half a dozen arms slam into the cage. Dirty, crusted fingernails scratch at the air between them. They almost have her. Wind tingles her skin as each swipe misses her by inches.

They push harder, their skin bulging as they try to force themselves through the barrier.

A hooked finger catches the edge of her blanket and pulls. Cover ripped from her grasp, the cold bitter air of the winter slices through her body like a hot knife. On instinct, she tries to pull her only protection back. A hand like iron snatches her left arm, and she is yanked forward.

Skull slams against iron, and her world begins to swim. She can smell their breath on her. Spit begins to drip down her arms, and she fights her eyes that want to roll back in to her skin.

Fire lances through her arms as teeth tear into flesh. "Ah!" she screams.

Anger and frustration surge through her veins.

The shriek forces the animal back. Skin flaps away from the bone of her right shoulder. Blood pulses out. Reaching up with her free hand, she grabs the one that has her by her left wrist and slams her forehead into cartilage and iron. Blackness swirls in her vision, but she is dropped. Monsters howl, and the blood lust is on. Her cage is shaken violently. Wool blanket rolling around, she cannot get her footing as the floor becomes wall and the wall becomes floor, and then reverses again.

Crawling away, she digs her fingers and heels into the bottom of the cage. The frenzy of hands and fingers is endless. Blood drips from arms and faces with eyes that scream for her. The cage lifts again, and this time drops completely on its side.

They are all around her now. Two jump on top while the others reach from the sides. Nails and fingers dig into her skin. One manages to spear her open wound with a finger, and she can feel it strike bone. Words she doesn't understand escape her lips, and her frenzied call increases their need for her. All she can see is them reaching for her. The cage is now her salvation, the one thing keeping them from her.

Shouts can be heard in the background, but she cannot distinguish between them and the thirst for blood as the four sets of hands try to tear her apart.

Metal screams as it is torn apart. The door to her cage is ripped off, and the howling around her reaches a level she can no longer comprehend. Crawling as far away from the opening is all that she can think of.

Pain lances through her back. Another set of teeth finds purchase as she reaches the back wall of her over-turned cage. She screams but no one cares. Arms reach for her through the open doorway. Her instincts tell her to swat them back, fight them until the last drop, but she does not have the strength. Blood soaks her body. A river of red gore runs down between breasts and over her stomach. A pool of it steams beneath her, and another set of hands pulls her back and slams her against the wall again.

Drained, she slumps forward, and hands wider than her shoulders pull her from her confinement by her damaged arm she can no longer move.

Her vision is cloudy. She sees men beating those that attacked her like dogs, and the whimpers and screams are lost to the roar of the fire. An iron grip wraps around her neck. She can't breathe, and the ground lifts away from her feet. Straining, she sees the face of the monster look at her. His fingers squeeze tight, and the bones beneath her skull begin to crack.

Blood trickles from her lips, down her body, and the darkness takes her away.

Chapter 6

Five Years Ago

"Awaken, my soldier," a voice calls from the void.

Warming, comforting, and soothing, the woman's words disperse into Merchant's mind.

His eyes flutter. The lids are as heavy as stone, and he cannot keep them open. Like a long summer's nap, he doesn't want to wake up.

"That is it. You are with me, and I am with you," the sweet song beckons.

Merchant lifts his head and lets it fall backwards onto his shoulders. He rolls his eyes, and the sleep breaks away. A bright sun burns high overhead, the golden rays broken by the thick canopy of a single oak tree that sits atop an empty hill. Birds sing in the air, a song of peace and joy. The breeze calls to him, its touch warm and soft. He can feel the small hairs on his arms move, and it comforts his body. He smiles and lets the feeling wash through him.

"Welcome back, my general. Oh, how I have missed you," her voice touches his ears gently, sending shivers down his body.

He wants more, and the smile becomes a soft nibble

onto his lower lip. Squeezing his eyes tight, he opens them to focus and look around. There is no one with him on this hill, his back pressed up against the solid trunk of the tree, its strength comforting as he sinks himself against it.

"I couldn't have chosen better myself," her words are a song to his ears.

But where is she? He turns to his right to take a peek around the tree, but he is held in place. An invisible weight sits on his lap, and he cannot move.

"Now, now. There is no need to rush things," she says from the opposite of where he looks.

A woman steps from the shadows, and his heart begins to race. Deep brown skin shines in the summer light. Legs that reach the heavens walk gracefully until she is standing in front of him. Hair as black as night weaves down from her head, wrapping her shoulders and looking deeper, he can see all of eternity lost in the richness and volume. She smiles down at him. Thick, luscious lips that burn the brightest ruby red he has ever seen stretch and part to reveal brilliant white teeth.

She kneels before him, her white cocktail dress hugging her curves tightly. She lets her eyes level with his. They are a blue he has never seen before. Lovelier than the sky above, there is a pureness in them, so genuine he almost wants to giggle like he would at the sight of a newborn baby. Swaddled and comforted in its first blanket.

"Who are you?" he is finally able to ask.

The words are a whisper, his voice a distant croak as if this was the first time he has spoken in a millennium.

"That is not as important as why I am here, my fine soldier," she answers.

Reaching her hand forward, she lets one finger, with its nails painted a glorious golden color, trace the outline of his cheekbone. Fire, not the kind that burns, but the stuff that brings you to life, erupts in his body. He is drawn to her like he has never been to a woman before. She is a stranger to him, so full of mysteries, and there is nothing he wants more than to delve deep into the pursuit of all that he can find within her.

"Tell me why. Whatever you want, you can have," the words come unbidden from his lips.

She smiles. Perfect white teeth bite down on that full bottom lip, and she pulls her hand back and begins to tap her own cheek.

"Oh, if only it was that easy. My good man, you haven't even heard what I offer yet."

"Anything!" he pleads.

A giggle lifts into the air to join the chorus of the birds, and she spins as she stands once again to walk away. Merchant struggles to follow but once again a weight he cannot explain pins him to the tree. A single chair waits for her, and she sits. Leaning back, she crosses one leg over the other and begins to chew on the index finger of her right hand.

"Be careful what you promise me, my good fellow. Do not let yourself get lost in charms your mind cannot possibly understand."

Merchant wriggles, but the bonds hold him tight. Inside, he can feel the fire spreading through his body. She pulls at him with an attraction he can't ignore.

Can't she feel it as well?

"I have fought and raced my way through forest and mountain. Cities and endless empty plains have never stopped me. Anything you want, you shall have. I give you my word."

A soft, beautiful hand, the skin bright with life, slaps down on the arm of the fold-out chair. Thunder cracks, shattering the peaceful balance of the sky.

"I will forgive you this once," she says while pushing herself away from where she is seated. The skies darken. A storm races in with a fury only the gods could create, and it begins to rain. Large droplets splatter the ground around her, yet she still glows in the coming darkness. "I am here to make you an offer. Rise and see what has been done to you. Choose to do what you will with what you find, and then when the job is finished, I will have one simple request."

For the first time, Merchant feels fear. She is now inches from his face, her beauty is overpowering, but inside those eyes, he can see a fury that crushes him. He recoils and the taste of blood begins to fill his mouth.

"What? What has been done to me?" he asks, but the tree will not let him pull any further away.

"Look around you. Remember who you are, Merchant."

The rain falls in a steady storm. Birds no longer sing, and the sun is lost beneath a ceiling of clouds that roll thick and gray. A mist stretches around the bottom of the hill. He is on top of a solitary mountain, surrounded by a dark forest on all sides, and the swirling of the dead holds him prisoner.

"Inside of you, Merchant. Remember everything," her voice calls from the distant air.

Pain sears through his mind like a hot poker branding his skin. He can feel his abdomen ripping apart, the bones in his arms splintering as the nails are driven through. He is still tied to the tree. His bowels are splayed across his legs, and blood pours from his mouth. He screams like a hot fire from his lungs.

A hand, searing the skin it touches, slams his head back into the tree. Bark splinters, and her face is now inches from his. He can smell sulfur mixed with blood and fear. Her skin is pale, and her eyes are as white as snow. Words chant from her lips, and black poison spreads from her mouth in spidery veins that darken her beautiful features that are now pulled taut against bone. She is a creature he does not recognize.

Terror seizes his heart, and his insides are torn from inside his body. He loses himself to the onslaught. He can feel himself separate from his body, rising above it as light fills his vision. The words she chants are now a calling. Dark and ominous, they echo from the voices of a thousand dead men. He cries out, the light fades and the shadows race to devour him. He cannot fight them.

He is defenseless. They tear at him, piece by piece. He can feel teeth and claws, severing who and what he is.

There is little left of who he was. He can't remember his name, or why he is here. The chanting is now a thunder, and there is so little of him left. Down below, a tiny dot on the horizon is the hill where his body lays tied to a tree. He is lost forever, his existence done and forgotten.

A tether pulls tight deep within him.

Falling.

The sensation sweeps through him as he plummets back to earth.

He wants to vomit, his insides rolling like a ship on the sea.

Success!

The taste of bile burns at his tongue, and relief washes over him to be replaced by the lifting of gravity as he continues to fall.

His body approaches. He can see the hill speeding at him like an out of control freight train.

Clawing at the sky, he tries to slow his descent like every cartoon he has ever watched. Speed picks up. He can already see the crater he is going to leave.

There she is, standing over his body, his head pulled back, the dark abyss of his mouth wide open.

Falling, crashing, he can see the blood on his face now.

Red.

Bright!

Almost there!

"Ah!" Merchant screams and falls forward onto his elbows and knees.

The air chokes his lungs, and his stomach heaves. Bile and undigested food hurls from his mouth, and he lets it splatter in the mud beneath his face. Fire lances through his skin and the steady rain from above taps against the wounds that steam into the darkening, early evening light. He turns his head to the solitary tree. Razor wire lays snapped across the ground, stained with gore and blood. It no longer holds him prisoner.

With slow, painful movements, he crawls to the other side of the oak tree. Weakness runs through his body, the bones of his arms shifting under his weight, but he pushes through.

Railroad spikes stick out. The blunt ends flattened and dripping with water from the storm. Two spikes piercing flesh, bark, and the wood beneath.

Merchant reaches for his belly, but it all remains intact. He is not bleeding. Breath fills his lungs, and the pounding of his heart throbs in his chest.

He is alive.

His eyes trace the trail that will lead back to the hidden camp the general and the men he used to call brothers once used.

He is alive, and there are answers he must have.

* * *

A bonfire of old broken furniture, wooden support studs ripped from the guts of empty houses, and useless worn tires burns in the center of a four-way crossroad at the center of a town with a name no one remembers. The smell of melting rubber is a stench that chases the wind and goes on for miles. Merchant waits and watches from the empty window on the second floor of the vacant Holiday Inn. Cold air whips through the room, and the curtains, long ago reduced to nothing but thin pieces of sheer cloth, lift like ghosts in the darkness.

"So how you gonna do them, killer?" Snake-Eyes asks.

The ghost lounges on his back across the floor where the bed used to be, outlined in black soot that stains the faded carpet of red and greens. His head is propped up on his hands with a smile revealing that same dirty tooth. Beneath his chin, those reptilian eyes continue their blinking.

"I've counted six of them so far," Merchant says.

The infected are not well-disciplined or organized. They mill about, coming and going into the buildings as the night continues to pass by. A weak storm has settled in, sitting above them and dropping a layer of snow in large, fat flakes.

He leans against the cold frame of the window and counts again. Two sit by the fire, warming themselves and sneaking drinks from containers they carry on their belts. The one who carried his pack all the way from the interstate lays sprawled face down in the snow. He has not moved in over an hour, and the belongings lay untouched beside him. Considering that one dead, Merchant still finds four moving in and out of the alleyways between the abandoned buildings.

"Six shouldn't be too hard for you," Snake-Eyes adds as he appears along the other edge of the window. "I say we walk down there right now. Call them all in and watch them beat your brains out."

Merchant looks up at the ghost, the specter's hollow eyes haunting above his shit-eating grin.

"What? Can't a dead man wish, for Christ's sake?"

Turning back to the fire below, Merchant tries to ignore the man.

Why are they here? What did they want with his bag?

He looks up at the sky. There is several hours remaining before the sun rises and the storm doesn't appear to be in a hurry to find itself another place to sit. He sighs and turns to the door that leads out of the empty motel. The damn ghost is correct. There is nothing else he can do, and waiting will get him nothing. But the dead asshole will have to suffer another disappointment. He does not plan on letting them beat his brains in.

Making quick work of the stairs that lead him to road level, he stays to the shadows as he eases his way around the front desk. The boards that once created the working surface have been removed, leaving the empty leg frames sprawled on the floor. He grabs one and hooks one of its nails into a loop on the back of his pants. It isn't held securely, but it will have to do. Closing his jacket tight around his chest, he puts his head to the ground and steps outside.

Cold, shrill air pinches at his skin, and he breathes a puff of warm breath into his hand. Secretly, he keeps his eyes on the dark shadows that fill the empty gaps between buildings. Broken windows watch as he moves slowly up the road, his feet crunching the snow, and the light from the burning fire casting a yellow glow across the ice crystals

His shadow follows him, growing into a taller, formidable presence in his passing, and he is now twenty feet from where the two who sit for warmth wait. They have yet to notice him. The fire in his blood begins to burn, his heart slowing, and his muscles twitch in anticipation. Eyes, beady and yellow, blink from all around him. None steps up to challenge, as if they had been expecting him.

"Hello there," Merchant calls out.

One of the infected cocks his head toward him, a piece of red, juicy meat hanging between teeth and rivers of blood running down his pale chin.

"I didn't catch your names back there by the inter-state," Merchant says. "I see that you found my bag. I was beginning to worry I would never see it again."

He can hear the movement of feet all around him now. Remaining in the shadows, he can feel their thirst as much as he can feel the cold that bites at his cheeks.

"You don't mind if I take this back, do you? I'll just check if everything is here, and I'll be on my way."

The second infected stands, and now both are look-ing at him. They are similar to those who found him days earlier. Infection spreading its way through their bodies, but curiously only on one side. These two men are strong, still young, but a hunger burns in their eyes. Whatever helped them fight the disease earlier has lost its touch. They will soon be out of control.

"We thought you were dead when we cracked your skull open," a raspy voice says from the alleyway to his left.

A tall one steps out. Two inches taller than even Merchant. Infection has cratered the left side of his face, and his right eye is yellow with jaundice and seep-ing pinkish blood. In his right hand, he holds an old Louisville Slugger with several nails hammered into the end. His left twitches uncontrollably, and his nails have grown into devastating claws.

"For your sake, you should have stayed dead. Now, we won't be so kind to leave you where you fall."

Merchant does a slow spin, his hands held up pas-sively as six others step out into a circle around him. That makes nine plus the dead one.

"Damn, where did those come from?" Merchant whispers to himself.

"Oh, this is going to be so much fun," Snake-Eyes giggles.

The ghost materializes beside Merchant's discarded bag and sits down. A box of popcorn resting on his crossed leg. He winks one of the eyes on his neck before popping a kernel into his mouth.

"Asshole," Merchant gets out before the two who watch the fire charge him.

He ducks forward and both men's momentums carry them past. Rising, he brings hand and broken desk leg up in an arc that shatters the jaw of the first who turns. Blood and teeth spin wildly into the air. Tumbling, the first hits the ground in time to watch the second swing widely and miss Merchant by a foot. Two quick jabs with the stick and a kneecap is popped and wood now juts through trachea and out the other side.

Merchant rips his weapon free, and a red fountain sprays across the snow. Thirst for blood and fresh meat overtakes the others. They attack in a frenzy, uncontrolled and in a mad rush that Merchant steps and slides through like water. One falls with a broken neck, another a skull that splits open from tip down through his nose. A red river flows its way down the Main Street. Another drops as she trips over the one with the broken jaw, unable to get up in time before Merchant's boot flattens her neck to the pavement.

"Roses are red, violets are blue," Snake-Eyes sings out.

One of the infected is able to get his arms around Merchant's body. He begins to squeeze, and Merchant can feel his ribs begin to crack.

"Oh, I wish you would stop playing and finish them, won't you."

Another rushes in, small blade in hand, the light of the fire reflecting off its surface. Merchant slams his boot down as hard as he can, and he feels the tiny bones of toes crush under his heel. A screech escapes the man's lips a moment before blood gushes out as his nose is crushed against the back of Merchant's skull. Spinning his weight, Merchant puts the infected in front of the knife that shoves forward to skewer him. Dark blood pools on the man's filthy shirt as two inches of shiv stick out through the man's liver.

Merchant slaps down on the blade and feels the tissue rip as the monster's guts spill out. With a kick, he sends the dead man tumbling backward into the one behind, and they both hit the ground.

Exploding pain erupts through Merchant's back as he is thrown to the ground. Fire races through his skin when he turns onto his back. Blood drips from the rusty nails while the tall one slowly approaches.

"A tough one, aren't you?"

He taps the end of his weapon in his hand.

"Fuck, I'm going to enjoy this," the man says as he lifts the bat over his head.

Red embers and yellow sparks kick up into the air around the infected's face. Merchant rolls out of the way, flaming log of wood in his hand as the bat cracks into the frozen ground inches from his body. Rolling back to his feet, fire and smoke swing out and crack the side of a woman's face, and her voice sings a shrill song into the night. He finishes her off with a kick to the face that spins her neck like a top, and now the tall one is all that stands.

Merchant stretches his back, and his joints *pop*. He

can feel the blood dripping down his skin, and the steam that rises from his body.

"I told you I only wanted what was mine," he says.

"That one there really isn't listening," Snake-Eyes adds.

A wicked smile stretches across the infected man's face. Blood trickles between his teeth and blisters pop where the skin and scales of his face are burned. Lifting the bat over his head, he lets out a scream like an animal gone wild a moment before the side of his head explodes in a gory, slush-filled mess. His body flops to the ground like an empty sack, and his blood begins to pool with the others.

"God damn, that took long enough. Though, I'm mightily impressed you could do that with only a broken piece of furniture," a young female voice calls out.

"Now, this keeps getting better," Snake-Eyes says as he wipes his hand over his head to smooth out his hair.

Merchant turns to the alley across the way, the flames of the bonfire separating him and the one who approaches. Snake-Eyes glides over to his side.

"Maybe these infected aren't as bad as we thought," Snake-Eyes whispers.

Merchant has no words as the stranger steps out from the shadows and points the pistol at his head.

Chapter 7

Warmth and softness.

Trickling water and the smell of soap.

This must be a dream.

Eyes flutter open. The pain of bruises comes to life as the searing light of a single light bulb sways above her.

"Shhh, don't move. It won't hurt as much if you don't move," a soothing voice whispers.

A damp cloth is placed on her forehead, and her eyes grow heavy. She lets them close and feels the stress of her body fades. More water is splashed and another wet compress is placed over her arm. A warmth spreads through her shoulder, which is quickly pushed away by a sharpness that sets her heart racing.

Eyes burst open at the pain, which quickly numbs as fast as it arrived. Pale blue eyes look down at her, a smile like a child warms the face that watches her from above. Soft brown hair spills gently over the young woman's face. Beautiful and simple.

Confused, she pushes herself up and the world spins in her mind. Stomach lurching, she falls to her side and dry heaves, but nothing comes out.

"Please, don't move so fast. You need to rest or you'll never heal," the young girl says.

Delicate hands grip her arms gently and try to pull her back down. Resisting, she slides away.

"Where am I? Who are you?"

The girl slides forward and places a reassuring hand onto her knee. The touch is soft and reminds her of a mother who left her years ago.

"My name is Alexis. We are in the birthing ward," the girl answers. "You were brought here after you were attacked in the judging circle. Usually, they don't bring you here after such an ordeal, but you were bleeding badly, and the Father's Chosen wouldn't take no for an answer."

"Father's Chosen? Birthing ward? What the fuck is going on around here?"

She tries to push this girl, Alexis, away, but she doesn't have the strength. For the first time, she notices the tubes running from her arms up to IV bags and the beeping of a heart monitor that is now racing with the thoughts that spin in her mind. There are so many questions, and she can barely keep up.

"Yes, he was our Savior's first child and greatest triumph. You are blessed that he sees you in such favor," Alexis continues.

"I can barely remember anything. One of them bit me, and then…then I was pulled out of the cage. He started choking me, his fingers were ripping through my throat."

"That is him. All the strengths of the gods were given when he was born to this cursed world. He did it to protect you," the girl says. "Once you were asleep, he punished those who hurt you, and then brought you here so we could help you get your strength back."

"Brought me here? Wait a minute. You think I'm going to be staying?"

Frantically, though her movements feel sluggish, she tries to rip the tubes taped to her arm. Soft, gentle hands quickly seize like iron, and she can't find the strength to fight them. Everything swims around her as if the air was really water. She is suddenly dizzy, and the urge to lay down is overwhelming.

"Just let me go. Give me a jacket and any food you can spare. I won't tell anyone, and I'll be gone before anyone notices."

The young girl places her warm fingers to her lips to stop her from talking.

"Please, slow down. You are still hurt. Take a moment and catch your breath. First, tell me your name, and I will fill you in on where you are and what is happening."

She looks around the room. They are alone other than a row of a dozen empty beds.

A hospital ward.

Clear IV stations run down to the vacant slots, and a dozen machines blink red and green lights.

"My name? It's Elizabeth," she answers.

The air in the room is suddenly warmer than she has felt in weeks, but it still sends a shiver down her spine. She feels like she is beginning to sweat. Her stomach turns, and an acid burp forces its way through her mouth. Alexis smiles, her light-colored eyes closing as the dimples in her chin spread and her brown hair falls around her face.

"Well, Elizabeth, it is nice to meet you. I want to be the first to welcome you to the city of Resurrection."

A pale arm stretches out and displays the empty

room as if it was a higher-class mansion.

"The city of Resurrection?" Elizabeth asks.

"Yes, our father has chosen this sacred place to start the world again." Alexis nods her head as the words are recited as if they were at church. "The prophecies told us of the coming of the apocalypse. God came to Earth, and in his graces, has chosen those of us here worthy of being his new flock. He even bore a new son for us, to lead us through the darkest days ahead."

"That freak of a man? That is God's chosen son?"

Short hair bobs up and down enthusiastically, the pale eyes lost behind a mass of loose strands.

"And by judging his current actions, I think you are something special in his eyes. I've never seen him take such interest in anyone, especially a stray from outside the city."

"A stray? Like a dog? Thanks, I think," Elizabeth says.

Alexis smiles genuinely and begins to pull her back to where she can lay down on the bed.

"Sleep now. You need more rest. Your wounds need time or the infection will spread."

"Infection?" Elizabeth shoves the girl away, her heart pounding and the drugs clearing from her mind.

She reaches for the dressing on her shoulder. The white gauze has the slightest of pink hue where the blood is soaking through.

"No, don't touch that!" Alexis orders. "There is no infection here. At least not like the kind that killed our world."

Elizabeth looks the young girl deep in her eyes. Breathing heavily, she realizes how hard it is becoming to catch her breath.

"You are one of the lucky ones, Elizabeth. The curse of this world has not touched you. Your wounds were savage, but our master's medicines are strong. You need time to heal. Now rest."

A soft pillow comforts her as she lays back down. The young girl raises her hand and turns a knob on the IV drip. She can see it begin to feed the medicine faster. Shadows from the darkest corners of the room fill around her. Alexis is talking, but the words are slurred, and Elizabeth does not understand them.

The light that swings over her bed is all that she can see.

Left.

Right.

Left.

Darkness.

* * *

Sleep breaks easily with the warmth of the morning sun. Golden rays, filtering through glass, shine into the room, the glorious light spilling across the empty beds. White sheets tuck in tightly with single pillows waiting for needy heads.

Elizabeth pushes herself up until she is seated. There is no pain. A little tightness pinches her joints, but the stiffness slips quickly away. There is no one else in the room. Running her hands down her arms, she feels the bandage that holds her shoulder tight, and the cloth is clean and fresh. A single IV runs into her hand, and the heart monitor next to her bed is on, but registers a flat green line as the green and red dials blink like those at the empty beds.

Pulling the covers away from her legs, she is happy to see she isn't bound, and slipping over the edge, ice cold tiles send shocks through her legs that threaten to spill her to the ground. Catching herself, she now feels how cold it is and pulls the blanket from the bed, white and fresh like all the others, and wraps it around herself.

Where is Alexis?

She realizes she misses the young girl standing alone in the empty room, her shadow her only companion. It is a strange feeling. Having been a loner for such a long time, that young girl is the first person to show her any kind of concern.

Maybe it's the drugs that are softening her edge.

Yes, it must be the drugs.

She shrugs the blanket higher and lifts her chin. There is no time for softness.

Bare feet tap cautiously against cold tile as she slips past the beds. A sharp pinch spins her and a few drops of blood splatter to the ground. The needle from the IV recoils across the floor.

"Damn it!" she swears, and grabbing a roll of gauze sitting beside a vacant slot, she quickly wraps her hand.

The door below the unlit exit sign is not locked, the window looking into the hall is too high for her to look through. Pressing her ear against the cold steel frame, she can't hear anyone out in the hall. The hinges make very little noise as she pushes her way into the hallway. Someone has been sure to keep this place working.

She is alone in the sterile tunnel. Left or right, she has no idea which way to go.

Reluctant to stop, she turns to the right and continues on.

Bright white walls line the path that is filled with dark, empty rooms all around her. Vacant chairs with single tables lay out like scattered islands. Waiting areas for families desperate for good news on the condition of family members who knock on death's door. She hasn't seen a working hospital like this in years. Memories flood her mind of them being overcrowded, the dead and injured laying in the halls, bleeding and spreading an infection that would kill the vast majority of them. All of that was after the devastating wars that tore this country apart, and if the reports she had heard were correct, the entire world fell apart with it. Deaths from bombs and poisons were in the millions. Those who survived this country's darkest days were vulnerable when the infection attacked.

No one stops her when she reaches the end of the hall. An L-shaped reception desk with a chair and unpowered computer sit empty. File cabinets are open, but there are no papers in them. The arms on the clock say 3:15, but she has no way of telling if it's am or pm and the second hand isn't moving anyway. Rummaging through the desk, she looks for anything sharp. A knife. A pair of scissors. A set of god-damn keys that she can use if they find her. There is nothing but a pencil. The point is dull, still able to write, but dull.

She grabs it anyway and tucks it between fingers that hold her blanket around her. Cold air pricks at her skin. Not freezing, but chilled and empty. As if she is the only person left in the world.

Moving, there is a stairwell at the end of the hall, the exit sign pointing at it with a big red, shiny arrow. It's not like they won't expect her to go that way. Reluctantly, she has no other option and follows where the instructions tell her to go.

Three levels down and the stairwell ends. She can hear voices now. Dozens of them. Talking, arguing, and laughing. If she closes her eyes, pushes away all memories of the bad things that have happened in this world, she can imagine what she knows of the world has only been a nightmare. Standing in an empty stairwell, with nothing but a medical gown and blanket, quickly helps her forget that crazy idea.

It must be the drugs. Really, it must be.

Crouching against the chilly concrete wall, there is a window ahead. Light filters in through dust and grime, not as strong as what came into her room, but at least it is something. Slowly, cautiously, she presses forward and takes a look outside. People are everywhere. Men, women, and even some children are heading in all directions. Each of them moves without a care in the world. Carrying boxes or sacks from one location to another as if the world had not ended in the twenty-first century but stopped and thrived in the nineteenth. Some people were pulling carts. Others working on food.

Real food!

Where is she? What year is this?

Elizabeth's stomach growls. Her mouth fills with saliva. She can see potatoes and other vegetables piled into wicker baskets. Fresh meat hangs from hooks, and buckets below are filled with the remains of the red work and sticky feathers.

How?

None of this can be possible.

"But it is real," a man's voice says as if reading her mind.

Elizabeth doesn't think, she spins, releasing her blanket she shoves the pencil out like a single-handed spear toward the source of the intrusion.

An iron like grip snatches her wrist long before the simple weapon can reach flesh. He stands in front of her, towering as he looks down at her. She tries to tear her arm free, but he holds it in place like he would a child's feeble attempts.

"Who are you?" she demands.

He smiles as he looks her over from head to toe. Dark hair, trimmed evenly, sits spotlessly over a tanned complexion. He's young, but not too young. The slightest of age lines extend from his bright eyes, which are filled with hunger and the darkest brown she has ever seen. Almost black as she tries to recoil away, but he won't let her go. A smile reveals a mouth of freshly white teeth and wordlessly he tells her he likes what he sees.

Giving no care for modesty, she swings with her other arm, but it is weak and slow. Her shoulder still tight beneath the bandage, he lazily wraps his hand around her second arm.

"Now, there is no reason to be so violent," he says.

She tries to pull away, but she can't. A soft stream of air picks up through the hall and pulls her medical gown away from her body and shivers prickle the skin of her bare back. The smile on his face grows wider.

Anger boils in her blood.

"Let me go, you bastard!"

"If you promise me you aren't going to try and kill me again with this pencil," he answers while lessening the pressure on her wrists. "You do realize how painful of a death that would be?"

"Then don't startle me like that again. Who the fuck are you, anyway?"

He lets go of her arms, and she quickly picks her blanket up and wraps it around her body, looping the top above her breasts so that she doesn't have to hold it so much with her hands, leaving them free to hold the pencil he never took away.

"Such violent tendencies, and that language. We'll have to work on that," he answers while tapping one long finger on his lower lip. "The name I was born with no longer matters. Who I am and what I mean to my people is the only important thing."

"And that is?"

She takes a step back from the man, his attention drawn to the window overlooking everyone that is outside.

"I am their father. Correction, I am everyone's father. These are my people, living and working together to bring this world back from the brink of extinction. To give what was promised to you all a millennium ago."

Ignoring her scowl and the pathetic weapon she still holds before her, he steps around her and takes a closer look at the window.

"Well, my father was a dead-beat drunk who like to beat my mom," Elizabeth says.

He turns to her, his smile now a slight frown as he glances once more at the pencil that shakes in her hand.

"And where is he now?"

"Pile of bones somewhere in Oregon I suppose."

"Infection?" he asks.

"Nope."

"The war?"

His face looks genuinely concerned.

"A steak knife through the back of his skull after he spent a night beating the shit out of my mom," she answers, and the grip on her pencil tightens until the skin of her knuckles are white.

"Let me guess, you aren't sorry you did it?"

A smile now finds its way across her face.

"I'm still alive. There is very little I'm sorry for."

"Pity," the man says while turning back to the window. "So much violence steals away your soul, piece by piece until nothing of what you once were remains."

"Shut the fuck up and tell me where we are."

"Do you remember, Elizabeth? Do you remember a time when you weren't so angry and violent?"

She takes a step back, and then eyes the stairwell. He couldn't stop her if she turned and ran, but where would she go?

"How…how do you know my name?"

His hands are behind his back, and he smiles, the whites of his eyes a brightness against the gloom, and his pupils as dark as the pits of Hell.

"I know all my children, Elizabeth. We are glad to see you've made it home."

Chapter 8

Five Years Ago

The rain is thinning. More mist and fog than droplets as Merchant enters the camp. Mud splashes beneath his boots and the grit of wet, heavy dirt squishes between his toes. Water runs down his forehead, stinging his eyes before continuing down his cheeks. He likes the feeling. It reminds him he is alive.

Part of him can't believe he is *actually* alive.

The small encampment is deserted. Shadows stretch weakly across the flooded ground from the gray light struggling to find its way through the lingering storm. He should feel cold with water dripping from his bare chest and shoulders while the approaching night cools the air, but none of it sinks in. He is on fire. His anger fuels him. He can walk forward, numb, but more alive than he has ever been.

Trash lays scattered, floating across the oily surface of tiny rivers. Crumbled bags and discarded wrappers. A single pair of boots drowns in a pool of dark water against a metal garbage can, scarred with soot from fire before someone put half a dozen bullet holes through the side.

Guard posts made of chairs sitting behind sandbags sit empty and deserted. Rusted chain link fence winds its way through trees soaked and heavy with water. The gate sits open, its arms thrown wide and welcoming.

Where did they run off to so fast?

Merchant heads straight for the central pavilion. The all too familiar sound of water dripping on an aluminum roof begins to call him home.

Tap.

Tap.

Tap.

His heart begins to race. He knows if he finds them, they will be there. What will they think when they see him walk right back into the middle of their realm of torture and treason? Come back from the dead, they'll scream. He'll be lucky if they don't shit their pants and run. A smile crosses his face, and he can taste the storm in the air. Putrid and rotten. The taste is unforgettable. Death lingers here thicker than the ghosts of those who deserted this place like the plague. Sleeping chambers made of plyboard and welded aluminum are nothing more than empty shells as he walks past. Forest green and brown rust, they blend in with the surroundings so well that Mother Nature will have to do very little to reclaim this as her own.

His steps echo through the constant hum of the fading rain.

Tap.

Tap.

Tap.

Merchant begins to slow. He stops at the crossroads of the camp. A breeze ripples through the trees, the leaves rustling and the torn American flag that sits high above the pavilion struggles to move its saturated body. Death, its very touch tickles the skin behind his shoulders. He cannot shake the feeling. There is something wrong here. Beyond what they did to him. He is not alone.

Sniffing the air, the stench suffocates him. Off to his left, beyond the pavilion, is where it is the strongest. Cautiously, he continues. Those he searches for temporarily forgotten, he cannot shake the feeling he needs to find his answer.

Wooden tables and benches are scattered around the only dry earth within the compound. Rats dart back and forth, hiding beneath the broken pieces, avoiding his movements and fighting over their next meal. The smell is stronger here.

Rotting food would smell sweeter than this. Even the rats do not seem to want to follow him. No, this smell is too much like shit. A steaming pile of human dung, left out to rot and fester in the rain. He is not far off.

Deep inside, he wants to vomit, hurl up anything that remains within him, but there is nothing left. Bodies are piled and exposed. Pieces drain into a hole where skin is gray and bones stick out bright white with marrow picked clean by birds. There are more than fifty soldiers shredded in death, disposed of worse than the trash his former team carried out with them.

This was the remnants of the battle he had heard. Whomever it was that attacked, they had been slaughtered to the man. Stripped naked, they didn't even bother with a simple burial.

A growl warns him as he takes a step closer. Reflecting eyes peer out beneath a pair of narrowed brows. Fangs are bared, and a dark red muzzle hovers close to the ground. The true feeding has begun.

Merchant lifts his hands in a show of indifference and slowly backs away. There are more of them out there. He can see their glares at the intruder who dares to step near the prize they claim. On practiced heels, he spins and makes his way back to the crossroad.

These were not the men he had fought with, bled with, and cried with. He has done many bad things in his life, most of them he regrets, but something has changed them. It's one thing to torture and split a man in half. Lie to him at the moment of his death about taking his wife and family away because you thought he has betrayed you. True or not, there was an accepted code for those who betray the men who fight and die beside you. They had all been professionals. This is sloppy. This is cruel. Soldiers respect those they fight. On different sides, they all fight for similar beliefs, but only of their own making.

Someone is teaching them hatred, and it is beginning to rot them from the inside.

Reaching the far end of their camp, Merchant can see what they used to call their barracks. A simple one room structure, the tiled roof is caving in and the front door is collapsing onto the ground. Black scorch marks show signs where someone has tried to burn it down, but the storm has thwarted their efforts.

Stepping closer, Merchant can see there is nothing left for him to salvage. Beds are piles of ash and warped springs. Storage lockers are nothing but broken pieces, the personal memories they held washed away with the flooding water or taken as the men moved on.

He shoves his way inside. His bed is always near the entrance. From the day he enlisted, he always sleeps near the door in and out. Stepping sideways, he keeps himself next to the wall. The roof seems strongest here, and he can see the last ten feet until he reaches the simple place he called home.

The floor has buckled, the walls bubbling where the heat was the hottest. Did they start the fire directly on top of his bed? Anger flares inside of him, and he shoves the cracked skeleton of his bunk as far as it will skid across the floor. Ash kicks up in to the air, and the wreckage tumbles as it stops near the center of the room.

Breath comes in large gulps as the urge to slam his fist through the wall threatens to overtake him. He wants to hurt someone, strangle them with his bare hands, but he is alone. Walking through the world as silent as the distant past, he is the only person left to hear or feel his pain. Looking around, the rage quickly begins to spill into desperation. What is he going to do now? He doesn't even know where they will report to next.

Kicking at the ash and pieces of fallen boards, the tip of his toe catches on a piece of canvas and pulls it free. A green Army bag somehow survived the arson. Merchant crouches down and begins to wipe it clean. One of the straps is broken, and the strong smell of fire clings to it like a perfume, but regardless, it is still functional.

"There is still more that you want to do," the woman's voice startles him.

Merchant skids a few feet away, and the roof above his head begins to *creak*. His hands are up defensively, but he now feels foolish as she stands before him.

She is more than a head shorter than he is now. Her dark skin somehow still bright in the gloom of the death and destruction that surrounds him. Her skintight miniskirt still hugs her curves, and her smile broadens as she catches his eyes roaming.

"Go now. Search for what you must and do what you know is needed. I will give you this time, but when you are done, I have a task for you."

Merchant puts his hands to his sides, the Army bag tapping against his leg as it drags itself through the ashes.

"And what must I do?" he asks.

Her smile becomes mischievous, and she turns away.

"Only you know what you have to do for yourself. As for me? I will tell you in time."

He watches her go. Not because her ass sways back and forth, one hip lifting after the other, but because deep down, he does know what he needs to do. He is going to have to walk a long way to get there, but it is time for him to go home.

* * *

The fire is warm, melting the snow in a three-foot circle around the pit and replacing it with dark slush that sticks like red mud. Blood streaks across the snow-covered streets, dark stains that stretch from the large black crater of quickly freezing gore to one of the furthest alleyways still marginally lit by the raging flames. Fresh wood has replaced old tires, and the stench of scolding rubber is replaced with a slight taste of oak and wood polish. Snow continues to fall, an unending layer of new skin replacing itself across the crust of America's wasteland.

Big fat flakes land on Merchant's arms and quickly melt into droplets of water as he sits by the fire. He can feel the warmth seeping into his body, but he doesn't need it. He is always warm. An internal fire rages within him that is fueled by his need to continue west.

"So how did you do it?" Cherry Red asks.

That is what she calls herself, Cherry Red.

Merchant looks up from the scars that run like deserted highways across his dark skin. Stretches of white that crisscross and travel clear across the terrain of his body. He ignores her at first, staring up at the empty buildings that close in around them. Their empty faces dance white in the flames, siding, brick, and mortar covered in grime and salt from years of abandonment.

"How do I do what?" Merchant asks, turning back to the only other living person in the entire town.

Cherry flips a few loose strands of red curls away from her eyes. She is surprisingly clean for an infected, the scales like the others ravaging the left side of her body and leaving the right unaffected. Scars and flakes crack across her neck, but the skin of both her cheeks is still soft and pink within the firelight.

The important end of her revolver taps on her knee, pointed at his gut from where she sits a few feet to his right.

"You stroll in here as if this isn't some deserted town full of monsters, and then you ask for your bag back."

Merchant shrugs his shoulders.

"It belongs to me. I wanted it back."

A small chuckle escapes her lips.

"Just like that, you wanted it back. I'll be damned. If I didn't see it with my own eyes, I'd swear you were as crazy as the others."

Merchant tilts his head, showing her that she now finally has his full attention.

"Others?"

"See, I knew there was another reason you were out here," she says.

Her smile stretches across her face. Droplets of puss leak out from the scales on her neck, and she slaps her empty hand against her knee. She all but jumps for joy before turning until she is seated and looking directly at him.

"You are out here for them, aren't you?"

She places her pistol on the ground by her leg, then both hands are steepled against her lips and her elbows pitch a tent on her knees.

"Who is *them*?"

Snake-Eyes materializes beside Merchant. The ghost sits down, stretches his legs, and begins to warm his hands near the fire.

"Damn, I had so much hope for this one. She is one fine piece of ass if you can get past the lizard scales," the dead man says.

Merchant fights the urge to slap him.

"That man-god and his useless sheep. They took your girl. I thought maybe now that you had your stuff you'd go looking for her."

"Man-god? They are the ones who took the woman

I was with? How do you know all this?" Merchant asks, his voice beginning to growl.

Cherry scoots back several inches and eyes the shadows that prowl around them. The tips of her fingers trace over the grip of her pistol.

"Look, it was never my idea. Hectar was the brains of this operation, and the man-god pays really good. This time, he gave us enough food for a month."

Her attention turns to a building two alleyways down. It's a broken-down gas station, the pumps fallen over and the canopy caved in, but the entrance looks still in place.

Merchant has had enough.

"What did he pay you for? How am I involved with this?"

The young woman sighs.

"His men pay those they consider undesirable to round up any non-infected we can find. They particularly like women, but men will do."

"Undesirable?"

"Rejects of their community or those who aren't completely infected."

She runs her hand over the scales on her neck. Noticing the puss on her fingertips, she wipes them clean on the leg of her pants.

"Why didn't you take me and sell me as well?"

The girl bites her lower lip.

"You fought back harder than anyone we have ever found. I thought you were going to kill us all until Hectar cracked you upside the head with a tree branch. Broke the damn thing on your back as well. We all thought you were dead," she answers, and then shrugs.

"We don't get paid for dead ones. Only those alive and uninfected."

Wood *crackles* and spits embers into the sky. Snake-eyes jumps up and tries to catch one with his tongue, but the searing piece glides right through him and down to the ground.

"Damnit," he shouts, but no one except Merchant can hear him.

"This man-god, what does he do with these people?"

With this question, she turns her attention back to the shadows. Scooting to the side, she is no longer looking at him, and her arms are wrapped around her body as if a sudden chill has overcome her.

Merchant decides to wait her out. He turns back to the fire. The flames dance red and yellow, tiny demons leaping from dark, broken pieces of wood grayed with ash and bright against the coals.

"He's building an army," she whispers.

"An army?" Merchant asks.

"Oh, this can't be good for you," Snake-eyes giggles. "I like it already."

"Yes, an army," she spits out. "The man is crazier than the infected themselves. He says he is God returned and is going to lead the people back from the brink of Hell."

"How does he plan to do that?"

She turns, and the anger burning in her eyes is brighter than the hottest coal.

"By creating people like me, but not failures. Monsters with the strength of ten men and obedient to the death."

Tears fall down her cheeks, and she drops her chin onto her risen knees.

"Creating people like you?"

Merchant looks over at Snake-eyes, who shrugs, and the eyes on his neck continue to blink.

"Yes, people like me. Do you think I was born like this?" She spits at him, her venom melting the snow between them. "I was pretty once, you know. Uninfected. I had men groveling at my feet, even out here in this wasteland. It was just my brother and I, ruling the world until the man-god arrived."

Her hand is back on the revolver, and she stares blankly into the firelight.

"Then what happened?"

"He lied. He lied to us all. Told us he was some savior, and through him we would all be saved." She wipes away the tears flowing freely down her cheeks. "And we fucking believed him. Had this medicine. Told us it would make us immune to the disease that killed this world. Give us the ability to finally be born into the mold that God had foreseen for us. Fucking liar."

"His medicine gave you the infection?" Merchant asks.

"So, people are manufacturing infected now?" Snake-Eyes adds, but no one cares.

"That's why he threw us out. It is supposed to stop after a day or two. Men and women heal ten times stronger than they were before. We could go days without eating, and the cold or heat does little to us."

"But?"

"Some of us, like my brother and I, the infection didn't stop. It is much slower than those who catch in naturally, but eventually, it takes you over."

"Where is your brother?" Merchant asks with a quick glance to the trail of blood that leads off into the shadows.

"He's not here. The infection took him too quickly. Hectar wanted to kill him the moment we noticed, but I got him out quietly."

"But you stayed," Merchant adds.

"Strength in numbers, you know. A woman needs to eat. Needs a safe place to sleep."

Both of them draw quiet as the fire continues to *crackle* and keep the storm at bay. Wind rustles down Main Street, a howl that reminds them they are alone in this world.

"The infection doesn't seem to be spreading for you any longer," Merchant says, his attention lost to the shadows of the town.

"It is slow, but still spreading," Cherry Red says. "A month ago, it was only on my leg and stomach. Now, it is all the way up my neck. I'll be lost soon, like my brother. Should have killed him when I had the chance. Would have been better off."

"She has that part right," Snake-Eyes says.

The ghost has himself spread around the fire, comfortably laying on the ground with his sights on the darkness above.

"You know, if you close your eyes, you could probably have her tonight. One of those, quick bangs and leave her. She'd probably enjoy it until she loses her mind," the ghost adds.

Merchant glares at him.

"Hey, I'm only saying what you are thinking, and I swear, I won't watch."

Merchant turns back to the fire, hoping for silence.

"Only for a few minutes, I swear," Snake-Eyes says, almost pleading.

"You know where this man-god and his people are?" Merchant asks, shifting toward the young woman so the ghost is no longer in his sight.

"Going after her, aren't you? I knew you had those crazy eyes," she says, a small smile returning to her face below cheeks as red as her name.

"It doesn't matter what I'm doing. Do you know where they are?"

"Maybe I do, maybe I don't. What is in it for me?"

Merchant sighs and turns back to the flames. Silence hangs like a dead man's weight between them.

"Okay, maybe I do know where you can find them, but I want something in return."

"Here we go, this girl likes playing with fire!" Snake-Eyes shouts.

He's on his feet and dancing a jig that is a cross between a drunk man and the swaying of a starving dog.

"Keep your requests," Merchant says with a wave of the back of his hand. "I have enough burdens to carry."

"Look, you want to get that girl back, I can lead you right to their front door. Without me, you'll be traveling west until you find yourself a mile into the sky, and you'll never see an inch of her."

Eyes glaring, Merchant turns back to her.

"See, you do want her. Do one thing for me, and she is all yours. Well, at least where she is."

"Here it comes," Snake-Eyes says.

"What do you want?"

"Do what I wasn't capable of. Kill my brother."

The joyous screams of the ghost as he dances around the fire are lost as the wind picks up and roars through the small town. Growling with thunder, the storm continues and Merchant turns back to the flames and wraps his hand tighter around the lone strap of his bag.

Chapter 9

Firelight crackles in the wind, the flames whipping back and forth. Tiny embers, orange and bright, lift into the air, floating on the wind as the wood *crackles* and spits. Bonfires scatter themselves along the main thruway of the small village, the smell of fire and fresh wood becoming an incense in the night. They are beacons of light with people huddled around for warmth and companionship. Ten to twenty people with smiles and happiness as fake as their safety.

Songs full of joy lift into the night sky. Like a practiced ensemble, the people of the town pick up the merriment. Women, men, and children alike, add their voices to the chorus. The sound is soft, harmonious, and yet gut-wrenching at the same time. Elizabeth scowls as the words form a crackle in her ears.

Alexis calls them all families, Elizabeth thinks they are full of shit. Resting in the shadows, she watches and waits for the inevitable to come in and wash them all away in a tide of misery. That is all that is left in this world. It is not a matter of if, but when.

Cold works its way in through fabric and anger. Biting into her skin where she stands against the corner of one of the empty buildings that is both within the flickering light of the fires but still hidden within the shadows. She watches from the sidelines like a child who refuses to be a part of the team. She can feel the heat from where she stands, enough to tempt her skin and send thoughts of comfort to her mind, but the brisk air at her back reminds her this is all an illusion. She cannot forget that.

The sky is clear, black, and full of stars. Moonlight shines like a second sun high above the eastern horizon, a blinding white as cold as the winter air. Shadows ten feet tall stretch below their feet, dark watchers who follow their every move. Bitter air fights with the warmth of fire. Elizabeth wraps the thin white shawl she wears tighter around her body and allows the solid frame of the house to take more of her weight. Made of cotton and hand sewn, the garment comforts the skin of her neck and helps with the stiffness of her shoulder that has yet to loosen. The remainder of her attire is borrowed as well. Loose fitting denim jeans and a thick sweatshirt made of some of the warmest material she has ever worn. The gift was a nice gesture. It hurt when she had to say so, but she knows sometimes a little pain is worth it.

A dog barks.

A rangy mutt with mismatched wiry hair and a blind right eye as white as the snow, jumps back and forth between fire pits. Its tail wags as it runs between the separated communities. Children giggle at the animal's antics and a few now chase it. Adults, presumably their parents, smile but keep a watchful eye as the young ones dart in and out of the shadows.

"This is a little piece of Heaven here on Earth, isn't

it?" Alexis asks.

Elizabeth startles and jumps away from where she is standing. Alexis' slender form steps out from behind the shadows of an open door. She wears a shawl like Elizabeth does, but hers is green, and the loose threads tell of a good amount of use. The sign overhead says Attorneys at Law in faded gold letters, but there are no lawyers here.

"Damnit, don't do that again," Elizabeth says.

The young girl smiles with a small bite of her lower lip and nods her head.

"This place is Heaven on Earth, isn't it," Alexis repeats.

"Heaven? Hell? What's the difference? If you ask me, I would say you are no freer than those assholes who lock themselves up in the cities," Elizabeth answers.

A gust of wind picks up, a sparkling of snow chilling the skin of her cheeks and her arms where the shawl is spread too thin. Paper scatters down the street, the people of the community huddling beneath thick winter clothing against the sudden intrusion. The song of the clueless begins to fade, and the million voices of the individual pick up.

"But we are free here. We do not suffer behind walls of concrete and the rules of tyrants."

Elizabeth pulls her sweatshirt and shawl tighter and takes a step away from the building where she had thought herself finally alone.

"Tyrants come in many sizes and shapes. Don't let a wolf in sheep's clothes fool you, Alexis."

"How can you judge so harshly, and without reason to do so? Our father does nothing but offer salvation and a life of love and happiness. He built this place with his bare hands, and gives it to us freely," the young girl says before placing a gentle touch on Elizabeth's arm. "The infected fear us, for the wrath of God will show them no mercy. We thrive. We are happy. Can you not see that, Elizabeth?"

Pulling her arm away, Elizabeth looks from fire to fire. She counts at least half a dozen groups as delusional as the one who now torments her. Even if there was no moon this evening, there wouldn't be enough darkness to hide from anyone.

"What I see is an entire host of lost and confused people. The world isn't coming back. No matter how much you want to try and believe that. We all went to Hell and the devil has its claws in each of us. Last time I was dragged to church, they told me he wasn't one for letting go."

"I really hate to hear you talk like that, Elizabeth. It hurts me so," Alexis says. The soft touch of young fingers presses down on her arm again, and Elizabeth fights the urge to rip the hand clear from the girl's body. "You have to give it time. Your strength will return, and by then, you will see we are all one big family."

"I doubt that."

"Have faith in our father. He will show you the way. Until then, remember you are in his son's favor. You should know you are blessed."

Dread races through Elizabeth's veins like ice, stiffening the muscles within her chest as she looks out for any sign of him. He watches her even now from the shadows like a ghost that haunts her. They call him the Chosen. To her, he is a giant from the pits of hell.

"Go sit by the fire, Alexis. Find someone else who wants to hear the lies you tell yourself."

The young girl doesn't move, but she also no longer speaks. Elizabeth refuses to turn and see the girl's reaction. She can't make herself see what she has done.

Why does she care?

A small amount of the drugs must still be in her system. She has heard of the good ones that stay with you for a couple days. That must be it. They must have used the good ones.

Snow crunches beneath light footsteps. Alexis begins the slow walk toward the nearest fire, her hands clasped before her and her eyes to the ground at her feet. Elizabeth watches her go from the corner of her eye.

Good, the girl finally listens.

Salty water burns at the corner of Elizabeth's eyes now that she is finally alone. She refuses to wipe away the drops, instead, taking a deep breath to calm her nerves that are finally returning to their sharp edge. The naive girl can stay here with her people. Death will come for them all. It is inevitable, and Elizabeth won't be a part of it. Too bad she can't take her with her. She deserves better than this fake dream. All of them will learn eventually. Nothing is perfect. Nothing is permanent.

She'll miss her for a little once she is outside the perimeter of this home for loonies. At least until the drugs finally wash from her system. By sun up, she'll be nothing more than a memory lost to the wind. But first, she needs to find that freaking giant, then make sure he doesn't follow her on the way out.

* * *

Shoulders like soccer balls are stuffed forcefully beneath his shirt. Muscles ripple and stretch thin fabric over skin that is streaked with white scars. Bare arms bulge, and veins pop out even in shadow and firelight as the monster crosses his arms over his chest. The Chosen waits in front of the hospital she has been resting in for several nights. All the windows are dark, the building towering empty and lifeless in the light of torches and the distant bonfires.

The cold has a firmer grip here. Elizabeth can feel its harsh bite against her skin though she is more bundled now than she has been in months. She pulls the sweatshirt and shawl tighter around her shoulders. Looking at the man is enough to freeze her in place. What will happen if he finds her before she can get outside the perimeter? What happens if he finds her *after* she gets away?

Demonic shadows dance and sway against the empty building face. Sharp eyes and emotionless features watch the shadows, waiting for her to return. One foot rests against the wall, back pressed against the cold stone. He remains motionless like a stature.

She can no longer wait. Turning back down the alley from where she watches, she tries to slow her breathing as she moves through the darkness with practiced steps. They have given her freedom to move around all she wants since the day she rose from her bed. They see her becoming one of them, finding her place in their community. She has never been more at home than when she is alone. Never part of the crowd, the simple walls of this community choke her like a noose, and she cannot get away any faster.

Turning around the corner, she follows the distant light of torches that mark the perimeter. A simple fence keeps everyone here safe. That, and more than a dozen armed guards who are miniature versions of their father's favorite son. Infection marks their skin, but only in small blotches. The men and women do not act wild, nor are driven to feed or uncontrollable anger. Controlled and obedient to their master, they are dogs, waiting for their next treat. Thinking about how they follow in step, taking orders without question sends disgust down into her belly and feeds the anger within.

She is her own woman. Nothing will take that from her. She would rather die out there. Exposure and infected can take her. This choice is hers, and she will make it.

Singing grows stronger as she slips from the alley and follows the edge of Main Street. There is only one exit through the fence without a set of wire cutters or hands that can rip through metal. She has neither, so pulling the shawl over her head, she tucks her hair beneath and continues away from the light and moves deeper into the darkness.

Two guards wait by the front gate. Rifles leaning against the chain links, they rock their chairs back and do not look her way. The music is a low hum in the background now. Wind whips over the snow, lifting waves of razor sharp ice. Mother Nature rules outside these walls. Inside these people feel protected, separated by what awaits them in the end. Elizabeth pulls the shawl tight across her mouth. Her eyes sting beneath the wind, but she has felt worse. She will always feel worse.

The soft steps of her shoes *crunch* the snow. Like a siren going off in her mind, she swears to herself with every step. Any moment, the men will hear her and turn before she has a chance to close the distance. Inside the sleeve of her right arm, she can feel the small knife she stole from the butcher earlier in the morning. A portly woman, she looks older than she is and, to be honest, her interaction with the chickens and hogs she kills is better than what she allows for those who depend on her work.

Rip-roaring mad, she'll tear the town in half the minute she notices what Elizabeth has taken, but that is for another time and will be several miles in the past if Elizabeth can only find a way through this gate.

Less than a hundred feet separate her from freedom. Both men sit silently with their backs to her. One on each side of the gate. They barely move, though the air here is a dozen degrees colder than it is by the fires. Thick jackets of fur and leather wrap their shoulders and torsos while denim jeans cover their legs. Dark boots tap to the soft rhythm that carries this far and white puffs of smoke lift into the air illuminated by torches burning in brands wrapped in razor wire above their heads.

Twins, if she didn't know better. They move in sync with one another. Now less than fifty feet sits between her and them.

The knife shifts its way from the tender skin of her wrist to where it now sits wrapped by her fingers, squeezing until her knuckles are white beneath the sleeve of her shirt. The first will go down quickly if she can get just a little closer. Her heart is pounding, and she can feel the sweat itching the skin of her scalp beneath the fabric of her shawl. Her lungs burn from the strain of holding her breath.

Close now.

Scales of infection wrap around the back of the red right ear of the man on the left. No hair pokes out from beneath a fluffy winter cap, while the one on the right is a few shades darker but still red with cold. Longer brown hair ruffles in the breeze where it breaks for freedom from the cap stretched over his skull.

Ten feet away, and her hands are as cold as ice. She'll have one shot at this. Quick thrust through the base of the skull and the first will drop without being able to get a word out.

Confusion.

That will be the only thing that will save her. If there is a god in this world, she needs him now. They have yet to notice her approach. She slinks into the shadows, trying to calm her breath and work her muscles for the strike. Once the first is down she will need to pounce like a cat on top of the other. He'll probably call for help, maybe even scream, but she'll cut his throat out as fast as she can. He'll die from his wounds, probably fast, but it won't matter to her. She'll already be on the run. Rifle in hand, she'll be lost to the wastelands before any of the others catch on and can follow her tracks.

They probably won't even try.

Confidence as high as it will ever be, she moves forward with purpose and on as quiet toes as she can produce.

Five feet now.

The man's scaly neck sticks out like a 'come stab me' sign, and she lets the blade inch out into the world. They still do not notice her. So much for being guards.

"How are you doing tonight, beautiful?" the guard closest to her asks.

Neither man move. She is frozen in place.

"Gets mighty cold this far away from the fires. You sure you aren't lost?" he continues.

Anger and fury loosens the chains that bind her.

Driving forward she screams and shoves the knife forward, killing edge aiming for his spine.

In movement lost in a blur, the man spins and the attack misses harmlessly over his shoulder. A stiff leg kicks out, and her feet are swept from beneath her. Firelight and darkness spin before her as the frozen ground races to catch her.

"Umph," she moans as the hard earth beats the bones between her shoulders.

The first man is on top of her now. Iron grip squeezing her wrist.

Pain and fire races through her arms. She can feel the bones begin to crack.

"Bitch is trying to stab me in the back."

Her hand shatters like ice as he drives it into the ground, and the blade skitters away.

The second guard watches from above. Smiling with eyes as dark as the night sky.

"Let go of me, you stupid fuck!" Elizabeth screams.

Lightning flashes across her face as the one who pins her down backhands her.

"Stupid fuck? Who's the stupid cunt who tried to

walk up behind me in clear sight and stick a knife down my back, huh?" the guard mocks.

His weight is crushing the breath out of her. She tries to shift and kick, but his grip tightens on her arms, and he pins her legs down with knees that are driving into her thighs like blades.

"Let me go!" Elizabeth orders.

Both men laugh.

"Oh, we'll let you go," the one on top of her says. He looks up at the other guard and winks. The second one sneers and nods his head in agreement. "But first, we are going to have to teach you a lesson for what you tried."

He squeezes her arms harder and pain erupts up through her shoulders. She goes to scream but another backhand snuffs out the words.

Thick meaty fingers are now covering her mouth. She can taste the dirt, the sweat, the infection. Nails scratch at the skin of her belly as her sweatshirt and undershirt are pulled up into a ball. Thick legs drive down into the pavement, stretching her legs apart as far as they will go.

She tries to scream, but her words are muffled. Her heart races, and she bites down until she tastes blood on her tongue. A look of pain pinches the man's face, but he won't be deterred. Fabric begins to stretch as the man struggles with the buckles that hold her pants tight.

"Fuck this shit," he says.

No longer settled with undoing the bindings, he begins to tear the fabric instead. Tears run down Elizabeth's face, and she tries to swing at the man's head. Dead fingers *crunch* on the guard's shoulder, and he swats her away like a fly. Excruciating pain pierces her arm as the other man crunches his thick boot down on her wrist. Her eyes roll into her head as her arm goes dead to the shoulder.

"Oh, come on, not going to fight anymore?" the one on top of her mocks.

He begins to undo the zipper of his jeans.

She is barely conscious. The sky is a black stream, and the fire light of torches is slowly beginning to slip away.

"You are going to enjoy this, you little bitch," the man says before the weight that holds her down is lifted from her.

Boots kick in the air and breaths come out in a gurgled choking as the guard hangs in the air by his throat. The Chosen holds him suspended beside her, his monster hands squeezing and crushing muscle and bones. The guard's face is cherry red, swelling, and he looks like he is going to pop. The other guard backs away. His face is as white as snow and his duty and friend are forgotten. Elizabeth rolls to her side. Vomit erupts from her mouth, and she curls into a ball.

Words she imagines were meant to plead for his life sound more like wet and squishy slaps of the tongue. The Chosen will have none of it. She can see fire behind his eyes, and it scares the life out of her. Fear begs for her to crawl away. Do anything that will separate her from his fury, but her body is useless. The numbing cold of the winter isn't enough to stop the pain, and her hand is swollen to more than twice its size.

Bones *crack* like rock candy, and the guard's body begins to convulse. The Chosen holds him like he is nothing more than a child. A few moments pass, and the man stops moving. The monster looks down at her, the fury in his eyes burning through her before softening. He turns back to the dead man hanging from his arm. With the slightest of grunts, he lifts the body over his shoulders, and with both arms, throws the guard over the fence like a used-up trash bag.

Dead weight hits the ground like a rock, and she watches as the arms and legs slap the hard earth as he rolls into the snow. The other guard is nowhere to be seen. She is alone with the Chosen. He turns and looks down at her. She couldn't run if she wanted to, her body wasted and broken. Arms thicker than she is reach down, and his meaty paws slip beneath her. Like a baby, he lifts her from the ground, and her head rolls until it is cradled by his shoulder.

Warmth pulses through her body and clothes. The man's skin is on fire. He says nothing to her as they make their way back toward the hospital. He does not carry her through the bonfires where her broken form will be on display for everyone to see. Turning down a side alley, he traces the steps she had taken herself. How had he known? Did he follow her? She can't think on the possibility that he had followed her without her knowing.

Pain pulses from her shoulders to her feet, so intense parts of her figure death would be much easier. But not her face. Warmth and the gentle softness of fur comfort her face as the rocking of his steps pushes her to sleep.

Chapter 10

Five Years Ago

A week passes by. Three hundred and fifty miles of walking, hitchhiking, and sleeping on the side of the highway, and Merchant finally arrives. The trip was not easy. Road blocks and military checkpoints. Though the insurgency of rebels has been pushed inward across three states, the government of the United States can no longer take any chances, and most of the people's civil liberties are a fleeting memory behind obedience and curfews. Here, in the western lake region of what used to be New York State, the war and its casualties can be forgotten. If only for a little while.

Stones crunch under the weight of his boots, the soles rubbed smooth and small puffs of dust lifting beneath his feet. The single strap of his Army bag pulls down on his shoulder as Merchant traces steps he has not taken in close to a year. Blue sky lights the way ahead, broken by scattered puffs of white pillows taking their time as they crawl across the day and the leaves dance in the gentle breeze that cools itself against his skin.

Merchant is home. A quarter mile of drive is all that separates him from what he needs to know. A tunnel of oaks and maples pull at him from both sides, the songs of birds that have never sounded sweeter welcome him as each step draws him closer. The memory of his own death, his guts spilling out, and the taste of that woman's breath is a distant nightmare. A voice deep inside of his head tries to remember the last words spoken to him, but walking here in the warm sun and cooling shade fills his heart with such a feeling he knows nothing can go wrong in this world.

A smile inches across his face. Pulling at the corners of his lips as he can already see in his mind's eye his boys running down the porch to see who can get to him faster, and his wife smiling as she waits for him to reach her. That bright brown hair, those ruby red lips. The blood in his veins quickens at the thought of holding her again and what they'll do tonight when he finally calms their sons enough for them to fall asleep. Her perfume is in his nose. Lilac mixed with the sweet smell of grass and fresh air that filters through the private forest edge they decided to let grow so that their home could be an oasis away from the dangers of the outside world.

Little more than a dozen yards now separate him from where the drive opens to the front yard and the beautiful view of his home and rolling fields of grass. Two dozen acres, purchased with hard years of military service, life out in the country is coveted by few as there are no jobs or amenities out here like there are in the cities. There isn't a store for miles, and the nearest town is over an hour away by car.

Private.

Serene.

Safe.

This is what they call home. Until the day they die, this would be theirs.

Inside, down in his belly, Merchant feels a tightening. A sharp pinch that races from his gut and causes his heart to jump. He grimaces and places his hand over his chest. He can feel the heat radiating from his skin. It is only excitement he tells himself. He hasn't seen in his family in too long. Shaking out his arms, he quickens his pace.

The sweet smell of late summer grass and the approaching change of fall begins to fade as it mixes with something that burns the inside of his nose. He can taste it on his tongue. Acidic and strong, he fights the urge to spit on the ground to clean it away from his teeth.

Ash!

Racing now, he drops his bag and rounds the corner where the drive opens to a gentle slope of lawn that ends at the wraparound porch of his house. The grass is there, green and swaying as the gentle breeze moves the blades, bending them until they are golden beneath the warm sun, but the house is gone. Gray support beams are charred and broken as they spear the open sky with contempt. Black soot and ash scar the open ground, the foundation and basement are gaping holes that swallow all that he has come to love.

Merchant runs forward.

The horror he finds worsens as he gets closer. There is nothing left. Every inch of the house is gone. No walls remain. The boards, the memories, all of it turned to ash and dust. Green grass fades to black dirt and broken pieces of wood. He falls to his knees where the front door once stood. Half of the left frame still stands, the broken piece cracked with heat and splintered as it stands against the test of time where all others fell.

Where is his family?

He looks for any sign of their Jeep, but he is alone. Maybe the house burned down in an accident and they are staying with friends up in Buffalo. Reaching for his phone, the knowledge that they are lost to him sinks in before he remembers he no longer has his phone. The wind picks up and swirls the smell of death into his face. Tears run down his cheeks, and his chest throbs with each sobbing breath.

Why?

He pushes himself off his knees. Walking around the foundation of the house, he looks for any evidence of how this happened. Deep inside, he knows exactly what happened, but he must prove it to himself. Around the back, where the kitchen opened to a screened in mudroom, he finds only melted plastic and scarred boards. One of the pieces of plywood, painted a lighter blue than the sky above his head, lies too far from the house. The bottom corners are scorched, but the panel is intact except for a hole punched through it.

Larger than his head, Merchant sees what he does not want to see. Small pellets, lead buckshot wedged between layers where the shot went through and took out a part of the wall. Dark stains of blood run along the underside. Streaks of gore telling the story of someone's gruesome demise at the end of a shotgun.

She must have fought back.

Merchant grabs the board and hurls it in to the yard. Picking his way through carefully, he steps closer to the foundation and looks to see if there is anywhere he can make his way down. There is no way he can reach the bottom easily. Heat and flames melted the stairs that had come from the central hallway of the house. He can see the bottom step, bent beneath the weight where the first floor has fallen.

Glass and other debris is scattered on the basement floor. All that is left of his life. Digging his fingers into the stained walls of stone, he lowers himself gently until his boots find the hardened cement floor. The smell of fire and dust is too heavy down here. He pulls his shirt over his nose and now all he can smell is sweat and ash. His eyes burn with tears and pollution. Small chunks of wood and cold embers break beneath his feet, and his skin is beginning to turn gray beneath all the dust.

The black scars of the fire are everywhere. He can feel the heat that destroyed his home. Like the pits of Hell, they never had a chance. Toward the back, he can see where the largest boards caved in. Maybe something he can save will be there. Burned and broken, the lumber rests against the basement stone at an angle, shielding whatever may have survived the wreckage.

Everything cracks and crumbles as he pulls the remnants of his life away. Piece after piece falls, and he can see that beneath, everything is dark and scarred like the rest of the house, but he continues. There has to be something that remains of his life.

Ice shoots through his body, and his lungs cough uncontrollably. Merchant falls to his knees and several broken boards fall against him, but he pushes them away like annoying bits of cloth.

His two boys.

They cling to their mother for safety.

His wife.

She holds her sons to her chest, trying desperately to shield them from the flames that took them all.

Their bones are charred and brittle. Empty skulls look at him. Vacant eyes begging to know why. He does not see the skeletons. Images of their last moments flash before his eyes.

Their fears and their screams. The tears that run down his cheeks are not his but theirs. Why did he let this happen to them?

Fury erupts inside of him, and he grabs the last few pieces of broken wood beside them and hurls it across the house. Dust and ash scatter to the wind, and he turns back to the only people in this world he loved. His father's shotgun rests against his wife's leg.

Yes, she did fight back.

The stock is burned away and the barrel is dented with heat, but he can see there are no more rounds left. She fought till the end, and then they left them down here to burn.

Fucking cowards.

Merchant reaches forward and touches the tips of his fingers on his wife's hollow skull, the indentation where her cheek used to be is cold and empty. He closes his eyes and can feel her soft hair fall across the skin of his arm and the warm smile she always had when she closed her eyes to his touch. Pain and tears burn holes into the backs of his eyes. He wants to die. Lay down and perish right beside his family, but he knows he can't.

Just like that woman had said, there was something he has to do.

Pulling his hand away, the bones of his family shift, and his wife's head drops to the side. Inside of her chest, still wrapped around her neck, Merchant notices the slightest shimmer of light. Gently, he lifts her remains and wraps a finger around the chain that still holds her tight.

The necklace he had given her the day he had left for his last assignment. He was going to retire. They had saved enough to live a long and happy life as long as the wars stayed to the west.

He unhooks the fragile silver and puts the simple chain and horse shaped pendant into his pocket. Looking to the sky, there is still several hours before the sun falls below the horizon. The men who did this have no respect for family or the dead. Merchant will not leave his loved ones to rest within the ashes of their home.

Three hours pass by the time he returns to where his driveway meets the front yard. Fresh mounds of dirt with piled rocks mark where his family waits for him to join them. A large part of him wants to go now, let his guts fall out one more time and lay beside them in the earth. But the woman is correct, there is still too much for him to do. Lifting his Army bag from the ground where he had dropped it, he pulls the silver chain from his pocket and looks at it in the evening light.

A red sky ignites fire along the polished metal, the horse on it spinning beneath his hand. It is such a simple beast, yet beautiful and full of power. A pale crystal reflects from the body of the animal, and the tiniest red ruby eyes look at Merchant as the pendant sways back and forth. Opening his bag, he drops the necklace inside and slings the one good strap over his shoulder. Fabric pinches his skin as the sack is much heavier than he remembers, but he will not be slowed as he walks back toward the highway. There is still so much for him to do.

* * *

There are no roads this far into the plains. There are no people and no towns. Rolling hills of white snow stretch for miles in all directions, and Merchant is no longer certain which way they are going. Inside, he can feel the pull of the highway, old Interstate 80 calls to him from behind so he guesses they are moving north. Cherry Red leads, her face bundled beneath three scarfs, and her red hair blowing in the wind. Dark glasses shield her eyes from the sun that shines across the white glass and burns their eyes raw. His bag sits heavy on his shoulder, pinching at his skin, and his jacket flaps open with every gust of wind as he follows.

Temperatures have dropped since they left that small town and continue to fall with every hour. He can see the skin on the girl's forehead going dry, and she is beginning to slow. Snake-Eyes glides behind them, his steps falling in line behind Merchant, but it would not matter. He leaves no tracks but, instead, leaves a wake of aggravation as his relentless chatter increases as the air grows colder.

"You may end up eating her anyway, demon," Snake-Eyes says. "I mean, I am pretty sure it would have been nicer while she was still warm and particularly if she was a willing participant, but if we don't find a way out of this frozen tundra, you are going to have a frozen popsicle leading you soon."

Merchant glares back at the ghost, who smiles back and licks his lips.

Damn ghosts are always right.

"How much further do we need to go? If your brother is this far out, I'm going to guess he hasn't made it even if you didn't kill him yourself," Merchant calls to the young woman.

His voice barely carries over the wind.

She stops, and he can see how the snow reaches her knees. Pulling the scarves away from her face, she blows out several puffs of steam from her bright red lips. Tiny scales now mark the skin between her ear and the corner of her left eye.

"Not much further. Judging by the sun, we still have half a day left to keep moving, and we will find my brother down by the river," she says before replacing the scarves and pushing her way forward. "Another hour or so, if we hurry."

River?

Merchant shrugs, positions his bag further up his shoulders, and follows her. A river in this frozen waste-land? He begins to wonder if she is as crazy as the idea of tracking down a single infected to kill him for mercy. Watching her move, he sees the pistol she offered him create a bulge in the jacket she has pulled tight against her. A gift for doing the one thing she couldn't do, but he did not take it. There are enough burdens weighing him down and enough ghosts following him and chatting without end. He does not need another, and this world will not cry with one less infected roaming around looking for its next meal. He will do this for free. A favor for a favor.

Snake-Eyes is, of course, not very happy about this arrangement. Rules are rules, he complains. For the first hour, the words ran endlessly through the wind, but out here there are no rules. He makes them as he goes along and does as he sees fit. She will see to it that he finds the girl who had been taken by this man-god after they kill her brother. That is all he needs to hear.

Within forty minutes the world begins to change before them. The sun is closer to the western horizon, and the sky to the east is darkening and chasing at their heels. The wind howls like a beast that waits for them to drop their guard, but there is also something else that roars behind the constant noise.

"What is that sound?" Merchant asks.

He cups his hand to his ear and tries to distinguish the echoes, but it is a sound outside of this world.

"That is the Platte River. Sounds like a fucking monster until you get to it," Cherry answers.

She keeps her head down against the tide of blowing snow and pushes forward.

"Water would be frozen out here. How can it still be moving?"

Cherry doesn't answer. Merchant looks back at Snake-Eyes, who is following the sight of the clouds that roll across the sky. When he notices that Merchant is looking at him, he shrugs.

"Don't look at me. I was never any good at that whole science thing. I was always better in health class."

The ghost's tongue sticks out, and he licks at the air with a shit-eating grin on his face.

"Asshole," Merchant mumbles.

"What was that?" Cherry Red asks.

"The wind," Merchant answers and closes the distance between them.

Ahead, he begins to see where the ground starts to drop off. Shadows lengthen in the late afternoon sun, but where the hill begins to fall, the darkness fills in completely. Drawing closer the sound of the river is a freight train going downhill with no brakes. The cresting of water over rocks echoes in the cavern with such thunder he can hardly think.

"How is this possible?" Merchant asks.

She ignores him again and turns west where the ground slopes less. Soon, they are on the edge, looking down as the water rushes past over a hundred feet below. A river as clean and clear as the afternoon sky rushes by, cutting its path through rock walls like a hot knife through butter. Rapids break the surface in dozens of places, churning the river as it snakes its way through the cavern.

"My brother is there," she says and points further up the ravine.

A building sits against the stone face. Cut into the earth itself, giant bricks stretch with dark open windows that follow all the way down to the river bed. Large gates create teeth that mimic a living face. Mournful in death, it stairs up at Merchant. Metal looks rusted and old from this distance, the structure cut from a different age, hidden from the world by the rocks and the shadows.

"Follow me. We want to be down by the river before darkness settles in or we'll never make our way safely."

Merchant follows as the young woman slowly moves along the cavern walls, delicately sliding her boots through the snow until she is all but hanging over the edge.

"We go down here. Follow my prints as much as you can. You're a big guy, but try not to act like one right now. It is a long way to the bottom."

Doing as he is told, Merchant steps into the small impressions left by the woman. There are steps buried beneath the snow. They descend along the side of the cavern, a sheet of ice covering the rocks like skin, and icicles as long as spears hang dangerously over their heads. Cherry Red moves slowly. Sure-footed, but cautiously, she leads them further into the ravine.

Merchant takes in the size of the hidden structure. They are not yet to the ground but already the ancient walls tower over him, and he can feel its history bearing down on his shoulders. A lot of people have died here. He can feel their souls lingering in these walls.

"What is this place?" he asks.

She shrugs.

"I have no idea. I found it when I had to bring my brother out here. Doors are rusty, and the place smells like stale piss, but the locks still work. I hate knowing that he sits here wasting away, but what could I do? They were going to kill him, and deep inside, I know my brother is still there somewhere."

She taps the side of her head and continues to lead them forward.

"But now you want him dead?"

They reach the bottom, and she wheels around and steps up until she presses her chest against his. The shadows rule down by the river and very little more than her bright red hair and face is visible.

"I do not *want* him dead. But I also do not want him to suffer any longer. I don't have the strength or the heart to do it myself," she says. A tear begins to make its way across her cheek and falls off the tip of a scale that peels away from her skin. "Every time I look him in the eye, I break down and can't make myself do it."

"But I can."

"That is why you are here, big man. Just make it quick like you did the others. Then I'll lead you to your lady friend."

Merchant nods his agreement and looks up at the colossal building that awaits their arrival. Teeth of metal bars and a mouth of darkness and death awaits them. Somewhere deep inside, her brother sits. An infected who is hungry and most likely very angry.

"Sure is sad that you two can't go skinny dipping before you go and throw some other poor schmuck from a window," Snake-Eyes says by the river bank.

Dark smooth stones line the water's edge, and Merchant begins to make his way over.

"I wouldn't do that if I were you," Cherry Red says.

Merchant stops and turns.

"Why?"

"This," she answers before she kicks at a branch of a long dead tree that is buried in snow and frozen to the ravine's wall.

Wood splinters, and she is able to pull it away. With a grunt, she heaves it toward the water. The river swallows the short log whole and water splashes high into the air before settling down again. Slowly, the wood rises to the top, but steam and smoke sizzle where the piece begins to melt away.

"Acid?" Merchant asks.

"Yep. A dirty bomb went off further up river about five years ago. There is so much poison in there it will never freeze again. Anything that touches it burns away immediately."

"That's why this ravine is here. It cut itself through the ground."

"Now you are catching on. Only thing it doesn't seem to touch is this dark stone and that building. Whatever it is seems to hold it back."

Merchant lets his eyes follow the rushing water. All of it poison, every drop of it deadly.

"We better hurry. Night is here, and we can't sleep out by the water," Cherry Red says and begins to make her way toward their first destination.

Hesitating a moment, Merchant eyes the deadly river and the ancient walls full of shadows and ghosts. Shifting the bag over his shoulder, he follows. There will be no turning back.

Chapter 11

Shadows broken by green flashing light and red buttons that beg to be pressed. Empty beds line both sides of the wall. Her heart monitor is the only one on. She begins to wonder if it is the only one that actually works. Down at the end of the room, light filters in from the hallway. Two bright windows leave yellow squares on the floor. The white walls on the other side are blinding and lifeless.

Elizabeth is alone. This makes her happy, but so do the drugs. And the pillows. The back of her head is so warm, and she can turn her face to either side and the comfort continues no matter what.

They did not give her as many of the good ones this time. She is mostly numb, but if she tries to move her arm or hand, the pain cuts in like knives.

Turning her head, she watches the little green line as it races across the screen, jumping with every heartbeat.

Boop.

Boop.

Boop.

She holds her breath and watches the tiny mountains speed up. When her lungs burn, she lets out the hot air and takes in a deep breath. The valleys increase and the sound begins to slow. A giggle like a little girl slips from her lips and out of her control.

Boop.

Boop.

She smiles. It is so much nicer to be alone.

"You did a silly thing back there last night," Alexis says.

The young girl materializes out of the shadows by the head of her bed.

"Holy fucking shit, girl!" Elizabeth exclaims.

The little mountains of green on the screen jump and rush. Her words are heavy and slow. Excitement runs through her body, but it is as if she wades through mud and the world is moving in slow motion. She tries to shift away. Razor wire rips through her shoulder and chest, and she lets out a scream that is more like a moan.

"Whoa, please be still," Alexis cautions.

Small, delicate hands help pull Elizabeth back to her spot on the bed, though she never successfully moved that far. Cold skin cools against the warmth of Elizabeth's neck, and the young woman straightens her blanket up until it is tucked nice and tight against her.

"You are badly hurt. It will take days before you are strong again. Thank God, the Chosen found you when he did and brought you back here. You would have died out there in the snow."

Tears are now running down the girl's cheeks. She brushes her hair away from her eyes.

"Those men?" Elizabeth asks, the memories crashing over the walls created by the drugs.

"It is horrible what they were trying to do to you. The Chosen one punished one of them when he found you. The other is awaiting his sentence."

"You mean he killed them with his bare hands."

Alexis does not answer.

Elizabeth can still see the man's life being choked out of him by a single hand, and then his lifeless body being hurled over the fence like a bag of sticks. So much power and fury wrapped into the body of one man. Wiggling her head, she tries to position herself until she is comfortable again. Her soft pillows now feel flat and cold.

"Did they do more than hurt you, Elizabeth?" Alexis asks.

She is seated on the closest bed, her hands folded together and her eyes watching her own feet as they dangle above the tile floor.

"More than hurt me? What the fuck is worse than this?" Elizabeth demands.

Moving her arms and shoulders sends a furious rage of fire through her body, and once again, the speed of the green line begins to race across the screen.

"I'm sorry if it upsets you. I'm just so worried about you and wanted to make sure," Alexis says before her words trail off.

"You want to know if they raped me?"

Alexis' brown hair lifts, revealing eyes swollen with tears. She cannot say the words, but nods instead.

"No, those fucks never got to complete the job. That giant fucker…"

"Our father's Chosen."

"Yeah, that bastard ripped them off me like a troll squashing hobbits. Waited till the last possible moment, too."

"Hobbits?"

A small chuckle rolls through Elizabeth, and she sighs.

"You really are sheltered here, aren't you?"

"Our father protects us from the dangers of this world. Soon, we will see peace again. He has willed that our way of life be spread to all corners of this planet."

Elizabeth turns away and watches the monitor beep, and the room falls to silence.

Why can't she be alone? For once in her life, just let someone realize she doesn't want them around and leave her in peace.

Long minutes pass. The young girl waits, her slippers swinging and her breathing shallow and slow. Elizabeth wants to sleep, close her eyes and wake up when all these crazy people have moved on, but the frustration now overpowers the drugs and all she can do is watch that little green line.

Boop.

Boop.

Boop.

The room lightens up as the door at the end of the row swings open. Glaring yellow light pollutes the dark solitude and the *father* steps through. Elizabeth eyes the bastard with contempt, but the Chosen is close behind. She wants to be angry, even furious, but the emotions die away as the memory of him pulling the men off her resurfaces. His shoulders and muscles bulge as he crosses his arms over his chest and does not take a step closer than the doorway.

"You can leave us be, Alexis. Our sister here needs her rest," Father says.

"But, Father, she needs care and—"

"No buts. We will make sure that Elizabeth gets all the attention she needs to make a full recovery."

A smile spreads across his face, and he presents the door with one sweeping arm. The Chosen turns to the side to let her out, and Alexis, with one final glance at Elizabeth, begins to make her way out of the room.

"She needs so much, Father."

"I know my child, and we are all so appreciative for your help. Now go, I will be with her for only a moment and soon she'll be resting again."

A half-smile creases the young girl's lips, and she disappears down the hall. The monster lets the door swing shut and positions himself in front of it, his wide shoulders blocking the light.

"Now, Elizabeth…" Father says.

He crosses one arm over his chest and taps his lips gently with a finger of the other hand.

"That was such a stupid and terrible thing you did last night," he says before seating himself on the end of her bed.

She tries to recoil away, but the pain and stiff covers force her into place.

"It's not like I asked them to do this to me," she says.

His smile says he can see the bullshit she spits from a mile away.

"I'm not here to talk about what those men tried to do to you. Our Chosen here made sure that our ugly situation with those two was appropriately handled."

The big man says nothing and doesn't move a muscle as he waits by the door.

"Then what the fuck do you want?"

The smile on his face disappears, and his eyes go hard as stones.

"You know exactly what I'm here to talk about, and when I'm done, we'll all be sure you won't make that same mistake again."

* * *

The soft, hazy light of a new day burns at her eyes. Filtered through heavy clouds, everything is gray and dull. The air is brisk with the approach of another storm, and yet Elizabeth squints as she walks down the main street of the village. Children race between stalls and through alleys formed by short, squat structures. Plywood nailed between the patchwork of scavenged boards create most of their homes. Where solid beams and rock could not be found, thick canvas and bundled field grass is tied tightly into place. Smoke rolls from openings in all the structures. Fires give the air a burning scent, both fresh and polluted.

She can see the outlines of the old city that this town used to be. Foundations and skeletal walls still stand in all directions. Sidewalks and broken asphalt break the surface of the snow where footsteps and cart traffic has melted everything into a muddy mess. A thick layer of the dark grime covers her up to her knees. The homes of hundreds are built around and over the remains of a people lost in the past. Guessing, she figures the old city stretched at least five to six miles. Now, within its fenced encasement, they cannot extend more than a mile in either direction.

He keeps his flock close. Always within his grasp.

Their father.

Her captor.

She spits on the ground. The saliva melts the dirty snow, and she kicks at it with her boots. They have given her thicker clothing now that she hobbles around like a cripple. Stiff padding and tight bandages wrap around stitches and a sling pulls her right arm in close. Her body is covered in a gray sweatshirt material. Her pants hang loose over her legs, and it is too easy for a stiff breeze to find its way in to her skin. Her shirt and coat stretch because of the extra padding. Her shoulders rub against the edge of her neck, irritation bothering her incessantly and bringing back thoughts of their damn Chosen.

He saved her, killing the man who probably would have done worse to her, but she can't help but hate the monster. She was so close to getting away. Now, she can feel him following her even more. Somehow, he hides in the weak shadows that linger in the hazy light. Big broad shoulders and hands the size of God's, and yet, she still cannot see him. But he is there. Watching and waiting for her to try and escape again. Fucking bastard will never let her leave.

The swollen mess above her left eye has finally reduced to a point where she can move her face without wanting to drive a stake through her eyes. Sometimes, she still considers doing just that. People in the village watch her. Their eyes following her movement as she stumbles between them. Her good left leg is stabilized by the help of a large crutch pinched under her braced shoulder. Easily a size too big, she drags her way over the stone, dirt, and icy road. It wasn't until the day they finally let her out of bed that she realized what those men had done to her body in their failed attempt to take advantage of her in ways that only nightmares would envision. Pulled the muscle that extended from her groin to her knee. So much bruising, far too much internal bleeding.

Alexis had said it would fade away over the coming weeks as she moved and the strength returned. Damn girl was too optimistic. Always looking at the bright side and following her like a stubborn puppy. She made Elizabeth sick, but moving through the crowds as they pushed between tiny houses and shops where goods were bargained for with time and services, she began to wonder where the young girl was. Like a shadow, she had always been a step behind, looking for ways to help and lead Elizabeth towards the belief and life they had all been promised.

Now, she has been missing since the morning after they last talked in the hospital. Elizabeth can still hear the desperation in her voice as she tried to convince their crazed *father* into letting her stay in the ward with her. Almost begging until she was shown the door. The next morning, their conversation had been hushed, quick, and about her injuries and nothing more. Since those early hours, the young girl has just vanished. Has something happened to her?

Elizabeth shook her head. Not her problem. They wouldn't harm her just for caring. She wants to help. See to it that Elizabeth become one of them. It was a foolish venture, but nothing to kill the young girl over. She has probably been given some other poor soul to look after.

Taking a deep breath, Elizabeth stretches the stiffening muscles in her back, adjusts her shoulders the best she can, and continues down the road. There is no pattern to the way people move here. No jobs to go to, no disease, or army to flee from. They are happy, content to live their lives without doing really anything. She watches them with a scornful look that burns away the stares they send her way.

Fuck them.

If they want to remain prisoners here, living and dying in the same place they were born, let them. This is the cesspool they created. Let them rot in their own waste. She spits on the ground again. Her mouth is full of phlegm and tastes like iron. God-damn drugs and their side effects.

"This way, it has almost started!" a boy yells.

He is half her height. Bright eyes and red cherry cheeks come running down the road, mud splashing up and immature limbs flailing like a fish out of water. A handful of other children are chasing him. All of them with smiles that reach their ears. Elizabeth tries to move out of the way. Skirting to the side of the path to let the locomotive of young adrenaline and carelessness pass.

Her luck holds out, and she doesn't even make it past the first child. Thick boots, at least two sizes too large, kick out and crack against the side of her crutch. She goes down. Hard turf cracks against her elbow. Lightning flashes across her eyes, and her mouth is warm and salty.

"God-damn it!" she screams.

Three boys and two girls skid to a stop, slush splashing beneath their feet. Elizabeth rolls onto her back.

The mud and water is seeping into her pants, freezing her ass cheeks, and she can feel the ice running up her spine. Wet, unkempt hair is now plastered to the back and side of her head.

"Hey, lady, are you okay?" the tallest of the boys asks.

Maybe he's ten, or he could be twenty. Elizabeth doesn't care. She hates him anyway.

"Do I fucking look like I'm okay? You tripped me, and now I'm fucking covered from head to toe in mud," Elizabeth answers.

Rolling onto her left side, she uses what strength she can to push herself away from the ground.

"Here, let us help you get up," the boy says.

"Come on, David. We'll miss everything," two of the boys plead.

Elizabeth shoots daggers at all of them with her eyes, and two of the girls keep their heads down as they walk over to help David. Their hands are tiny, and the word gentle is not in their vocabulary as thin, pointy fingers dig into her body. Pain has become her closest friend and, at the moment, they are lovers. She grits her teeth and swallows back the blood that fills her mouth.

"She's fine, David. We have to go, now!" The others plead with their friend again.

"Are you sure you are fine, lady?" David asks.

A wad of phlegm filled blood splatters in the mud by his feet.

"No thanks to you and your pack of brats here. Go on, get out of here," Elizabeth replies and waves him and his friends off.

They do not hesitate. With rockets in their shoes, they race down the road. Taking a deep breath, she watches them go. Looking around, she realizes more than just the children are heading in the direction opposite of her own. Parents carrying younger ones. Adults walking in small groups or couples holding hands. All are making their way to the south end of the village.

Looking to the north, a small hope begins to burn within her. If everyone is gathered on that side of the village? Maybe, just maybe?

Blood, a deep red, and fresh from the cut in her arm, splatters once again at her feet. Anger and frustration wells up within her, forcing her to push the idea away. Even if she could somehow find an opening in their fences, or an area unguarded by distracted men, what would she do? Hobbled like a fucking cripple, she won't even make it a hundred yards before one of these assholes shoots her in the back. Or knowing her fucking luck, the Chosen will stomp his way out to her and carry her back like a damn child.

Elizabeth pivots on her good leg and watches the sea of heads and shoulders moving their way down the street. Might as well see what all the excitement is about. Mingle with the locals, you know. Fire races down her spine, bringing pain while ice shivers the skin of her back where the mud and dirt reminds her that this really is Hell.

Growling, she begins her slow dragging steps to follow.

Fuck them. She'll never be one of them.

Chapter 12

Five Years Ago

Old American Diner.

Like the 1950s have returned, the florescent orange light shines into the evening hours, and the open sign dangles behind the glass door on a beaded metal string. Cars line the sidewalk. Bumper to bumper, they stretch down both sides of the street, ending at red lights that click when they turn and sway in the evening breeze. Sports cars and family sedans, trucks and a few motorcycles. All hug together as the city closes in for the night, finding refuge in homes or within the confines of bars and diners. No reason to be out at night. Only bad things happen after sundown.

Music *thumps* down where light streams out of The Green Room at the corner of Market and 21st Street. Flashes of strobe lights and the appropriately named green rays flicker across puddles from the rain that ended an hour ago. Dark mirrors shine along the pavement. Looking glasses into the souls of those who walk over them.

A bouncer, shaved head and a T-shirt two sizes too small, stands outside the bar with his arms crossed over his chest. He is no taller than the girls who shimmy their way in on heels with skirts that scream to roll back up over the skin they are stretched across. The streets of Rochester no longer feel like the home he once remembered.

Merchant stands in the shadows with his back against a brick wall, a hoodie pulled over his head more for cover than warmth. The air is thick with humidity the storm left behind. He does everything he can to hide his tall frame standing in the shadows, silent and still. He watches the short security man. The girls walk by with smiles and tiny touches of fingers with painted nails on bald head. The smile is unmistakable, and unprofessional. Doesn't even bother to check their IDs until the boys move up. Then it's shoulders back, chest out, firm lips, and a growl until the little pieces of government issued plastic are handed over. Desk jockey with a night job. Common place when all the real men are off fighting the war.

Some things change while many others stay the same. He guesses that is the way life and the times always are. But he is a stranger on the streets he grew up on. These are different people, with lives he doesn't understand. They see a future with friends and family. The war pushes far to the west, the dangers and the panic pushed behind walls of alcohol and daily living.

Turning back to the diner, all of what was once his life is behind him now. His future is no longer certain, nor is it pleasant. One thing remains for him to do, and he intends to start it now.

Stepping from the shadows, Merchant crosses the street. Boots splash in puddles and a woman down at the corner whistles at him. He keeps his hood up, shoulders drawn and makes no contact with eyes as he heads directly for the glass door.

Bells chime when he pushes his way in. Warm air, filled with grease and warm coffee, escapes through the door. He can taste it on his tongue. The grease is so thick he can feel it on his skin. Some things never change.

None of the patrons turn to look his way. Old-style booths that match the feel the establishment tries desperately to give line the windows that follow the streets outside. Red vinyl upholstery squeaks as people shift in their seats, all of them talking as if they are the only ones there, their voices filling the half-empty establishment. Polished bar stools, all but two empty, line the front counter, where a middle-aged woman wipes away at the counter. Her gray stained towel swirls in a storm at a stain he figures has been there for years.

Music plays in the background, some `50s song he doesn't recognize. All big band and multiple singers wooing girls that are now older than he is. The banging of pots and plates fills in with the rhythm of the beat. It's as if he's been transported back in time, not only in outward appearance, but a lost reality that is sealed within the aluminum framing of the building itself.

"Seat yourself, honey," the waitress calls.

She smiles at Merchant. Her lips are too red for her pale skin and bleached hair. Lipstick stains the white of her teeth, and there is little she can do to hide the liver spots on her arms. Candy-striped blouse and skirt finish off the ridiculous outfit. The men who sit at the counter pay more attention to their steaks and coffee than the woman working for pennies.

Merchant nods but doesn't say a word. He keeps his hood up and begins to make his way toward the back. Boots squeak on polished linoleum. No one notices. He is nothing but a blur to them. Empty booths pass by, the two he finds occupied spare him only a momentary glance before turning back to their coffee or meals. Old men telling tales of time gone by or bitching about their wives.

The drunk crowd hasn't made its way in yet.

Good, he still has time to get this done.

He approaches the final booth. A man sits alone, his head down, dark wet hair disheveled as it plasters to his forehead. His jacket is as dark as the mood that surrounds him. Desperate, angry, and dangerous. A spoon swirls coffee as dark as Merchant's skin. Stopping, Merchant waits a moment, drawing the anticipation out.

"Find yourself another seat, partner. There are plenty of them, and this one is taken," the man says, his voice a low growl.

His head doesn't move. Too angry at the world or the shitty liquid that cools in front of him. The spoon continues to swirl, the stainless-steel tip tapping against the ceramic in an endless pattern of its own. Thick jacket pulls away from the hand that holds the cup of steaming coffee. Tattoos and scars follow thick bones with skin stretched thin from knuckles to wrist.

Powerful hands.

Murderous hands.

Merchant steps forward, turns back toward the door he entered from and shoves his way into the seat beside the man.

"Hey, what the fuck?"

Merchant's hand wraps around the other's wrist, twists until he feels bones crack and shoves both of their arms underneath the table. Some of the other patrons lift weary eyes in their direction. Merchant gives each one of them a nod, and they go back to their own lives.

"Quiet now, or I'm going to make a mess of this right here in the diner," Merchant threatens.

"What the f—?"

With another twist, there is a *pop* and the man goes limp as his head drops against Merchant's shoulder.

"I said be quiet or this is going to get ugly really fast."

The waitress turns the corner of the front counter and begins to shimmy her way over. Blonde hair tied up in a beehive, she smacks on gum and holds her ticket book out in front of her. Flat shoes scratch at the floor below ankles that swell through the fabric. Her hips sway, and Merchant notices that the front of her blouse is too low for someone who's lived far too long.

"What can I do for you tonight, honey?" she asks, already writing something on the ticket card.

"I'll take a coffee," Merchant says and gives the man a squeeze on his wrist as another warning.

"Anything to eat tonight?"

A bubble of gum pops in her mouth.

"Probably not. I'm here for a few words with my friend, and then I'll be on my way."

"Okay, honey. Roast beef is tonight's special if you change your mind." She scribbles some more on her notebook. "Do you need a refill as well?"

She looks over at the man sitting next to Merchant. Color has returned to his face in the form of a fiery red that makes her lips look dull and flat.

"He's good," Merchant answers.

Her eyes dart between them both. She shrugs and heads back to the counter.

"You are not a hard man to find, Travis," Merchant says.

"How the f—" Travis begins and Merchant tears into his arm again.

The smallest of screeches escapes the man's lips as his head drops against Merchant's shoulder once more.

"Quiet now. No need for these nice people here to hear what you did to me or my family."

Travis nods his head. A drip of saliva stretches from the corner of his lips as Merchant relieves the pressure on his arm.

"You are supposed to be dead. But… We all heard what the general did to you," Travis whispers.

Fire rises inside of Merchant's belly, and the uncontrollable urge to slam the man's face into the table until there is either nothing left of his skull or the table is barely held in check.

"Looks like you got your information wrong. Do I feel dead?"

Merchant wrenches on the man's wrist again, and he falls face first against the table. Spoon rattles in coffee cup, and the entire diner goes quiet. Everyone begins to turn their way. Lifting his other hand, Merchant waves and gives them all a smile. Travis sits back up. They all go back to their food and drinks.

"How is this possible?" Travis coughs out.

"No time for that. I need to know where I can find the others."

"What others?"

A slight squeeze of the wrist has the man putting his other hand up, begging for a moment.

"Okay. We were all given some leave that ends at the end of the week. The general wants us at our new HQ outside of Baltimore by sunup on Saturday."

"So, he's going ahead with that foolish plan?"

"Bastard has it all mapped out. Said you were the last leak on the boat. His ship is tight and the mission is a go. We are going to be heroes," Travis says.

He reaches for his coffee, his hand shaking.

Merchant eyes the drink, and then the man. The tattooed fingers slowly slide back under the table.

"You don't seem so certain sitting here in a diner late at night by yourself."

"Can't a man enjoy some alone time?"

"Travis, we fought together for what? Ten years? There is a bar at the end of the road filled with more women than your dick could point at with boys who couldn't stand in a puddle of our piss if they begged us. But here you are. By yourself, wallowing in pity over a cup of coffee. Are you having second thoughts?"

The skin beneath Merchant's hand is becoming clammy, and Travis turns to look out the window.

"Never. When it is all done, people will realize it was the correct choice."

"What about those who try to stop you?"

"Some will try. Those who do will end up like… like you were supposed to be. They'll never believe you, though. It's too late, Merchant. There isn't enough time. Besides, not all of us wanted you out. Most of us still believed you were one of us."

Travis looks down at the table. He picks at the nails of his fingers with the thumb of his hand. He does not look up at Merchant.

"Didn't seem to help me any," Merchant says and smiles as the waitress comes over with his cup of coffee.

She smiles at both of them, and this time Travis even does his best to fake something other than a grimace.

"It was that bastard Dog Breaker. If you listen to me, there is something not right with that one."

Merchant releases the soldier's arm. Travis lets out a sigh and brings up his mangled wrist. The fingers of his twisted hand are white and curled unnaturally.

"One word to the others that we had this little talk and that bastard mutt won't be the worst of your fears. You got that, Travis?"

Merchant puts his fists on the table as he stands and looks down at his former teammate. There is no fight left in the broken shell of a man. His eyes are weak as he looks up, and his face is pale.

"Yeah, you got it," he replies.

Turning, Merchant heads for the door. His coffee untouched.

"I'm sorry about your family. I heard about it in the news," Travis calls out.

Merchant doesn't stop. He hits the door hard, and the open sign falls to the floor.

The night air is sharp and the shadows are bright. There is too much to do and so little time. Merchant turns down the street but stops at the first alley. Now it is time to wait.

* * *

Oil lamp sizzles and a ball of orange light pushes back the darkness. The air is thick with mold and rust. Tiny feet scatter over ancient metal. A thousand of them, running and screaming in tiny voices. The river outside is thunder confined to travel within the walls barely more than two men wide. Churning, rolling, and echoing like the fury of the gods above.

Mildew stains everything green and white. Paper is piled on the ground in dark wet mounds that move as the light draws near. Sprouting short legs and long hairless tails that sweep dangerously behind them, and the paper hisses in warning as it runs away. Hinges crack and shriek as Cherry Red pulls the door shut behind them. Dust and mold kicks up into the air. Outside it is cold, the storm settling in over the ravine and dropping more snow by the minute. Inside, the air clings to Merchant's skin. It is a disease, and the whole building is alive with infection. He can feel its heart beating. Slow and steady.

They were expected.

It wanted them to come.

"Quiet now. No need to make this harder on ourselves than we need to," Red says. "Give me the lamp, and are you sure you don't want my pistol?"

Merchant shakes his head.

"Suit yourself. Hope you are as good as you think you are."

She steps around him, takes the lead, and begins to creep her way down the first corridor.

They move deeper into the rock. The sound of rushing water moves higher and further with every step. The wailing of the wind is still around them, torturous and hollow as it sings and calls to them. Bared steel doors line the walls, rust and cobwebs holding them shut. The floor creaks, and the mountain shifts with every step. A ghost couldn't be quiet here. But Merchant hears nothing save for themselves, yet he knows they are not alone. Red's oil lamp is their only window into the gloom. One quick puff of air and they'd be lost to darkness deeper than the pits of Hell.

"There are infected here," Snake-Eyes says.

Even in the absence of light, Merchant can see the bastard. He has an internal shine, soft blue and the bastard glorifies in his ability to always be seen. He does nothing to help light the way.

"I can feel them watching us," the ghost adds.

Merchant spares him a quick glance. Eyes angry, the silent command to be quiet is easy to read.

"Okay! They are watching you. I've never felt hunger like this. My god, they are hungry. I am in Heaven."

"How much further is your brother?" Merchant asks, turning back to Red, who moves them through a second corridor that turns to the right and continues farther into the stone.

"He is on the bottom floor. Three flights down," she answers.

Nothing about this place feels natural. Man did not make this, for living things would not venture down here. Apocalypse or not, people would not have created this. Merchant stops where he is, and she continues down the path a few steps before she notices. The golden light forms a halo around her head as she turns back. Her red hair is a fire that is both dark were it is still wet and ablaze where it flows behind her body.

"What? Okay, look. I knew he would grow more dangerous the more the infection took hold of him. He could hurt himself if he got out, so I made sure he was too deep to escape once his mind was gone."

The muscles on Merchant's face tighten.

"Oh, now she is lying. God, I love it when bitches lie to me," Snake-Eyes says as he licks the non-infected side of her face.

She doesn't notice.

"I know, I know," she says. The stomp of her foot echoes throughout the chamber. "It wasn't the smartest idea now that I look back at it, but sue me. I'm his sister, and I was doing the best I could with what little I had. God damn-it, can we just get this over with?"

"Bitch with a heart of gold is hiding something from you," Snake-Eyes jeers.

He floats behind Merchant, who hefts his bag further up his shoulder.

"Keep moving. I want to be out of here before the night is through," Merchant says.

Cherry Red nods, the smile returns to her face, and she turns back down the corridor.

"Trust me, there is nothing I want more than to be out of here as soon as we can be," she adds and begins to lead the way again.

A hundred feet passes, and a half-dozen sealed doors bar their way before they reach one that will open. Rust has punched its way through the metal. A sign, held on by a single screw dangles beside the failing frame.

Stairs.

Cherry Red puts her shoulder against the barrier and dust and cobwebs fall like rain as it slides open.

The scratching of metal echoes loudly up and down the stairwell that goes deeper into the earth. Making their way up is no longer possible. A dozen steps separates them from where the wood and tile of the floors above have rotted through. The light from their lamp shines into the shadows above their head, but it is quickly choked away beneath a smothering gloom that sits heavy over their shoulders.

"It is down we go then," Snake-Eyes says. "Hell. At least this way you'll get home faster when they eat you alive down there."

Merchant growls, and Cherry Red looks up at him.

"Something wrong?" she asks.

"Keep moving," he says.

The look on her face goes cold, and she turns to lead them down toward the lowest level.

With each floor that passes, the smell and the air get worse. Spoiled, sweet, and wet, the must is thick. Cherry chokes into her own shirt, her breaths nothing more than quick gulps. She is drowning in the death that has found them. Merchant slows his breathing. He has smelled this before. Bodies piled and left to rot. Exposed to air and gnawing teeth.

"How much farther?" he asks.

She doesn't respond. Her coughs force her to fall against the wall.

"My god, it wasn't this bad the last time I was down here," she struggles to say.

His big hand squeezes tightly against her shoulder, the fingers pinching against the bones beneath her skin. A grimace crosses her face and quickly fades away as she does her best to strengthen herself up. She steps away from the wall, the knees of her legs visibly shaking underneath her pants. He does not let her go.

"How much farther?" he asks again.

Her eyes are red with blood. Snot runs down over her lips, and the infection has spread over her left eye. Down here, in this sickness, she will turn faster. A squeeze forces her to shake her head.

"Down the hall, there is a final gate. He was inside there the last time I was here. It is locked from this side."

Merchant looks into the darkness that surrounds them.

"Give me the key and stay here."

"No, I want to go with you."

He lets go of her shoulder and sticks out his palm. The lighter skin under his hand is still a thousand shades darker than the ghostly pale she has become.

"I will do this alone. Now, give me the key and stay here."

Cherry Red steps back. A sudden surge of strength finds her backbone.

"Look, he is my brother, and I am the one who brought you down here to kill him. I want to see what I have done to him. He deserves to see me one more time. I deserve to see him."

Anger builds up within Merchant. She is being stubborn beyond reason. Giving him the key to a locked cell would be the smart thing to do. Snake-Eyes hovers behind her. His shit-eating grin is larger than ever below his empty eye sockets. Merchant stares at him, but the ghost has nothing to say.

"Have it your way. Stay out of my way, and we leave the moment it is done."

She nods her head. The courage that holds her up begins to fade. A pistol dangles from her limp fingers. Grip first, she holds it up for him.

"Last chance," she says.

He pushes her arm down and does not take the weapon. Lifting the strap of his bag away from his shoulder, he puts it in the corner by the stairwell.

"Show me where he is."

No more words. Only action is required now. Holding the lamp in front of her, Red takes the lead and moves them down the hallway. Her steps are short and slow. Every creak and echo stops her in her tracks. The flame and light sways in her loose grip.

Merchant can see the gate ahead of them. Dark steel bars thrust their way into ceiling, floor, and wall. A single door, a jailer's door, remains locked. Brown rust tarnishes the surface, but the metal is strong. Staring back at them is the keyhole that will unlock their protection.

Large and silent, it waits for them to bring the key to their doom.

Cherry Red reaches into her pocket with her empty hand. Her entire body is shaking now. A rat screeches back near the stairwell, and the young women damn near drops the lamp. Merchant reaches for the light, but she shakes her head and turns away enough to keep him from her.

Slowly, she pulls out a long stick of twisted metal. A skeleton's key. Tarnished with age, it is a perfect match to the bars that block their way. A long-lost sibling returning to find its way home.

Inserting the key, the lock makes no sound. A turn

to the left, and a *click* echoes through the hall. She looks up at him, and he spares her a quick glance. Her eyes dart back to the floor.

"Please, God, forgive me for what I have done," she whispers.

"There are no gods down here," Merchant says.

He pulls on the door, and the hinges scream but are as solid as the rock they are buried under. Stepping in, the shadows quickly move in to swallow him. Merchant turns back to Red with his hand out.

"Give me the lamp and stay outside," he says.

She does not look up. Her hands are shaking.

"Did you hear me?"

Something moves behind him. A shuffle. He is not alone.

Merchant tries to step back through the door. Metal slams with the finality of death as Cherry Red pushes the door shut and twists the key to the right. The lock clicks and there will be no opening the cage from this side.

"I'm sorry," she whispers. "I can't do it. He needs to eat, and I am all he has."

Tears are running down her eyes. She leaves the lamp on the ground by the gate. Her feet kick up dust as she begins to back away. Dark red hair is plastered to her face where she tries to wipe away the pain.

"I'm so sorry," she says again.

She is now down the hall where the stairs lead back to safety.

"Told you she was lying," Snake-Eyes says from behind the bars.

Merchant turns around. The movement is getting closer. He can feel their hunger now. Warm against his skin, he begins to back his way into the corner where the light is the strongest. A dark figure begins to form in the darkness. It moves slowly, with limbs that are out of its control.

"Oh, and another thing," Snake-Eyes adds. "I also warned you before and you didn't listen."

The monster is closer now. Merchant can see the full outline of his shoulders, a black hole against the light.

"There are definitely more than one of them down here," Snake-Eyes says, and he pops a piece of popcorn into his mouth. "Have fun."

Merchant can feel the cold hard steel of the bars against his back. His skin burns, and he can smell the infection deep inside his nose and taste it on his tongue. Splitting like cells, the shadows slowly fade from one to two, and then to three. There is more shuffling now. There are dozens. A moan moves through them. There is nowhere to run, no place to hide.

They surround him, and as the light reveals the scaled and pealing face of the first, they all attack at once.

Chapter 13

There are more people here than she could have ever imagined. The darkness of night and the business of the day has hidden the truth from her. Hundreds of heads flow like a brown and golden sea of hairy mops under the hazy light of the afternoon. Inside a bowl, they circle around in chairs and benches. The younger ones stand or sit on the ground. Those older or hobbled like she is are given priority, but she refuses take anything from them other than her freedom.

A stiff breeze, cold and sharp, brings with it the stench of body odor and piss. Elizabeth wipes snot away from her nose onto the back of her sleeve and finds solace in leaning against the railing of a bench that climbs ten rows high. The wood frame is hard and cold, stiff against her skin, and it vibrates annoyingly with the movement of a hundred pairs of feet. Flags flap in the wind above them all. Cone shaped and bright, a robin's egg blue pennant ripples and snaps to the south of the human coliseum while three red ones with black trim follow suit in the three opposite directions.

Words of excitement echo through the village. Hints of judgement and God's make their way to her, and she hates it all.

What the fuck is going on here?

She can see the open dirt arena they circle. The snow has been shoveled away, the soil turned up. Dark and muddy, the earth has seen the feet of a thousand people. Single cages sit beneath each cloth marker. Elizabeth recognizes them.

The judging circle.

Itching radiates down her shoulder, and she can still feel the teeth tearing into her flesh. The taste of disgust, warm, salty, and rank, begins to fill her mouth. She can't believe what she is about to watch. Looking around, all the villager's eyes are wide with excitement.

They can already taste the blood.

Lies. All of it is lies. These people are no different than the other bastards who remain in this world. Talking of peace and prosperity for all mankind, they are savages like the rest. One drop of blood and they become animals. Even the children.

Those as young as toddlers race between chairs and those who are forced to stand. Giggles and happiness fills their world as they play and wait for the inevitable slaughter.

Elizabeth has seen enough and the event hasn't even started yet. She straightens herself and turns to walk away. Kill the weak and timid. She isn't one of them. They may have made the mistake of thinking this was her when she first got here, but that would be their final mistake. She will show them. She will leave them behind to die and rot behind their own walls.

Pain greets her wholeheartedly as she puts her weight back onto the crutch and tries and push her way through the crowd. Men, most of them young, block her way. They do not even notice her. Eyes, bright and strong are locked to the show below. They want it to start. Their need is so thick she can feel it on her skin. Revulsion bubbles in her stomach, and she bites her tongue to hold it down. God knows, she doesn't care if she vomits all over them, but no reason to start a war she can't win.

Not yet anyway.

"Move it, asshole," she barks at the closest body blocking her path.

She doesn't care who or what it is. They need to move now.

Attention drawn away from the awaiting spectacle, the man looks down at her. Wide shoulders stiffen, and a head with a wide set jaw tilts down to her. Scales of infection have inched their way up the left side of his neck, but there is no crazy in his eyes. Only anger at a hobbled woman demanding he step aside like a summer breeze does to a thousand-year-old oak tree.

"Did you hear me or is the infection clogging those useless ears of yours as well?" she asks.

Pushing the man is like trying to move a pile of stone. Muscles tense, and he doesn't even tilt. Elizabeth grits her teeth and snarls. He smiles back. Tuffs of light brown hair poke out from underneath a knitted cap of red and blue like a fucking hipster from twenty years ago.

She turns back toward the spectacle.

He chuckles.

"Have it your way," she says.

A spin on her good leg sends razors up her back but does less harm than the crutch that crushes the side of the asshole's knee cap. A loud *snap* of bone and wood sends the man to the ground. He begins to yell. Curses and threats, but the noise of the crowd rises from a slow heartbeat to the roar of an ocean.

"Ladies and gentlemen!" the Father begins.

Elizabeth ignores him and tries to step over the fallen asshole. He clutches his knee and continues to say things she can't hear, and his lips are moving too fast for her to care. Her crutch wobbles when she puts pressure on it, but it holds.

One long painful step has her over the living log and three more quickly step in to fill the gap.

"For fuck's sake, let me through."

"I am so glad we have come together as a family today," Father continues in a voice that vibrates like he is a thousand feet tall.

The clapping is a thunder that shakes the ground.

Two of the bodies blocking her ignore her attempts to push through. Standing in the middle, the tallest looks down at her and shakes his head from side to side. No words given. No attempt to communicate with her like a normal human being. So be it.

Stepping back, she firms her grip on the crutch and turns like she did before. Whatever he gives these people sure does make them strong, but it does nothing to improve the gaping pile of stones that rattles between their useless ears. With a deep breath, she tries to slow her heart. The pain in her back has subsided, and she is ready to swing again.

"Today we will see the judgement of God himself," Father continues from down within the makeshift arena.

People are on their feet now. Hundreds of bodies

swaying and jumping in excitement. Hatred for it all burns within Elizabeth like an ember that threatens to burn itself out of her guts.

Fuck them all.

Closing her eyes and gritting her teeth she takes a deep breath to steady herself.

"Hi, Elizabeth," Alexis says.

Air jets out of Elizabeth's lungs like she's been gored through the belly by a charging bull, and she begins to cough. Tiny, soft hands, wrap themselves around her shoulders. Arms like a bird's rest across her back. There is no meat to the girl, just skin and bones yet so much warmth comes from her petite frame.

"Hi…Alexis," Elizabeth gets out between coughs.

"Are you okay? Do I need to help you back to the birthing ward?"

Elizabeth forces herself to straighten and then looks the young girl in the eyes. They are sad and tired. Dark circles shadow what were once bright and warm. Her hair is limp and it sticks to her skin where it isn't held up within her own knitted cap of light blue and pink. Red blotches of scratches and cuts line the side of her neck and the skin of her arms are paler than snow where they are not showing signs of bruising.

"Do I look like I'm okay? Fuck, girl. What did they do to you?"

Alexis looks back to the arena, but her attention is not with the excitement down below.

"I've been busy doing things to help people. There are so many people that need help," Alexis whispers.

"For the first time, you are telling me the truth," Elizabeth says.

The young girl looks back at her. One eyebrow is raised, and her lips part to say something, but the words do not come out.

"Come on, Alexis, let's get out of here. I've already seen enough."

Elizabeth turns back to the men blocking them, but they have not moved. She sighs.

"We should really stay and watch," Alexis says. "From what I have heard, this may be one of the most exciting ones we've seen in a long time."

"You are fucking kidding me, right? I've seen enough. Let's just get out of here and find somewhere to rest and be alone for a bit."

Alexis smiles, and then it fades away faster than the dark marks on her face.

"There is nothing more in this world that you want than to be alone is there?" she asks.

"Pretty much. Maybe a house full of food, as well, and a young stud who doesn't speak and knows when to move when I tell him to." Elizabeth growls.

She looks back at the men, but they do not pay attention to any word she says.

"Join me for this," Alexis says. The grip of her hands is tighter, and she is leading the way back toward the bleachers. "It will be good for you to watch. I think you will understand in a moment."

Both women step over the man who groans and rolls like a turtle flipped over on its shell.

"Fucking bitch. Look what you did to my leg," he says with a hiss.

Elizabeth jams the end of her crutch into his groin, and he howls in pain. He tries to grab at her with the hand he isn't using to cup his crotch, and Alexis kicks the feeble attempt away. A look as cold as ice solidifies on the young woman's face, and the man rolls back the other way.

"What have they done to you, Alexis?" Elizabeth asks while tracing her eyes between her friend and the fallen asshole.

"This way. We don't want to miss the best part."

Both women shuffle their way between bodies and around children until they are at the front of the bleachers. Alexis says a few words and several of the people on the first bench slide over or stand to give them enough room to sit. Alexis finds her spot and pats the bench next to her. Looking at those who are now forced to stand, Elizabeth relents and lets herself drop down.

The pressure on her feet fades instantly. With all the aches from the bruising and cuts, she hadn't taken the time to realize how much her feet hurt. She places the crutch by her side, keeping her hand wrapped around it for strength.

"Do you recognize that one?" Alexis asks.

Her slender arm points to the arena below. A single man walks circles around the Father. He wears no shirt, and tattoos and infection weave their way around his torso. A long-wicked knife sits tucked into his belt. The blade is ink black and the edges are jagged and sharp even from this distance. His arms are up in challenge as the people boo him and hiss as he draws near. A smile as wide as the village itself stretches across his face, and his head is shaved clean.

Elizabeth recognizes him from the guard post. This is the one that the Chosen did not kill. She had thought they punished him already, but now she realizes she was wrong. He is different from what she remembers. The defiance in his eyes masks the crazy bloodlust that burns bright. Infection does not only take hold of his chest and arms but half of his face. He growls, and the audience shouts back.

"Ladies and gentlemen, standing before you is one of your own. Accused of the horrible crime of attempted rape and murder, we are here to see how the heavens above judge him. As the Almighty given form, I have decreed we will let this man prove his will in the judging circle," Father says from where he stands in the center.

The sentenced man does not look at him. His attention is drawn and locked by the hundreds of hungry souls who want to watch him die.

"By our graces, his punishment will be decided here," Father finishes and walks himself out of the arena.

"Do you recognize him, Elizabeth?" Alexis asks.

Elizabeth doesn't answer. The crowd has quieted down, the anticipation of a thousand souls so thick she could feel the collective heartbeat. The banners ripple in the wind, their fabric snapping sharply as the doomed waits in the center, his feet buried in the mud.

Metal creaks as the gate furthest from him swings slowly open. Nothing moves, the crowd does not breathe.

A man steps out. Stooped and pale, the cloudy afternoon light burns at his skin, turning it red and popping blisters in between the scales. He shields his eyes with his burning arm. Infection has run its course throughout his body. Muscles have atrophied, and the bones are swollen at the joints. He twitches as he tries to protect himself from the sun, and he sniffs at the smell of a thousand meals that surround him.

"Come on you maggot, fight me!" the man in the center challenges.

The infected lifts his head. He sees the creature yelling at him. His head cocks to the side with a *pop* that is audible all the way to the first rows of the audience.

"He's going to fight the infected?" Elizabeth asks.

There is no time to answer as the creature charges the man. Faster than a starving creature should be, the infected is on top of the prisoner in a flash. Dirty nails and snarling teeth rake and snap before they are lifted into the air. The monster throws itself at the condemned, and thick arms and legs help propel the hungry beast into the air where it flies head over heels into the mud with a sickening *thud*.

No hesitation, the former guard jumps and comes down on top of the body with bone-crunching force. The infected howls, not in pain but in hunger. It tries to bite his opponent, but meaty fingers wrap around its throat. Blood begins to flow as fingernails dig into flesh. A swing of the arm sends a geyser of amber liquid into the air as the man holds his trophy of triumph in the air.

Men and women boo as he parades his way around. Dark liquid pools where the infected dies, and Elizabeth wants to hurl the contents of her stomach at her feet. Alexis has an iron tight grip on her arm, and the pressure is beginning to hurt. Looking at the young girl, her skin is almost translucent, but her eyes will not pull away from the carnage.

The two other metal cages open, and the condemned man tosses his gory treasure into the shadows of the first gate. Without hesitation, the infected charge out of their bindings at the smell of blood. One woman and one man barrel across the boggy arena. The guard pulls his knife and prepares for their arrival. The male infected reaches him first and is greeted with polished steel across his chest and abdomen. Blood and guts spill, but he continues to fight. His weight pushes the guard back. The woman reaches him now, and she leaps on his back like an enraged jungle cat. Claws rip into the guard's skin, and she bites down where his shoulders end and his neck begins.

He howls in pain, and Elizabeth joins him as Alexis' grip becomes a pinch that draws blood beneath her sweatshirt.

Bringing his knife up, the guard jams his blade through the male's chin and into his useless brain. The infected spasms, grips at the guard's shoulder one more time, and falls over dead. One danger down, the guard reaches up and rips the woman off his back by the thin hair still attached to her head. She tumbles forward and splashes in the blood saturated mud. Dark streaks waterfall down the guard's chest. He rolls his shoulder and more blood spits out. He no longer has a weapon, the knife still logged in the dead man's head.

She growls as she circles her intended meal. Blood and dirt cake most of her body and the little cloth she wore has been torn away. Her flesh is bare to the wind but covered in so much infection that puss and other liquids mix with the grime from the arena.

The two combatants continue to circle one another. The crowd is going frantic. People are jumping and shouting. Curses find themselves thrown into the arena along with rocks that splash in the mud. Elizabeth hears and feels none of it. She can only see the hunger in the woman's eyes and the desperation growing in his.

This is madness.

She spares a quick look back at Alexis, who sits so silently she would be dead if it wasn't for the terrifyingly strong grip she has on Elizabeth's arm.

Elizabeth turns back to the fight as the crowd goes into chaos. The guard now has the woman in his arms, her back pressed against his chest. She scratches at his skin and bites at his arm as he squeezes his muscles around her neck. Blood is pulsing out of the woman's ears as fast as it is leaking from the tear in the guard's shoulder. Bones pop, and the woman's arms and legs kick out frantically. Dark bits of dirt are sent into the air. Elizabeth can see them splatter on some of the children and women who sit too close to the killing ground.

With a final shout, the guard snaps the woman's neck, and her body falls limp. He is breathing heavy now. A hundred scratch marks drain blood over his body, and he carries himself with a limp. The crowd begins to quiet. There is a feral squealing like a rabid pig coming from the opened cages.

The guard turns to them. He backpedals toward the corpse with his blade sticking out like King Arthur's promised sword.

There is not enough time.

More of the infected make their way into the arena. Three at first. All of them men. Bigger, stronger, and fresher. The guard eyes his weapon. It is too far away. All three men charge at once. The smell of blood draws them in like flies to shit. Four more women charge in after.

Villagers are no longer human as they explode into jubilation as the first reach the man fighting for his life. Elizabeth turns away, dragging Alexis with her. She can hear the cries from the arena as she swings her crutch in front of herself, battering bodies out of the way as she drags them through the crowd. People ignore them, and Elizabeth fights to keep her stomach in check. She can smell their lust and stench as she pushes through.

The world is spinning and the air is as hot as a humid summer day. At least Alexis is no longer fighting, and they race for the exit.

Free of the last row, Elizabeth falls to the ground and pain erupts through her leg. She vomits on the ground between her hands, and her stomach spasms. Alexis is saying something. Words of comfort most likely, but Elizabeth cannot hear any of them. The village behind them is a madhouse of insanity and more deranged than the cursed pits of Hell. Elizabeth looks up at the young girl who kneels beside her, and then up at the fading light of the afternoon.

She has to get out of there, even if she has to die trying.

* * *

Knees wobble. Elizabeth shuffles forward along Main Street. Alexis wraps her arm around her, giving her support where the crutch has given up two blocks ago. Voices of jubilation carry on as the villagers move past. Too much adrenaline, too much excitement for any of them to care about a crippled woman and the one who cares enough to help. They stagger like drunks, leaning heavily on one another but with legs that work without pain. Songs of triumph and cheer are sung into the air as women whisper secrets among themselves, men boast about their strength in the arena, and children slash imaginary swords at one another, chasing away the bad guys and infected before them.

All of it makes Elizabeth sick. They all make her sick.

To the west, the sun is nothing but a sliver of red fire burning the horizon, pushing out long shadows that grow darker every minute. As bodies pass, the air stays warm with the heat of excitement and the radiating animalistic wants for blood. So many people crowded into such a tiny space, they cannot feel the cold, but she knows it is there. The most recent storm has passed. Tonight, when the moon and stars are out, the temperature will drop and the bodies in the arena will freeze.

The vision of herself laying there in the mud, her guts torn out as the people cheer wildly twists her stomach, and she belches another acidic burp.

Elizabeth takes in an unsteady breath. Her stomach is twisted, and she can only hold in enough breath to prevent herself from coughing. Weakness holds back the pain, but she can feel it gnawing at her nerves, and the anger builds as people pass, recalling the battle in all its gory details.

Torches and lanterns burn as both women continue their slow pilgrimage back to the hospital. Alexis is correct. She needs to rest. Her body is not ready for so much motion, but she can feel her time running short. This is not where she belongs. Unless she died a long time ago, and this is her unending punishment, there must be a way for her to free herself. Even the devil himself can't be this cruel and sadistic. Elizabeth spits on the ground at their feet, her mouth full of bile and the taste of blood.

Splashing in the dark, cold slush at their feet, she can see her boots lifting red with each step. That man's blood is on her skin. Killing someone for your freedom, she is okay with. Time only knows how many she has had to kill before to stay alive. But that guard's death was not for her freedom or with mercy. These people secretly live off this shit. Their souls burn with vigor as they watch others torn apart in the name of their god's will.

Fuck them. They can all rot in Hell.

"We are almost there, Elizabeth," Alexis whispers. Her voice is soft, reassuring, and almost back to the strength Elizabeth remembers. "We'll get you tucked in and a few more medicines in you. A good night's rest will see you stronger in the morning."

"How can you sleep after that?" Elizabeth asks.

She looks at the young girl whose arms are supplying her with the only strength that she has.

"God sees fit to give us a way to our salvation. Those who choose to break away from his teachings must see to it that they seek forgiveness," the young girl says. Her eyes are locked forward, and the words are recited with no emotion. "If he had been found worthy by our Father, he would have survived in the ring and we would have accepted him back into our family."

Elizabeth stops her feet and is almost pulled to the ground as Alexis continues forward.

"If he would have survived? You unleashed ten hungry and wild infected on him. Seven of them at one time. Only a fucking monster could have killed their way through that. Who knows how many more were waiting for him after?"

She takes a step back from Alexis. A family with two young children stop, a boy hugging the father around the waist and girl with her chubby arms wrapped around her mom's knee take notice of the two crippled figures as they stand in the middle of the street. Alexis smiles at them and waves them to continue. They eye Elizabeth, their attention drawn to the bruising and the bandages, their children pulled close to their legs. Without saying a word, they eventually turn and begin their way further down the street.

"Father's Chosen once fought off twenty and survived. He is as blessed as we are. If God had wanted that man to live, he would have. Please, Elizabeth, don't get yourself so excited. You need to rest."

Alexis steps forward and takes a soft but firm grip on Elizabeth's arm.

"I told you, only a fucking monster could survive," Elizabeth adds before allowing the young girl to pull her along.

Both women remain silent as they continue down the street. The voices of villagers fade, and the long shadows grow into a cloud of night. Stars, those brightest and able to fight their way past the flames that line the street, watch silently overhead. Elizabeth can feel the chill in the air quickly becoming a brisk cold. Painfully, she wraps her arms around her chest. White puffs of smoke cloud up before her eyes, and she can feel droplets of snot pool on her upper lip.

"We are almost there, Elizabeth. I will be happy

when I see that you are resting," Alexis says.

The lights of the birthing ward are bright across the third floor. Open braziers burn at the bottom of the stairs leading to the front door. Their bright orange glow casts shadows that dance like demons over the empty front walls. No one waits for them. Even the Chosen is nowhere to be seen.

"It will be nice to lay down again," Elizabeth says.

Alexis smiles and gives her a slight hug.

"There is our beautiful!" a man yells out from behind them.

The muscles in Alexis' body go taut, and her steps quicken. Elizabeth tries to keep up, but begins to stumble and forces them to slow.

"Wait, don't you want to celebrate?" he calls again.

Elizabeth looks at her friend, and the young girl has closed her eyes and a couple of tears have already made their way down her cheeks. Seeing the pain on the girl's face, Elizabeth turns to see there are three men steadily walking towards them.

Shoulder to shoulder, they could be copies of the guard they just watched slaughtered in the ring. Wide shoulders, bright eyes, and shoulder length hair. Infection peppers one's arm where he walks sleeveless through the cold night air. The middle one, the tallest, has a smile from ear to ear, and he taps the other two across the middle of the chest with the back of his hand as they slow their approach. The one on the right eyes Elizabeth, slits half-open and fire smoldering behind his stare. His dark eyes do not move when they meet hers. They are hard and determined. If this was fifteen years ago, these would-be hippie college punks would be more dangerous for the air pollution they caused with their overused cologne, but not these days. Somehow, the world ending infection helped them grow into even larger pricks.

Elizabeth snarls, and the smile on the tallest one grows.

"Honey, didn't you watch the show?" the middle one asks.

Stepping forward, he reaches out a bare hand, forcing Elizabeth to step in-between. Alexis makes no move to look at the three pricks.

"Look, shit for brains. My friend here is helping me back to the hospital where I can get some medicine and rest for the night. I'm not sure what you three have been able to get your pea-sized brains together for and come up with your plans for the night, but I believe you should be looking somewhere else."

The smile drops off the middle one's face like a rock. The other two step to the opposite sides and flank the women. Elizabeth fights the anger that flares to life like gasoline on a weekend cookfire. She doesn't have the strength to fight, not all three of them.

"We are looking for some fun with a friend tonight. That is all," the leader says. He balls his fist and cracks his knuckles. Several flakes of infection puss out where the skin pulls tight. "Alexis here has been more than accommodating the last few nights, and with tonight's excitement, we thought she would like to join us. Isn't, that right?"

Alexis drops her head down, and the other two step forward with chuckles echoing into the night. Both reach for her arms. Elizabeth moves as fast as she can and pulls her friend in close.

"Fuck off, ass-wipes. She isn't going anywhere with you."

Rough hands grab both women by the arms and pull them apart. With the last strength she has, Elizabeth keeps hold of her friend with everything she has.

"Let her go, you little whore, before we smash that other leg of yours," the leader says as they are wrenched apart, and her only connection remaining is the last few fingers that stretch the thin material of Alexis' thick shirt before giving away.

Elizabeth can't see anything as her mind goes berserk. She slaps at the man, raking with her fingernails, but his reaction is faster, and he pushes her arm away. Thick fingers that reek of puss and metal wrap around her neck and all air is closed off immediately. The heat of his fingers is fire against her skin. She can feel the muscles in her neck stretching as she tries to force her airway open.

"Cat don't have many claws left, does she? Maybe we'll have to see if she has any lives left either," the man says.

Elizabeth tries to growl, but her tongue clicks dryly in her mouth.

"Please, Elizabeth, let them be," Alexis pleads. Her head is still down as the other two men hold her by the arms. "I will be fine. Father has seen to it that I help these men with their aches and pains. If they want my assistance this evening, who am I to deny them?"

The grip of the man's hand releases, and Elizabeth tumbles to the ground.

"Oh, all three of us are in a lot of pain tonight, beautiful."

"Alexis, you can't…" Elizabeth stammers.

The cold slush of the ground sends shivers through Elizabeth's body as she tries to lift herself off the ground.

"Tell your crippled friend she best make her way to the hospital before she slips and falls again in some gutter where no one will find her in this cold. Wouldn't want anything to happen to her, would we?"

"You fucking asshole." Elizabeth growls, and she throws a handful of mud that splatters across the man's back.

He turns. There is fire in his eyes, and both hands *crack* as he balls them into fists.

"She is just trying to help," Alexis pleads. "Please, I will be happy to help all three of you men this evening. Just let my friend here make her way back to where she can get some rest and medicine. The pain clouds her judgement. You'll see she won't be any further trouble. Will you, Elizabeth?"

Reluctantly, Elizabeth looks the young girl in the eyes. There is so much pain hidden behind those dark circles that Elizabeth can feel the burning of tears threaten to fall across her face. She glares at the three assholes who now have her one and only friend laced between their infected fingers.

"Go fuck yourselves," Elizabeth says and swipes her hand through the snow and mud.

All three men laugh and turn with Alexis between them.

That is right, they can go fuck themselves. She eyes the hospital with its burning eyes and judgmental stare. Ice cold fingers race through her skin, and she refuses to move. Night has only started, and she isn't tired, but the pain is a constant drumming throughout her body. What else is she to do? She follows the silhouettes of the monsters taking Alexis away. She can't stay here even a single night more. She can't possibly stay here another moment.

Bones *crack* and *pop* as she forces herself back to her feet. Something has to be done, but maybe she has given all she can. There must be some way she can slip out of here. Taking a shuffling step away from the medical ward sends piercing blades through the muscles of her legs and hip. In the silence and darkness, she screams out in pain.

This is really it. There is no way for her to escape. She spits and growls at the people of this fucking place.

"You won't have me. You'll never take me alive, fuckers," she yells.

A dog barks in the distance.

"Fuck you too, bitch" Elizabeth mutters with no conviction.

Pain pulses through her body, and depression sinks its vampiric teeth into her soul. She will not cry. She will not give in. With shuffled steps and the dragging of her right leg, she begins to make her way back to where she can rest for a few more days and, for once, be alone.

In the shadows of night, with no one around, a tear falls and mixes with the blood-colored slush on the ground.

Chapter 14

Five Years Ago

Music pulses deep enough to change the beating of the heart. A rhythm rolls into thunder, and the crowd cheers the man with the cupped ears as he beats his head up and down with the pounding of the bass. Green light dances with the techno music, strobing across hundreds of sweaty bodies as they dance across the floor. Arms up, bodies jumping, breasts bouncing, and a hundred peckers standing at attention. The clueless keep their adrenaline pulsing and the alcohol drowning as they dance, and Merchant watches.

No one notices the shadow hasn't moved from the corner for the last thirty minutes. A few stray eyes turn his way but are quickly disinterested and back to the lust of youth and sexuality that is the dance floor.

There is no distinguishing one from another. The entire pool of people is shadows moving in mass, yet going nowhere in time or space. He has his eyes locked on one individual. Travis, slumped at the bar. Unless he has missed one, this shot of clear liquid poison is his sixth since he walked in here shortly after leaving the diner. Hair plastered against his face, his skin is paler and his cheeks sunken beneath the rays of green sunshine. He pushes away the next patron who steps too close, the young brat falling to the ground as Travis tips a finger to the bartender for another.

Full of bravado and inebriation, the fallen fellow stands with fists balled and chest out. Travis turns, a big 'Try it Fucker' in his eyes, and the college kid quickly changes his mind and slides himself back into the mass that sways like the waters of the ocean.

Another glass is slammed down in front of the drunk soldier. Movements slowed, he picks up the thumb-tall drink and pours it down his throat. He turns back to the bartender with his index finger up. The server shakes his head from side to side. Broad shoulders, and shaved head, he is a match pound for pound with the teetering drunk. A look of his own 'Fuck You' crosses his eyes, and Travis slams the shot-glass down.

No one notices the staggering man at the bar. A wad of money is pulled from a rear pocket and a single bill hits the table. The lips of the bartender lift his ears as he slides it into his own pocket before turning to the women off to his left.

Travis moves into the crowd. His eyes are cloudy, the tilt of his walk uneven, but Merchant recognizes it immediately.

A predator on the prowl.

Sliding between bodies, the drunken soldier rubs up against every female he can find. Hands sliding over asses and bellies. Cupping a few breasts, he makes his way to the center of the pile and begins his own wild gyrations. They do not notice him. The mass has claimed him as their own.

Smelling of alcohol and stale piss, he loses his form in the shadows that grow wild as the DJ changes the song without a hesitation in the beat. The lights pulse faster. Whites and greens send system shocks through the young minds being eaten away by drugs and liquid poison.

Merchant makes his way into the crowd. He does not dance. He does not have to. Shoulders rub and pelvic thrusts push him toward the center. He catches glimpses of Travis as the shadows fall to the ground and loses him as the featureless demons are lifted back into the air.

His ex-teammate has picked his prey. A blonde, hair as straight as a bullet and as wild as field grass. She rubs her ass against him like it's on fire. He has one hand on her shoulder, and the other slaps the cheeks with enough enthusiasm to be a drum itself. A drunken smile is stretched across her face. Cheeks red, she is as aroused as they all are with the pressing of young bodies together in a giant non-penetrating orgy.

Merchant watches from behind a ring of bodies. Two more girls try to slide their way into position where the blonde has found her mate. Travis rears back, arms thrown up and pecker pushed out. He roars like a lion claiming his pride. Bodies begin to separate between dancers and bar. Shadows stretched and torn, three boys step through, fueled by alcohol and hormones.

The two girls separate from the drunken soldier and his copulating blonde. Mischievous glints reflect in the strobes of whites and yellows as one bites a nail while the other wraps a strand of auburn hair around her finger. All three males are barking. Merchant can't hear what they say over the pulsing beat, but it is clear what they intend. These are their women. They own them, they paid for them in expensive cars and too many drinks. Travis has stepped into their territory, and they will have nothing of it.

Alcohol deaf, the soldier pays little attention. His hand is up the blonde's shirt. His clumsy fingers are fighting with her bra strap, and she barely notices anything but the floor at her feet as she pushes harder against him.

The girls are shoved into the mass. Swallowed by the shadows, they are gone. Pride swells larger than dicks as the three step up to the couple who do not give a fuck.

Merchant slides from the darkness, an invisible spectator. More words are exchanged in one direction, all following on deaf ears. Travis is all sweaty hair and hard cock. The closest man reaches forward, grabs the girl by the arm and pulls her away. Travis tips forward, moment of thrust lost and balance drowned in liquor.

Fist connects with chin, head rocks back, and the soldier falls. The young fool, brazen enough to throw a punch, continues to yell, his words heard by no one and cared by even less. His two friends give each other a high five and slap their leader on the back.

Merchant continues to watch, the show not done yet.

Travis begins to climb his way back to his feet. Unsteady, he hesitates and falls to his knees. Blood drips from his lips and a smile is stretched over his face. The dancers do not notice. Those who have stopped moving are swallowed and forgotten.

Filled with pride and confidence, the young man squats down to the kneeling soldier. Anger burns in his eyes, and he goes nose to nose with his broken prey. As fast as a cat, Travis grabs the boy's skull and drives his forehead into his nose.

Blood fountains out, and the asshole falls backward. Friends in shock watch as the injured squirms on the floor, a worm baking in the heat. Moment of hesitation gone, the first steps forward and meets Travis' fist with his belly. Toppling over, a knee greets his face and blood and teeth scatter to the floor.

Leader back to his feet, the crowd is pushed back, but the flow begins to fill back in. The music is a soundtrack. Fighters stepping as the beat orchestrates their combat.

Merchant keeps his distance, both men flank Travis, who is rolling his shoulders. His adrenaline is running now. A fire behind his eyes.

Both men jump forward. Arms wrapping, they try to tackle their target to the ground. Travis is too quick. Hands sliding past, he has them falling with bruises and bleeding.

Bouncers push their way through. Men with shirts too tight, and egos too large, they bark orders and pull everyone apart. Enemies them all, Travis is in his glory. He swings and men fall. No one knows the monster they have unleashed.

Merchant does. He was only waiting for the best moment to step in and stop the carnage. Moving from the shadows of dancers, the screams of men and women fall and move with the music. Two sets of arms have swallowed the drunken soldier. Teeth bite and draw blood. He struggles to get free.

Two slow taps on the shoulder from Merchant turns the first guard's head. Only a glance, he struggles as

Travis continues to fight. Merchant's fist rolls eyes back into skull and the bouncer drops like dead weight. Arm free, Travis cracks the other bouncer first in the neck, and then into his ear.

Dazed, the man falls. All three of the young men who valiantly defended their women are tangling with the remaining bouncers. People are beginning to notice. Some cheer, some push their way toward the door. Bodies begin to pile.

Travis pays no attention to Merchant and grabs the first person his fingers can hold onto. Skull into face, a young man in stripes and glowing shoes drops with a screech higher than a prepubescent girl.

Little bouncer is next. Diminutive to Merchant, he eyes Travis with contempt that would fill a man twice his size. He approaches slowly. Fists up, he keeps the soldier at a distance.

The man has training.

Merchant knows it means little.

Foot slipping on blood, Travis falls forward as Merchant is forced to push the crowd away to fight the swallowing mass as they drive for the door. It's a feint, and the little man falls for it. He sends his fist flying, but misses the face that turns easily to the side.

Two cracks under the armpit and lower ribcage have the man on his knees. Stepping back, the soldier readies for the kick to send the man to another world.

Merchant grabs the one he follows and spins him around. Anger hides his identity. Travis swings, and Merchant dodges. He does not swing back. Fury burns below the surface of the drunk who dives forward.

Merchant shoves him away, and he slides across the

floor into the sea of legs. Young asshole who started it all is back. He swings at Merchant. Fist missing its target, it clips shoulder and knuckles still crack. Attention the young man did not want is drawn, the asshole rears back and goes for Merchant once again.

This has gone on long enough. Merchant sidesteps the blow and catches the arm at full length. He lifts, turns, and pulls down at the elbow. Bones snap, skin tears, and blood sprays to the ceiling.

Women and men scream, drowning out the bellows as the boy passes out and hits the floor. Merchant stalks over to where Travis finally reaches his knees. He's laughing, blood dribbling from his chin.

"Did you see that asshole? Crying like a fucking baby," the drunk mutters.

He doesn't look at the one who stands over him. His eyes are glassed over, his smile permanently etched to his face. Merchant eyes the soldier with contempt. This is a fellow patriot. A man he once fought with. Once bled with.

What has changed him?

Why has he fallen so far?

The man laughs. Sirens roar in the distance, and the tiniest hints of red and blue reflect off street signs and windows. Anger flares deep within Merchant. He has no time for this.

Driving his fist into Travis' chin, he watches his friend fall, and then begins the slow drag out the back door.

* * *

The body of an infected, not those just beginning their fight with the disease or these half-mutants created by the one she calls the man-god, holds as much blood as a healthy human, though their body is shriveled and starved. Evidence of this theory displays itself in undeniable form around him. Dark rivers of gore flood through the gates of Merchant's underground tomb.

What evidence lacks in current, it makes up in volume. Thick, sticky, and filled with the horrid stench of bile and shit, the bloody remains of the infected pile against the locked jailer's door. Pale limbs, and bones brittle with disease press against the bars.

Twisted in death, the screams echo through the stones. Wails of anger and pain, the monsters throw themselves at Merchant with no thought of their safety or lives. Only the need to feed and the anger within them for those who still live drives them forward.

His muscles burn. His skin is covered with a thousand scratches, but he continues to push through them. The smell and taste of death is lost beneath the salt of his sweat and the iron in their blood. There could be one or there could be a thousand more. He has no way to tell, and he does not give a shit.

Betrayal ignites a rage in him so primal there is no other thought than what he will do when he finds her. The gate is locked but there must be another way in. Two more bodies fall beneath his hands. Necks twisted and backs broken, they bite and scratch, but he kills with no remorse and less hesitation.

Death has finally come for them, and he is happy to give them their overdue sentence. Shadows have almost swallowed him whole. His eyes are beacons of anger and white against the backdrop of darkness that is the holding cell. The lone lamp burns, its light poking between steel bars and twisted limbs, yet he has not hit the farthest wall.

A pin prick of guidance against the darkness ahead, he keeps moving. Each step is fought against the push of more bodies.

Where are they coming from?

Screeching from the darkness, an infected drops from above and lands high against Merchant's chest. Momentum stopped, Merchant sways but does not fall. The monster bites down on his shoulder, teeth tearing into flesh and Merchant howls, not in pain, but anger and over-fueled rage.

He rips the man from his body like a little puppy snagging on his clothes. Grabs the back of the head, long stringy hairs clinging to the blood staining his fingers, and he drives its face into the wall. Bones *crunch* and a wet *pop* snaps as the body goes limp. Rearing back, he drives the skull into the wall again.

Solid barrier cracks and chips away. Hollow, rotted wood falls and splashes in the gore. The infected is dead weight, its body swaying like an overweight fishing line. Merchant releases his grip and two more monsters are ready to oblige his need for something that will crumble more of the structure.

Agony and hatred echoes through the darkness as the dark wall explodes. Broken limbs flap around, twist, and roll as the second body passes into the passage behind.

Merchant steps through.

The air is now cleaner, the stench of death behind him, though it follows like a shadow.

The smallest of outlines flickers in the distance. This is a hallway. Long and silent, he can see gray, or what is only a slimmer shade of darkness, where else there is only black.

"If I didn't hate you so much, I'd say that was one hell of a show back there," Snake-Eyes says.

The ghost materializes behind Merchant. Soft calls of hunger and moans trail out from death's playground behind them.

Merchant does not stop. He begins to track his way down the tunnel. Wooden doors line each side at regular intervals.

Silent.

Empty.

He cannot waste any time. Every minute he spends down here is a minute she will have to separate herself and leave him behind. The hallway ends at a doorway of solid oak and aged steel. The top of his head reaches the apex of its frame, and there is nowhere to go but backwards.

Thin, cold air snakes its way from beneath the wooden slabs that bar his passage. It tickles his skin like the first chills of a winter morning after leaving the comfort of a warm blanket. Anger flairs hotter and burns a hole within Merchant. He steps back. Growling, he unleashes his fury into the wood, and it splinters into a thousand shards as the handle breaks off and the barrier swings open. Dusts lifts into the air, and cobwebs swing around where they hang from all over the ceiling.

Stairs. Twisting up, the lighter gray begins to grow. He moves quickly. The heavy leather of his boots pound an echoing song through the empty corridor.

Climbing, the path twists around itself over and over. Locked doors appear at regular intervals, but he ignores them all. He follows the light and the cold. Each grow strong as the shadows fall back. The life and anger he once felt as they approached this hellhole begins to fade. White puffs of steam form with each breath. Ice nips at his bleeding skin, but he ignores it.

"We going to climb our way out of the ravine?" Snake-Eyes asks.

Merchant gives no response. One step in front of the other, he pushes ahead.

Fuck the infected. He has a score to settle, and there is a redhead who has come due.

Countless levels pass. Sweat runs from his skin faster than the blood that smears against the wall as his arms and shoulders rub the stone structure.

Birds begin to sing. He can hear them over the roar of the river that is still a background noise that lost itself behind the screams of the dying. The surface must be close. Adrenaline pulses through his veins, and his pace quickens.

The stairwell ends abruptly with a wall covered in frost and a door made of frozen stone. Frosty tendrils snake through the door's frame, ice crystals locking themselves between door and wall.

Merchant places a hand against the rock. Skin and blood freezes instantly. He grits his teeth and pulls away. Tissue stretches and rips. There is no other choice. He puts his shoulder into the work and feels the chill radiate through his arm. The fight is short lived. His internal fire fights back and the cold and pain is gone. He shoves with all his strength.

Stone scratches against stone. Light, bright and clean, beams in like lasers as the slab of rock slides out of the way inch by inch.

Snow spills through. A few flakes at first, but then inches pile at his feet.

The morning arrived and is now long gone. It is closing in on midday. In the east, a golden ball of fire is well above the top of the ravine that is still dozens of feet above his head. The rays of sunlight are warm against his skin, fighting the chill that melts away against the fury that fuels his anger. He stands near the top of the structure that tried to seal him in. Ice crystals as wide as his shoulders hang from the rock ledge above. Jagged spears of trapped water, ready to fall and break anything in their death plunge to the stone below.

Merchant looks to where the water of the river rages through the unrelenting rock. Hundreds of feet separate him from the bottom. A wind carrying the screams of a thousand souls wails through the canyon. It does not fade. This place does not want him to leave. He was destined to remain here. This place had claimed him as part of itself.

Death and entrapment will have to wait for another day. No place can hold him. He cannot be stopped. Not until he reaches the city that touches the sky. He balls his hands into fists. Drops of blood squeeze between angry fingers before falling to the ground and cooling in the perfectly white snow. Off to his right, there are more steps. Snow, more than ankle deep, sits undisturbed.

Merchant turns and begins to climb. The wind rocks the wood below his feet, and the screams grow distant but frantic. The ugly, scarred face of the ancient building moans for him. This is a place of death and life is its only food. He growls at himself and the hunger he feels pulling him.

The top of the ravine slips below his feet. The stairs end, and he reaches flat ground. Light burns his eyes where it reflects off the fields of white like mirrors.

Where is she?

Would she have crossed the river?

She wouldn't have. Merchant pulls his ripped coat tighter. She would return to where she came from. Hoping to hook up with another group of lost souls, she would wait to find more prey for her brother. If she even had one.

Boots pounding through the snow, he follows the cut in the ground and the sound of the raging water below. It does not take long before he spots the snow-covered markings that give way to the stairs they used to reach the bottom. A single set of prints lead away and back the way they came.

She did not leave slowly. The holes in the snow are stretched apart. She was afraid, but a wide cut in the snow drags behind her.

Merchant smiles.

He knows what slows her down. The weight of what she has done pulls on her shoulders. By now she can barely walk. He does not chase. There is no reason to. Taking a deep breath to fight off the stench that clings to his skin, Merchant begins the slow walk back the way they came. With each step, he draws closer.

She could not have gotten far.

Chapter 15

Five Years Ago

The smell of blood and lies is hard to wash out of the car. Cool air from the night sweeps in through open windows as fast as the scenery. Trees and signs, highlighted by bright bulbs and blurred into the darkness of speed, pass by.

Interstate 81 going south.

Merchant knows this path. Exhaustion fights for control behind his heavy eyes, but he cannot let it slide. Time is running out, and the distance is not going by fast enough.

Leather along the steering wheel is warm against his skin and the smell of fresh cotton blows in through a cheap gas station vent clip that dangles from the center console. Red amber light from the dashboard and radio casts everything in a bloody glow, a menacing look for the dark work ahead.

Traffic is light, the road wet and covered in flashing mirrors of puddles from headlights as the vintage Impala barrels down the road. Trucks, engines rumbling and exhausts blowing out poisoned air, swerve in and out in their travels. Merchant keeps his pace fast but uneventful. This is not a time to bring attention to himself. Cops and onlookers would only slow him down.

It is Friday night.

Little time is left for him to make his way down south of Baltimore. Red lights flash and the truck in front of him jams its breaks before swerving to the left. Yellow and red warning lights flash. Merchant slows, and his passenger slumps with a moan. There is an accident or a drunken ticket being given. He does not care. Blinker begins to tap.

Click.

Click.

Click.

Merchant shifts to the fast lane and begins to slow down further. The cop is out of his car. Bastard has his ticket book out and the turned over pages flip in the air. Merchant drives by without a second look.

"You'll never get away with this," Travis mutters.

His words are slurred. Saliva drips from his lips and his head slumps against the window where fresh air dries the sweat from his hair and keeps him awake. Keeps him alive, for the moment.

"They took my family," Merchant says. "I begged them to leave them out of it."

Travis lifts his head. His skin is pale, ghost white in the passing headlights of cars as Merchant swings back into the slower lane.

"I told you I was sorry to hear about that." Travis grunts. A fresh line of blood drips down from his nose. "I had nothing to do with any of that. I'm a soldier, just like you were. We follow orders. Do the jobs no one else is willing to do."

Merchant glares over at him. Pain racks the man's face, and he falls back against the seat and his head then tumbles to the window sill.

"You killed me," Merchant says.

"But you didn't die!" Travis shouts and begins to cough before wincing.

His body shakes, and the smell of fresh blood overwhelms the little cotton clip. The nails driven though Travis' hands and into his thighs tear deeper into his flesh. His pants are soaked dark and caked against his legs where his life's blood has dried.

"Something happened up on that hill. They tortured me. I gave up. I gave in," Merchant says.

He does not care what he has done to this man. Even if he was once a friend, he is only a bump in the path he needs to follow.

"Another mole. I heard rumors there was another mole," Travis says.

There is very little strength to his words. His coughs are wet and weak.

"Yet they still killed my family," Merchant adds.

A slap of his hand on the spikes driven through Travis' legs sparks electricity behind the dying man's eyes, and he screams into the night. No one hears him, his words lost in the rushing wind.

"An example had to be made. That way no one else would even dream of betraying the squad. You fucked up, Merchant. Should have kept your mouth shut and just did your fucking job. For once, just kept that mouth of yours shut."

Merchant does not talk back. He continues to drive, and the car falls silent behind the hum of the reworked engine. For a car older than he is, it is in miraculous shape. Travis always worked wonders with engines, and he cared about this vehicle. There wasn't a scratch in the paint, and the interior was refinished with the highest quality leather a person could get beneath the government rations. Too bad it was all soaked with the remains of his life.

Four hours pass, and the sun is a kindling haze in the eastern sky. Not yet above the horizon, there is still time. Traffic is building and cars and pickup trucks swerve between the unending flow of tractor trailers that swat at them like cow tails. Baltimore, the city and its skyline, are lost to the north. People are making their way toward Washington DC, but Merchant does not follow.

He exits an hour away from the city. Indistinct exit sign points the way toward the point of no return. Some cars follow, even a few trucks, hoping to skirt the traffic of the city on a Saturday morning, but none of them will follow where he is going. Travis murmurs incoherent words with his head bouncing against the door frame.

Thunk.

Thunk.

The sound is hollow and echoes with a wet, squishy sound. Blood and saliva is dried to his face, and his pant legs have crusted over completely where his hands have not moved in over an hour.

"Where is this place?" Merchant asks.

Travis moves his lips, but the words are slurred and sloppy. He can't understand them at all.

"Fuck, just a little longer. Hold it in, soldier. That is an order," Merchant barks.

Pale skin is loose against bones as Travis' head rolls forward, and he tumbles into the dashboard.

"God damn-it." Merchant pulls over.

Dust kicks into the air, and the sound of tiny stones hitting the bottom of the car sound like a pinball machine going berserk. Slamming the car into park, Merchant gets out and tastes the dry, dead earth on his tongue. The heat of the day is approaching. He can feel it against his skin, and the cicadas buzz between the sound of trucks rolling by in the distance. Throwing the door shut, he storms his way over to the passenger side.

The smell of death is overwhelming, and it hits him like a bat as he nears the passenger side of the car. Blood has leaked its way down the door. Dark rivers that drip down before being pulled into long rivers across the black paint. He swings the door open, and Travis rolls onto his side, the belt holding him up and his arm dangling where it ripped through the nail that points upward from his leg.

He is still alive, but barely. Eyes are gray and move as slow as the blue lips that flap in the wind, silent and empty.

"Wake the fuck up!" Merchant screams.

He slaps the man across the face. Travis' head cracks off the frame of the car, and he rolls uncontrollably forward. Fresh blood drains from his face and stretches into a sticky string as it reaches for the ground at Merchant's feet.

"Fuck this shit." Merchant stomps his way to the back of the car.

He flips open the trunk. Buried beneath an armory of rifles and other weaponry is his bag. Hauling it out, he returns to Travis and drops the Army bag onto the ground.

"Mer…" Travis mutters.

"Keep your strength, asshole," Merchant says. "You'll need it for the next few minutes."

Inside there is a medical kit, and Merchant pulls it out. Travis' head rolls in the wind as the syringe is prepped. Clear liquid squirts into the air and splashes in tiny drops on the dry soil before evaporating as quickly as it arrived.

"This might sting just a little," Merchant says before stabbing the needle into Travis' chest.

He jams the plunger down, and the clear serum pushes its way into muscle and blood.

Nothing happens.

Birds sing in the distance. Trucks roar by, thousand-pound tigers rampaging down the highway. The sun breaks over the horizon in its bright golden glory.

"Come on, you bastard!"

Merchant grabs Travis by the chin and shakes his head back and forth. The man's eyes roll around sockets like loose dice.

Another minute passes.

"Fuck!" Merchant yells and kicks at the dirt as he spins on his heels.

Rocks skirt across the brittle, patchy grass and cracked top soil.

"Ah!" Travis bellows out.

The dying man tries to jump backward, but the belt holds him in place. He's only successful at ripping his other hand through the nail pinched against his leg.

Blood fountains up against the windshield, and

Travis' screams scare birds into flight, and the sound of insects is lost.

"Listen to me!" Merchant orders as he throws his elbow into the man's chest and presses him roughly against his seat.

The soldier fights. His muscles tight and as hard as steel, he pushes against Merchant's pressure, but he doesn't have enough strength in his beaten body.

"Fucking stop it, Travis," Merchant orders again.

The soldier begins to settle before he snaps his teeth and tries to bite Merchant's arm.

"Now that wasn't very nice," Merchant says.

He grabs a hold of the man's face and pinches hard. Skin goes red, and the man's eyes bulge.

"You are not going to like this, but you're a dead man and you know it."

Travis' eyes burn, and it takes Merchant all of his weight to hold the man down.

"I've injected enough adrenaline into your system to jumpstart a fucking jet and you've bled out all over your car. I'm rather surprised you've made it this far, but I still need you for a few moments."

"Go to hell, asshole," Travis says.

Merchant smiles.

"I'll get there eventually. But it's time for you to make amends for your crimes."

Travis spits in his face.

"Suck my cock. You're a dead man, Merchant."

There is nothing left to hold back the rage that burns in Merchant's chest. He lets it loose. Elbow drives deeper into breast bone, and he can feel the cracks beneath his arms. Blood bubbles around the edges of

Travis' lips, and his eyes widen as far as his skin will stretch.

He tries to say something. His lips moving, but nothing comes out as he tries to melt into his seat and get away from the man crushing him alive.

"P…ple…" Travis is able to get out.

Merchant backs off and a spew of blood erupts from the soldier's mouth as he coughs, trying to pull in more air.

"You've only got a couple of minutes left, Travis. Be a man. Tell me where the others are. I know you weren't there when they killed my family."

Merchant kneels on the ground and looks at his teammate's face. A glossy film is moving across his eyes, but there is still a little recognition there.

"Tell me. Let me get back what has been taken from me. Tell me where they are."

A smile tries to inch its way across Travis' face. The left corner of his lips twitch and pull up while the right side remains dead.

"You'll never get what was taken from you," Travis whispers, "but I'll tell you what I know."

Merchant listens. Secrets are revealed, and a hundred cars and tractor trailers roll by across the highway, unaware of what is going on in the Impala parked on the side of the road.

In the east, the sun is now a blazing ball of fire, the heat of its rays already warm against the skin. Merchant shuts his door and taps on the air freshener and gets a tiny burst of fresh cotton. Death and lies may be hard to wash out, but no longer having a dead boy sitting next to you makes it a lot easier.

Pulling back onto the road, he looks down at the clock. It is seven in the morning. His time is running out, but he still has just enough.

* * *

Blood trails behind the prints that dig into the snow. Boots are dragged, the individual holes are one long path cut beneath inches of precious flakes.

Light blinds off the endless fields of white, brighter than the yellow ball that flares in the clear sky. It is directly overhead, casting no shadow from snow-covered boots.

Single, lonely clouds move hazily through the sky, faster than the prey that struggles through the fields. Ice cold air bites at the skin. Death coming slowly and sleepily. None of it touches the anger that burns beneath betrayal and fury.

Shards of ice pick up and pinch at the skin, washing away gore that drips from clothes caked with blood and bowels. A hell-risen monster, the dark figure pushes forward over the fields.

Merchant eyes the blood trail of the one he follows. He is getting closer. The ditch created by his bag is now deep enough to reach the ground below. Cherry Red bleeds, trying to drag it along, but she can't let it go. No one ever can.

This is his burden. His curse to carry. Many have tried to take it from him. The draw of the secrets held within too great to leave it behind, but it kills them all. Like flies to the stinking carcasses he leaves in his wake, they have a need to possess it. A voice that calls to anyone who has the strength to try and take it. There are no words, no embodiment of why they must have it, but all succumb to their wants. Secrets held closed for all recorded history and before there was a time to remember. The desire to possess it kills their mortal minds.

He reaches down and picks up a small handful of snow. The cold ice melts against his skin, and he rubs the red droplets between his fingers. Still fresh, and much heavier as her life bleeds away. She is close. He can feel his curse pulling for him. It is out of his reach but cannot be past the short hill that breaks the flat horizon and disappears in the bright, eye-piercing glare of the sun above.

A sharp wind cuts across the plains. Its voice harsh and brittle. The air is razor-tipped and cuts through skin and bone. Tainted with something metal, a taste of rust and ruin. Adjusting the shoulders of his jacket, Merchant follows the trail.

He still can't see her. The world is an endless floor of white covered in robin egg's blue for as far as he can see. His eyes water with the torture of cold and light. Pain he can repress, he uses it to fuel the fury from what she has done.

The steps are drawing closer. An indentation and pooling of blood shows where she has fallen. Merchant smiles. He can feel the weight of his curse on his shoulder. She is close. Hiding somewhere out here in the middle of nowhere.

Silly girl.

He follows the trail. The stench of death follows him, and he is alone. Even Snake-Eyes has not appeared since he left the trap she sprung. A killing ground of hungry infected that did nothing but piss him off.

At the top of the next hill, her steps quicken. Mounds of snow are kicked up where she has fallen again, and a sledding path where she rolled down leads the way. Blood smears over white snow, and his bag is dragged toward an oasis lost in a desert of ice. Trees, barren and dead, stand with jagged limbs that cut into the sky above. Broken fence posts with snapped razor wire lean against the dry bark, the barrier cut years ago and rusting against dead wood.

Merchant trudges forward. She will be here. Hiding and waiting for him. The trail of red is now a constant stream. One of her legs drags behind her. The weight of his curse now cuts into the soil and slows her every move.

Tension releases inside of Merchant, and he feels his shoulders relax. He has found her.

Most likely dead, or close enough for it to no longer matter.

His steps are even, and calm. There is no reason to hurry. The trees grow closer. Twin trunks twisted together in life and death. The dual bases are one large stump separated by a gap where the plants tried to force themselves into individual beings, going at the world their own way. But life and Mother Nature's bad decisions brought them together in a knot of torture and pain.

Soaked red around the strap, his burden leans against the base, the single remaining strap pulled into the open gap between tree trunks. Blood pools at its base, and dry yellow grass sticks out where the snow thins against the dry bark.

Where is she?

Merchant stops and looks down at the old Army bag. The top seal is still buttoned shut.

She hasn't even tried to open it. A gust of wind crackles the branches above his head. A handful of twigs give up their fight with death and fall into the snow. Laced between branches, a bird's nest sits empty. He eyes the dead home. Trying to imagine the ingenuity of two animals capable of building something that has lasted longer than buildings made of steel and stone.

In the end, death always wins. It is the only equalizer.

"Ah!" Cherry Red screams as she shoves a hand-length blade through the opening between the trees.

The attack is slow and misguided. Merchant steps aside, and the dull end of the rusted steel falls short by half an arm-length. Fury and blood trail down the young woman's face. Red rivers run from her nose, ears, and the corners of her eyes.

"Die, you fucking bastard!"

Red spins around the tree. One leg drags, and she keeps her shoulder against the solid bark as the blade arcs out and comes for Merchant's shoulder.

Blood loss and delirium has taken her. He moves half a step back, and the weapon cuts air before slapping against the dead tree. Chips break away, but the metal is dull and *clangs* into the lonely afternoon.

Lost in rage and confusion she bellows out the pain that shoots through her arm. She drops the weapon, and it goes silent as it slips into the snow. Merchant draws closer.

Hissing like a cat, she swings a backhand that is meant for his face. He grabs her at the wrist, wraps his thick fingers through the loops of her belt at the back of her pants, and throws her away from the tree.

Limbs go sprawling, and her voice screeches into the air before the thud of bone against ice cracks the sky, and she cries out.

"Kill me now, you monster!" she demands.

Her strength is gone, and she is a mess from head to toe. Dark, wet hair is plastered flat against her skull and caked with blood and sweat. Her jacket clings to shoulders of sharp bones, and her tits poke out like darts behind a shirt stained dark brown with blood and dirt.

Knees wobbly, she tries to stand, but her bad leg gives out. She falls back into the white powder and rolls toward the tree.

"Do it, you fucking demon," she insists.

All the anger and fury within Merchant fades with the breeze that cuts through his jacket. She is broken and dead on her ass as she looks up at him.

Her eyes are bloodshot, her breaths shallow and rapid.

"I'm not going to kill you," Merchant says.

She spits at him, and a ball of phlegm hits the ground at his feet. Red and sticky, it melts the snow.

"Do it!" she screams and begins to cry. "Put me out of my fucking misery, just like you did all those fucking monsters back there."

He watches as the tears are thick with blood and salty water.

"Not much to look at now, is she?" Snake-Eyes asks as he materializes next to the burden that kills them all. "Too bad. Could have been a good fuck. Damn bitches always make the wrong decisions."

Red takes a deep breath when Merchant doesn't move. "Why not?" she asks.

She closes her eyes, her breathing slowing to mix with the sobs that shake her body.

"I held up my part of the bargain. You now have yours to keep."

A chuckle that sounds more like a cough rolls her onto her side.

"After what I just did. I'm fucking dying here, and all you are worried about is that fucking woman?"

Hacking until she is on her knees and elbows, blood drips from her mouth as she tries to smile.

"I couldn't help you if I wanted to. I'm fucking dying, and you have a hard-on for that bitch. Go find their camp on your own."

Anger flairs behind Merchant's eyes, and he picks her up off the ground with his hand wrapped around her throat.

"We made a deal. I take care of your brother and you show me where she was taken. I've done my half, now you will do yours," Merchant says the words like rolling thunder through gritted teeth.

Cherry Red tries to spit, but her lips barely move. Her face is turning red, and she kicks out where her feet no longer touch the ground. Eyes roll back, and he drops her to the ground where she crumples like old clothes.

"Plus, you aren't dying here. Not anymore," he says.

Turning her head, she looks up at him. Questions and anger burn behind her eyes. She smells of body odor and the iron shackles of death. He can feel her anger, but he doesn't care.

"Look at me," she says.

"I've already spent too much time doing that," Merchant answers.

"Not enough in my opinion," Snake-Eyes adds.

"You aren't carrying my bag anymore. You'll heal, at least enough to get me where I need to go. Then you can die if you want to."

"And if I decide to go back on my half of the deal? Leave you in another fucking cesspool of infected. This time with a thousand to gnaw away at that hard-on you have for the bitch?"

Merchant squats. Her left eye is two-thirds blood, and he guesses it is probably blind and useless.

"The question you should be asking is how I got here in the first place after you locked me in there with your brother and his friends."

"He wasn't my brother!" she screams. "None of them were. I was just supposed to supply them with…"

"With what? Food?"

Cherry Red tries to clamp her mouth shut.

Cheek bones drop, and her jaw hangs low, and she shakes her head from side to side but doesn't say another word. Merchant stands and offers his hand down to her. She'll recover once she has some rest. His curse is back in his possession. She'll still want it. Even at times thinking she needs it to survive, but she'll live.

Pulling her from the ground is as simple as lifting an empty paper bag. That is all she is now. She has had a taste of what is his. A part of her trapped now to the temptation.

She steps away from him and hobbles on her one good leg. Yes, she'll need some rest, but she'll live.

For now.

Chapter 16

Five Years Ago

Darkness has set in. Complete and stifling, the sky starless and the moon buried behind a thick layer of storm clouds. Rain threatens in the air. Thick and heavy, it sits against the skin and is carried with the wind that blows constantly to the east. Time draws near. Thunder rolls in the distance. A small shaking of the ground. A chill running down the spine.

A few droplets splatter against the hood of the Impala. Big fat drops that splash back into the air, and then end as miniature craters on the warm metal. Leaves rustle in the nearby trees. Twigs and trash swirl and roll across the ground. A low moan calls in the wind. It is almost here. Merchant lets the rumble of the Impala's engine vibrate beneath him as he sits comfortably on the hood above the car's engine.

The team's compound is exactly where Travis said it would be. Thick, prison razor wire surrounds an endless row of storage buildings, all of them black and solid voids against the reflection from the clouds above. Cold structures of concrete and bent sheet metal as soulless as the men who fill them.

Guards stand watch both in front of the entrance gate and behind it. Snipers crouch in dark nooks atop the corner buildings, silent weapons ready and waiting where they sit upon their empty, shadowed structures. Their slight movements are hard to catch if you don't know where to look. Bright beams of light follow the fence line in regular patterns, cast by angry eyes atop towers along the perimeter gate. Yellow balls trace the ground and skim over the soldiers before following the outline of the boundary the traitors are calling their own.

A military compound if there ever was one. Right in the middle of suburban Washington. Fifteen years ago, this would have been unheard of. Merchant shakes his head. He remembers the plan. No one will see it coming. There is no way to expect it, or worse, to stop it. Unless he does something now. His time is running out. He shrugs. Better not keep the Devil waiting then.

Merchant puts his night binoculars down onto his lap. Regret balls in his stomach. He was once one of them. Fighting right beside them in a war he once understood. Running his fingers over his stomach, the thick material of his uniform jacket bunches where he searches for the scars that should be there.

He doesn't understand what happened, but there is no longer time to question. He should be dead like his family, rotting beside that tree, but he isn't. Seated on the hood of Travis' car, he banishes the questions into the back of his mind.

Whatever the reasons are, whatever the cause, it has given him the chance to settle this once and for all. Not for him, or the pain they inflicted on him, but for his wife and his babies. The picture of their torched bones is vivid and inches from his fingertips every time he closes his eyes. Black with soot and fire, he can still see his wife's dead eye sockets searching his for any reason he can give her for the death that took them. An answer he doesn't have. That chance was taken from him, and he is here to repay that debt.

Thick plastic and glass lenses begins to crack under his grip, and he releases before his binoculars break in his hands. He'll need them for a few more minutes. Then after that, all Hell won't be able to stop him.

Hopping off the front of the Impala, he makes his way to the trunk. Popping it open, he looks over what he has to combat an entire platoon of traitorous soldiers with. Travis was good with his cars, a mechanic by pure nature, he always kept his in engines and body in top shape.

Merchant smiles.

Good thing he was the same anal asshole when it came to his weapons.

Rifles, knives, enough magazines to spray bullets until the sun rises, and more unaccounted munitions than he could possible carry, lays across the trunk. Merchant can't take it all, nor will he need it.

He straps an M-14 over his shoulder, two Glock pistols into his belt, and as many magazines as he can fit into his pockets. Knives are strapped into his boots, and for good measure, he clips several grenades beside the pistols. Why Travis needed grenades, he'll never know. He can't talk to the dead, and Travis won't be talking to anyone for a good time now that he sits beneath a pile of rocks pushed up against the slow lapping waters of the river. Buried unceremoniously within the tall reeds of river grass and mossy soil that sits in the shade all hours of the day.

When they were friends, Travis had talked hours about the times he spent fishing. Sitting on the shore, drinking enough beers to fill the Potomac. Maybe somewhere deep inside, he would find peace knowing his remains rest next to a river where someone will come in the morning and fish. They may even sit on that same pile that buries him.

Merchant doubts it. The sight of his family burned beneath their house rekindles in his mind. That bastard can go fuck himself.

Closing the trunk, Merchant makes his way over to the driver's side and slides himself behind the wheel. The road slopes downward toward the camp, and there is only one way in, and that same path is the one way out. Gravel and stone skip and crack as the heavy metal beast inches forward. He can't go too fast. Door still open, he lets one foot skip along the road. Rubber catches the rocks and kicks his leg out. A little more and the car begins to pick up momentum.

He leaves the transmission in first gear. The gear box fights the increasing speed, but the Impala continues to roll. Grabbing a fist-sized stone from the blood-caked passenger seat, he throws it down on the gas pedal and rolls out of the car.

The engine revs, and the solid earth sends shivers through his bones as he bounces on impact and springs back to his feet.

There is movement by the gate. Men scurry as their attention is drawn to the road. Lights swing around.

Orders are shouted, and a dark shadow grows as dust kicks into the air. Merchant follows at a safe distance. Black cloth decorates his attire, and he has added dark paint to his skin. They cannot see him. In the dead of night, he moves like a ghost.

Shots ring into the still air. Glass shatters. Muzzles grow hot, but the Impala does not stop. It has no mind. It has no conscience. A full tank of gas keeps the pistons pumping, and two thousand pounds of steel rolls toward the front gates.

Merchant jogs along the side of the road. A wraith between trees, he does not watch the men at the gate firing frantically at the charging vehicle. The snipers above are now involved. Their shots are hollow thuds that explode through aluminum and steel.

A tire explodes, and the car veers violently to the right. Engine roars. It is too late. Spotlights watch uselessly as the front grill smashes into the barbwire fence and bends the steel poles buried in the ground.

Bullets continue to fly. More glass falls to the dirt surface below the tires that spin. The Impala is stuck within the fence. A hole ripped through the cage, creating a second opening, this one not capable of being closed.

Shadows of soldiers approach the ensnared metal beast. Rifles ready, they flank.

Merchant can hear the radio calls. Signals of the disturbance, but there is no panic. Alarms do not sound. The threat is under control.

So they think.

Less than one hundred feet separate him from his target. Four men surround the car. At least eight have their eyes trained on Travis' prized possession and not the shadow that detaches itself from the tree line.

He must be fast.

No hesitation.

No delay.

Any of them mean death, and that is a mistress he does not want to meet again.

Twenty-five feet now separate him from the front gate. An opening large enough to squeeze through yawns and awaits his approach. The Impala has done its job. Engine still revving, it continues to distract. He smiles. For once there is something still willing to fight alongside him.

He readies his rifle. The guards do not notice him pass through opening in the gate. Their mistake has already cost them their lives.

* * *

The river is miles in the past, yet Merchant can still hear the roar of its waters between the screams of the wind. Snow swirls in the air. Tornadoes of ice and snow scratches at their skin like little needles, forcing them to cover their face and wipe tears from watering eyes. Darkness is almost complete. The western horizon holds on for dear life to the fading gray that can push through the clouds as night sinks its teeth in deep.

Cherry Red leads the way. A thick cloth wrapped around her mouth, hair dark and plastered against her head with dried blood and fresh sweat. She walks bent forward against the weather. Her leg no longer limps, through a small visible wobble works its way in with the occasional step as she pushes through the snow. She does not speak to him. A quick glance every mile or two is all she will spare. He does not care. She brought this on herself. Anger and frustration can fuel people to incredible heights. But fear can keep them in line.

Up ahead, as they continue their way west, the horizon breaks into dark, featureless shadows that leave the ground and stretch for the blackness above. The snow is a muted gray, reflecting the last bits of light before they plunge into the void of a stormy night.

Buildings.

Or at least what used to be buildings pepper the approaching wasteland. Tall squares and rectangles lose their tops in the shadows of the night sky. The wind picks up and whistles as it wraps itself around the structures and sings of the lives and world lost to the battles of the past. Dark shadows grow ominous as they approach.

Red does not hesitate. Shoulders rolled forward, she continues on. Merchant does not say a word. He feels no fear. She won't lead him astray again. At least not yet.

"We will need to stop here for the night!" Red yells back, her voice broken against the wind.

Merchant shifts the weight of his bag on his shoulder. They are close enough now to see the empty buildings. The closest are old brick homes. Two stories with shingle roofs. All of them are in bad repair. Some are nothing more than piles of rubble that stick out of the snow like ancient tombstones. This is the outer edges of an old town. Darkness shrouds the path ahead, giving him no indication how long the empty skeletons extend, but the nearest one looks sturdy enough for them to wait out the night.

Cherry Red stops waiting for him to respond, pulls her jacket tight around her neck, and turns to the nearest shadowed box to their right. Open windows of black watch them closely as they force their way through the swirling snow. A hole, punched through by rocket or crane, has decimated the second-floor wall, piling bricks and mortar beneath the snow, threatening to twist their ankles as they climb for the first-floor entrance.

Wood creaks but does not give as his guide pushes her shoulder against the door, which has remained shut against all odds. She grunts, and yet it still does not move.

"Some help here would be appreciated," she says.

Her boot to the door *cracks* into the night, but does little else to the barrier.

Merchant steps forward. He puts his hand against the door. Cold. Ice freezes it solid to its frame. Putting his hand on her shoulder, he gently pushes her away and puts his ear against the building. There is no movement inside he can hear. The wind picks up, howling as the last bit of light dives below the horizon. Merchant grunts and jams his shoulder into the wood. Slivers of wood crack off around the corners, and ice splinters into the air. The door moves a few inches into the house but does not open completely.

Another crash of his shoulder and the door swings wide and slaps the wall behind it.

Stale, cold air hangs in the darkness. Animals once made this their home. He can smell the piles of shit and stains of urine beneath the brisk winter air.

"Fucking dump," Cherry Red mutters and kicks at the snow.

Snake-Eyes materializes across the room beside a set of stairs that lead to the second floor. Debris from the wreckage above blocks the way, but the ghost has no problem sitting down.

"I wouldn't call this a five-star hotel, but I've slept in worse," the ghost says. He eyes Red who settles in the corner closest to the door. "Now that she's had time to heal up a bit. I would say I've slept with worse as well."

The asshole puckers his lips and blows a kiss at the young woman. Merchant turns and heads back to the door.

"You can't leave me here, we still have a bit to go," Red says.

She doesn't look up at him. Her knees are pulled up to her chin with her arms wrapped around her legs. Her voice is softer and struggles to hide the tremble beneath the chattering of her teeth.

"I wasn't planning on it," Merchant responds.

He takes firm grip of the door and pushes it shut. The wind fights him, but the barrier seals and holds. For assurance, he slides down against it and places his bag off to his side.

"I'm sorry, you know," Cherry whispers.

The words float on the wind like dry leaves. She does not look at him, though he doubts she could see him. The room is lightless, only the sound of their breathing and the cursing of the wind echoing beneath the empty walls. Snake-Eye's glow gives the room a soft, ethereal look. Only Merchant can see it. He stares at where she sits. She seems frail for a woman who has survived as long as she has.

"Your brother would have died quickly," Merchant says.

Red stirs and sniffs. Silence hangs between them for long cold moments.

"I don't have a brother," she admits.

Judgement hangs between them like the executioner's blade. Merchant doesn't say anything. He can feel the darkness begin to strangle her.

"Look, I was promised, if I brought people down there on a regular basis, I would be taken care of. He said he could cure me."

She sobs twice, and then growls in anger.

"You are full of promises, aren't you?" Merchant asks.

Snake-Eyes walks his way down the stairs. The broken pieces of wall and brick do not impede his travels.

"Told you that bitch was a lying cunt. You should smack her around a little. Show her that bag of yours isn't the only thing that can hurt her," the ghost recommends. "I would."

"Fuck off," she says. "You don't know how it is knowing this shit is inside your body. Growing. Feeding. Watching your skin turn, feeling it inch its way up and losing control of your own fingers. I'd do anything to stop this. He promised me!"

"That why you were with Hectar and his group? Leading them one by one to be fed to those monsters down there?"

Cherry Red shuffles so she isn't facing him. She doesn't want to be judged in the darkness. Not by him or anyone.

"Man was a fucking moron anyway. He'd be dead in weeks if I didn't set him up the deal with the man-god."

"Ooh, she works both sides of the fence, does she? God, I love women like that," Snake-Eyes says as he sits beside her.

He runs an index finger through her hair, and she doesn't notice.

"Who is this other one you made a deal with, the one who can heal your infection?" Merchant asks.

"It doesn't matter," she answers with frustration lacing her words. "Whatever deal I had with him is lost because of you and that fucking whore of yours. He'll never help me now. Not after you killed so many of his pets."

"He keeps them as pets?"

"Enough with this shit. You want to know more about where we are going or not?"

Merchant doesn't answer. He sits and waits quietly. Cherry Red grumbles a few words under her breath. They both sit and listen to the wind pound against the door at his back. Pieces of stone and rock settle with the storm on the level above their heads. He doesn't know if he should dig deeper or follow the trail where she would rather go.

"Go ahead. Tell me what you can. Do not think you can trick me again," Merchant warns. He reaches over and shifts the bag that sits by his side. "I will find you if I have to."

"I got it, asshole. I hope she's fucking worth it. You don't have any idea what you are walking into."

Reaching into his pocket, Merchant feels the edges of the cards scratch over the pads of his fingers.

Wherever she is, Hell or worse, he needs to find her. He cannot stop until he does.

Chapter 17

Morning has arrived. Bright, warm light shines its way through the square dusty windows near the rafters, and tiny strings of dust filter lazily through the air. Cutting through the golden rays, they dance in and out of the beams like leaves caught in the wind. The sound of a heart monitor beeps in the background.

Boop.

Boop.

Boop.

Elizabeth takes a deep breath. The sterilizing stench of a clean room burns her nose. She lets her body relax. This is a place for the sick and infirm. Something she refuses to let herself agree to become.

Most of the pain that racks her body is gone. Stitches and cuts are still covered in bandages, but if she tries, she can rotate her shoulder with only the slightest of pinching. Warmth wraps her body tight as she looks up again at the windows high upon the walls. Frost and tiny cracks of ice climb their way up the glass, but she can see the blue sky outside.

The storms have passed. The world is free. If only she could sprout a pair of wings, lift herself from this prison and fly carelessly into the sky. She takes a deep breath and ignores the burning reminder in her nose that she is still tied to this earth.

Clouds pass by, soft and as thin as cotton as they filter through her fingers. Freedom. It feels so good. It feels as it is meant to be. For a moment, she lets the feeling of contentment filter through her body. Enjoying its warm embrace upon her skin.

"You have such a beautiful smile," Alexis says.

Her words are no more than a whisper but enough to shock Elizabeth back to reality. Blankets fly into the air, and the heart monitor beats like a pounding garage band drum.

Beep. Beep. Beep. Beep.

"What the fuck!" Elizabeth shouts.

She scurries her way to the top of the hospital bed. Looking around, she sees that Alexis is alone. There is no one in sight.

"I'm…I'm sorry," Alexis adds, her face looking to her feet.

The young woman's hands are held together before her at her hips, and her hair falls about her downturned face. The strands of bright brown are darker now, thinner, and the skin of her scalp is red as if she has been scratching at something that just won't go away.

"Damnit, Alexis. There is nothing to be sorry about. You scared the shit out of me, that's all," Elizabeth reassures her. She reaches an arm out and beckons the girl forward. "Let me take a look at what those bastards have done to you."

Alexis steps closer but doesn't say a word. It has been over a week since she has seen the young woman. Bruises mark her arms around the elbows, and her skin is as pale as snow where it isn't a rainbow of colors from healing wounds and irritated scratches.

"Our father takes care of me, Elizabeth. I am fine, and I have been a good servant for our lord's family," the young girl adds with no conviction. "I am here to see how you are doing. You haven't ventured out of this ward since the last judging, and I was beginning to worry."

Elizabeth lays her head back and sighs.

"You worry about me? Fuck. I'm here, high as a kite in drug-induced lala land, but you are worried about me? We need to get you out of this shit hole before one of those losers decides you aren't worth his time. Once I'm strong enough, it's the road for both of us."

Alexis pulls away from the bed but keeps her fingers laced between Elizabeth's firm grip.

"Leave the home our father has built?" Alexis looks around the empty recovery room as if there is someone listening. "Where would we go? Why would we want to leave?"

Elizabeth squeezes the young woman's hands tight. There are tears around red lids swallowed by black circles, and it breaks her heart. To be honest with herself, she has been thinking about this very moment for the last week. The vision of Alexis being led away to help *soothe* those three men has put such a fire in her belly that she can't stand the taste of the idea of leaving the poor woman here to rot with the rest.

"It doesn't matter where we go, Alexis. Any place is better than here," Elizabeth says. She gently pats her hand down on the thin bones that make up the girl's hands, amazed at how cold they are between her fingers. "Look what they are doing to you. I have been surviving on the streets and open fields by myself for years. With you, we could make a team of it. Two heads are better than one."

Alexis' head shakes left and right. Her lips moving but words are not coming out as her eyes race from corner to corner.

"A time will come that I leave this place, Alexis. I want you with me. Ha, I'd never thought I'd say that, but maybe this world would be a better place if it wasn't so empty."

"I…" Alexis stammers.

Doors slam shut down the hall toward the stairs that lead to the exit into the village, and the vibration is enough to feel it through the metal frame that holds Elizabeth's bed. Flat hair sways as Alexis' gaze drops down to her feet, and she steps away, this time, removing her hold on Elizabeth's hands.

"I came up here for two reasons. First, I was to check on you, Elizabeth. To see that you were feeling better."

"And the second?" Elizabeth asks.

"To let you know it is time for you to venture out again. Our father has said that plenty of time has passed for your recovery. I am to lead you around and begin the process of seeing how you will fit in with our family."

"See how I fit? You mean, put me to work?"

"Everyone is expected to do their part, Elizabeth. The community is only as strong as its weakest part, and we all have our own responsibilities," Alexis says.

Her hands cup the small part of her abdomen below her bellybutton.

"No freeloaders, I guess. And if I don't find a place where I fit in?"

Alexis eyes the door and shifts her weight from one foot to the other. Elizabeth can see her bite down her lower lip.

"There is a part for everyone here. If you and I cannot find a suitable situation for you, our father will be able to with his unmatched wisdom."

Elizabeth groans and throws her hands up over her head. The sunlight burning its way into the room is no longer warm and welcoming. Cutting through the air like knives, she can feel her eyes water, and she is forced to squint to see through the shadows of black and red growing from the corners of the room.

"Unmatched wisdom, my ass. Go be one of his slaves or get myself raped every night by infected frat boys. Nice fucking compromise."

Alexis' face melts, and her eyes go wide.

"I never said…"

"Don't fucking lie to me. You've said enough," Elizabeth cuts her off. "Help me out of this bed and let's go see what little Suzy homemaker you can make of me, because I can promise you this, if one of those pecker heads tries to lay a hand on me, they'll be lucky if your Chosen is the one who finds them first. You ever seen a man bleed to death from his cock?"

Alexis' face is deathly white, and she recoils back into the nearest bed.

"Exactly. Let us hope you don't. Now, how about we don't waste any more time?"

The young girl nods and straightens her shoulders. With gentle hands, she begins removing some of the wires from the heart monitor and other equipment that does nothing more than hold Elizabeth down. Taking one more look at the windows that lead to her future, Elizabeth can't help but let the amber of anger in her belly fire once again.

* * *

The cold is bitter, and Elizabeth's attitude is even harsher. What warmth she felt from the sun and the blankets while wrapped in the folds of cotton and thread is lost as the harsh touch of old man winter sets his grubby paws over her arms and up her legs. Her toes wiggle in boots that are too big, and the skin of her calves chaff against the laces that struggle to keep the heavy soles from falling off her feet.

Muscles tense and injuries tighten as the wind swims by, cutting through the thick material of the coat that wraps her body tight. Surprisingly, Alexis has found something more suitable for the weather for her to wear, and after a spattering of grumbles and curses, the girl successfully walks her out the door.

Blinding light reflects off snow and white building walls across the village. Standing atop the stairs that lead into the medical ward, she takes in the breadth of just how big this community has become over the years. Black smoke from cookfires and work buildings stretches down Main Street for as far as she can see, and the dark marks of structures housing everyone stretches layers deep as small roads spring up like trails through a forest.

This is becoming a city of its own.

A gust of wind carrying the smell of shit and rotting food, mixed with the aroma of burning wood, wrinkles her nose. A cough racks her body, and Alexis wraps a thin arm around her to keep her upright.

Yep, just like the fucking cities.

"Stay strong, Elizabeth. We'll take it slow, but I know a few families that could use some help around their little shops. They don't need someone with much skill, just a pair of hands to help out. We could start there unless you think there is something else you could do," Alexis says as she leads them down the steps one foot at a time.

"Wouldn't happen to need someone to fill a gap in the perimeter guard, would you?"

"How could you think of doing something like that?" Alexis asks.

There is genuine concern in the girl's voice. Elizabeth shakes her head with a small smile and looks away.

"You said if there was something else I could do, and that is it. I'm pretty good with a gun. I could help keep the village safe."

And run the first chance someone isn't looking.

"Guarding the fences is for men, only," Alexis says. "They are the strongest and fastest after our father has given them their blessings. Our responsibility is to stay here, and serve the community."

Elizabeth sighs.

Fuck.

"Well, lead on then. I have no idea what else I can do."

"There will be something," Alexis says but her attention is quickly drawn away just as Elizabeth's is.

Three young boys go running down the street, fire behind their heels as both women reach the end of the stairs.

"Come on, it's approaching the front gate now!" one of the boys shouts.

Elizabeth looks at Alexis' face, but the girl's eyes are wide with wonder.

"Maybe we should go see what they are all excited about?"

The dark circles around the young woman's eyes shift as she looks up and down the street. More people are filtering out of houses as rumors of something approaching spreads like wildfire. From the shadows, in between the village homes, more families filter out and make their way down the street.

"I was instructed to find you a place not to…"

"Doesn't look like there are going to be a lot of people to talk to unless we follow them where they are all going. If you don't mind, I'd recommend we ride the tide on this one."

Alexis gives her a look of confusion, and then turns back to the groups of men, women, and children making their way down Main Street toward the western entrance to the village.

"Seems you are correct," Alexis says. "Can't miss the show, can we?"

A shy smile quivers at the edges of the young woman's lips before the muscles of her face tense, and she straightens to lead the way.

Shivers run down Elizabeth's spine as she thinks a quick thought about their most recent *show*, but she can't do anything but hope this one will turn out better.

"Lead the way," Elizabeth says.

With a quick nod of the girl's frail chin, both women make their way down the street. Walking is easier, her legs stronger, and her hips less achy, but Elizabeth still lets her weight fall on her young friend. She is enjoying the comfort of having someone to lean on. She thinks back to what she offered back in the hospital ward. It has been so long since she had someone to call family. Another living soul to rely on other than herself and her wits.

Skin, pale as a ghost, and a body as thin as a reed, she isn't much to look at, but just maybe she can find enough courage buried in that small body to risk leaving this hellhole and making a life for herself outside these walls. Elizabeth gives her friend's hand a squeeze and tries to push her own need to leave into the soft, cold fingers that wrap her own.

Alexis smiles and gives her a quick glance before looking back at the path ahead.

Dozens of heads shuffle for a better look as the razor wire of the protective fence looms ahead. A crowd that neither Elizabeth or Alexis could hope to push through blocks any chance they have of seeing what has brought close to half the village running from their everyday lives.

"For Christ's sake, what has gotten into everyone?" Elizabeth asks.

"Watch your mouth, Elizabeth," Alexis whispers and squeezes her arm.

The young girl tries to stand on her toes to look over the sea of people but she is no more successful than Elizabeth is standing there and cursing. Men with rifles push their ways through from the edges, and two rolling structures of wooden stairs and flat platforms spread the crowd out.

Positioning themselves on each side of the gate, two men climb each of the stairs and set themselves with rifles ready like portable castle turrets.

"What the fuck is—?" Elizabeth starts.

"Everyone, move out of the way," a deep voice rumbles with authority over the crowd.

Bodies shift and do not hesitate to clear a path. Alexis grabs Elizabeth's arm and pulls her off to the right. Forced to move, Elizabeth stumbles but catches her feet to prevent herself from falling.

The Chosen, his broad shoulders covered in glistening sweat, strides down the road and makes his way through the crowd. Elizabeth can't take her eyes off the man who dwarfs all that he stands next to. His skin is bronzed, and the wolf fur that straps itself over one shoulder, and across his chest, rustles in the gentle wind.

She swears he glances at her, his eyes judging and dangerous, but he is past her in a single step and moving through the crowd. Whispers move through the crowd like an STD carried by the wind, and it infects them all.

Is there a monster approaching the front gate?

Why are there so many men with guns?

Has the infected gathered to attack the village in the middle of the day?

So much bullshit filters its way through that even Elizabeth can't tell what the fuck is going on. Holding tight to Alexis' arm, she does her best not to find herself pushed to the back of the crowd or worse, to the ground where she'll be stomped to death for nothing more than a quick glance at whatever the hell is approaching.

"Can you see anything?" Elizabeth asks.

"State your name and purpose!" the Chosen's voice bellows as the gate swings open.

"Shh," Alexis hushes amid the rising voices of the crowd.

Metal gate and razor wire swings shut without another word. Men prep rifles and position themselves in expectation of war.

What the hell has gotten them like this?

"I have ordered you to state your purpose," the Chosen's voice calls out again.

Elizabeth looks over at Alexis, who stares ahead, though she can be no more successful at seeing what is going on.

Silence from the Chosen hangs in the air as people whisper of walking death and a monster that approaches.

Wouldn't they be shooting if it was a monster?

The Chosen wouldn't have just walked his way out of the gate for no reason, would he?

Moments pass and nothing happens. Rifles remain aimed, and men stiffen as the time grows longer. Feet aching, Elizabeth eyes the people around her.

This is far more boring than it should be and, in her mind, she begins to beg for a return to the medical ward. The comfort of a bed and drugs is more attractive than this.

"Make way!" one of the men on the platforms orders.

Bodies shuffle backward, pressing bodies against Elizabeth as she struggles to stay on her feet.

"What is going on?" she asks.

No one answers, but the crowd begins to part like the Red Sea. Elizabeth grips Alexis' arm and squeezes tight. The young girl looks over at her.

"Someone new has been brought home," Alexis says. There is a smile on her face that is an expression warmer than the cold that reddens her cheeks. "A new child has come to find the father."

Elizabeth has no words as the gate swings open. People gawk and words are lost behind numb lips as the Chosen makes his way through. Following him, striding in step behind the monster of a man, is a dark figure she can smell before she sees him.

Death, gore, and the stench of blood reeks like poison from the creature who stands shoulder to shoulder with the Chosen like no one she ever thought could. Families whisper of the Devil, and two babies scream in horror.

Words are lost to Elizabeth. The people of this village are shocked, horrified by what they see, but she can only stand there stunned. She knows this thing, this man who has found his way into the village that holds her prisoner. Dried blood covers him from head to toe. Bits flake off his jacket and pants as he walks. Scratches mark his skin, and people give him a wide berth. Over a shoulder, a single strap holds itself to a green Army bag that pulls heavy against his muscles.

He never gave her his name, nor did he share her bed, but he did find her in the middle of a raging storm. Hungry, but hiding the stash of food she had been carrying, he had willingly given her some from his own without question or request.

The dark skin of his shaven head reflects the light of the sun overhead as he passes the rest of the crowd, and she watches him go. When she was taken, captured by dozens of the half-infected men, he had torn through them like an unstoppable demon. She had done all she could do, but even with a rifle, he had torn the life out of more in a few moments than she could in the entire fight.

Here he is. Walking up to a guarded sanctuary like it was an everyday thing, stinking of death and destruction.

What does he want?

Could he have possibly found her again?

Elizabeth takes a look over at Alexis, who cannot be any paler at the sight of a man covered with enough blood to fill an arena twice the size of judging circle. If the man has come looking for her or not, she does not care. A spark of excitement warms her blood as she watches his figure follow in step with the monster that holds her here.

Maybe, just maybe, she has found her way out of this hellhole.

Chapter 18

Five Years Ago

Orange and yellow firelight shines through windows, casting dark shadows that dance throughout the hallway. Emergency lights flicker, and the electricity struggles to sustain a consistent power. Glass crackles under boots, crushed into a thousand tiny diamonds that sparkle in the fires of war.

The smell of spent gunpowder fills the air, and the screams of men dying in the field echoes into the night. Radios crackle with calls for reports and commands that will not be followed. Dark smoke filters through the hall, closing the walls in tight around the shoulders, narrowing the path forward into a tiny tunnel of death. Broken tile flakes from the dropped ceiling overhead, rat's nests of wires hanging and sparking.

Merchant can feel the cold embrace of steel against the skin of his hands and the hum across the nook of his shoulder. The comfort of combat cools his anger as he moves step by step through the hall. Men run frantically around the base, chaos driving them wild as they search for the army that has torn a hole through their defenses.

His vision is trained down the sights of his rifle. Little notch sits calm between the arch that tells him where his next bullet will go. They do not know where he is. Blood drips from his head and arms, cooling slower than the bodies he has left behind him.

"More of them must be coming…" A soldier says as he rounds the corner at the end of the hall.

Three rounds explode into his chest. Like a machine, the spent rounds ping on the floor and roll into the shadows. Blood puffs into a mist over his falling body, and his weapon crashes onto the tiled floor. Another target turns the corner, rifle rising, but it is too late. One bullet shatters the right orbital socket of his eye and decorates the wall behind him. A second shot opens a clean hole through neck and artery, creating a work of modern art across the sheet rock and molding.

More voices scream orders from the dark as the emergency lights go out and a canister is rolled into the hall.

Merchant pulls his jacket over his eyes and drops into a crouch. Light a thousand times brighter than the sun erupts and ringing silences the screams of the dying in his ears. He releases more messengers of death, like little bees pissed off and swarming, into the bodies that charge from around the turn of the wall.

Blood pools as his enemies trip over themselves. Six lay dead at his feet as he reaches the corner. Silence hovers in between the damage to his hearing and the death that follows in his wake.

Taking a deep breath, Merchant turns the corner.

"Got you now, fucker," a soldier yells as he turns Merchant's rifle to the side with one arm and reaches for his neck with his other hand.

A head-butt to the nose sends the man reeling backward. Distance created, Merchant raises his rifle and pulls the trigger.

Click.

Click.

Jammed. Anger explodes behind the soldier's eyes to fill the gap where the blood drains from his ruined nose. Driving forward, he tries to wrap his thick, bloody hands around Merchant's neck.

Rifle stock meets throat, and the man drops to his knees. Breath chokes out in wets coughs. Glock unsnaps from belt and gray matter sprays across the floor as the next bullet exits the back of the man's skull.

Merchant continues down the hall. He can hear boots coming from behind the wall to his left. There is a stairwell nearby. A sign hangs from the ceiling pointing in big red letters.

EXIT.

Picking up his pace, he reaches the door before anyone else can come piling through. Voices give orders as the steps draw closer.

Boots echo between words. A half-dozen pairs judging by the cadence.

They are a floor level below.

Merchant throws the door open, scans with his pistol, and unleashes a grenade down the descending ramp. Travis may have had a reason to keep them, but Merchant has a good reason to use them.

Metal rings like music as the explosive rolls over concrete steps. Men scream but are silenced with the sound of thunder that shakes the building and leaves pieces of rock and plaster sitting suspended in the air.

Stepping into the stairwell, Merchant can hear coughing mixed with the moans of the dying. The wall leading to the levels below has caved in. A gaping hole reveals piping and open spaces that fall onto the first floor below. There is no way down, but he does not want to go down.

His target is one more level up.

Sirens wail in the distance. Army or not, the sound of war so close to the capital and the cities has brought the attention of the authorities. Gunshots pepper the night between the wails of sound and light.

Merchant can feel his time running short. The blood in his veins quickens. He doesn't need that much time. What he wants waits for him up these stairs.

Calming his breathing, he begins to climb. Boots coated with blood squeak with each step. He cannot quiet them. He does not want to.

Let them hear him coming. Death is inevitable for everyone. It cannot be stopped. Tonight, he is the Grim Reaper, and they are at the top of the list.

A large number three sits painted in blue against the steel door. They are in there, waiting for him. Travis has laid the entire base out for him, pointing out every last detail. This was their central command building, home of the general and his damn dog.

Merchant checks how many rounds he still has in his pistol. Twelve bullets and one more magazine in his pocket. That is enough for him. One will shatter brains and do the job if it needs to.

Bloodstained fingers wrap around the cool handle of the door. The edges cut into his skin like fire and the barrier feels like it weighs a thousand pounds. A shiver ripples through his body, and he presses his shoulder against the stone frame.

This is it. Vengeance will be his, and his family will have the peaceful rest they deserve. The sound of his children laughing and playing in the yard calls to him from beyond the shadows. He can see the smile on his wife's face and when she bites her lower lip as her mind turns to things too naughty to give words.

She was so beautiful.

Blood drips into his eye, and the salt sets his vision on fire. Merchant literally sees red. There will be no stopping him. Another explosion rocks the ground, and he grits his teeth.

With a yank, the door flies open, and he steps through. Pistol held close and ready, he scans as he moves, preparing for the fight that comes.

Nothing but smoke and mirrors.

Silence.

Merchant can't believe it. He spins on his heels again.

"Looking for me?" the Dog Breaker asks.

The voice is behind him. Merchant goes to roll, willing his muscles to twist and turn toward his target. Pain and light erupts through his brain, and the floor rushes up to greet him.

Darkness spins throughout the room. Fire dances on the horizon. Vomit fills his mouth. Merchant tries to lift his pistol. Hard, heavy boots crunch into wrist bones. He screams, and his fingers release.

Metal skids across the carpeted floor. The Dog Breaker smiles down at him. His eyes are darker than the night sky. Black streaks his face and shadows hollow out his face.

Merchant tries to rise. A boot to his chest puts him back down.

"Not this time, asshole," the Dog Breaker says.

The next kick hits Merchant square between the eyes.

* * *

A cage and a thousand eyes. Merchant sits, resting against the back of his confinement in quiet solitude. The cold bars create pressure points between his shoulders, and the chafing wet of slush and mud soaks into the fabric of his pants.

The shadows of the day grow long, and the enthusiasm of the onlookers grows short. Three boys, no older than ten, look at him and whisper between themselves. They stand beside a pile of open crates full of stuffing made of yellow grass and piled snow. Their feet itch behind the barrier as they watch him.

He peels away some of the dried blood from his jacket and flicks it into the snow that piles around the cell. A stiff breeze whispers of the coming night. He can smell the aroma of burning meat and cooking vegetables. Stomach growling, he lets his eyes scan those who still wander by for a glance.

He has seen none of them before, but he knows she is here. She has to be. Merchant reaches into his pocket and runs his fingers over the cards that draws him to her and eyes his bag that sits outside of the cage. They promised not to take it away, leaving it within reach but not giving him the privilege of possessing it until they are certain he is not here to hurt them.

That decision will be theirs. He wants her. If they let her go, he will care even less for them. If she is a prisoner here as Cherry Red is certain she is, then he will do what he needs to so that she can be free.

One of the boys approaches. Long brown hair waves across his round and uneven face. He pushes it back over his shoulders. His steps hesitate. Dark stains reach wobbly knees of thick wool pants frayed under the soles of boots, which dwarf his slender frame. He looks back at his friends, who are now behind the crates and waving him forward. Another gust of wind and the youngster pulls his coat of denim and fur tighter around his shoulders.

Light brown eyes pass over Merchant and quickly turn away. They stop at the green Army bag that sits against the bars. Merchant can smell his fear. Sweet and strong, it mixes with the smell of body odor that the child has not had the opportunity to wash away.

"Little bastard is going to come and get it," Snake-Eyes says.

The ghost sits down next to Merchant. Pulling one knee up, he rests his chin and taps his fingers on his shin.

"They really can't resist, can they?"

Inching forward, the child is no more than a half-dozen feet away from the prize.

Merchant does not move, but the ghost whistles a funeral tune that is picked up by the souls of a thousand-restless dead.

The little thief turns to see if anyone is watching. All onlookers have vanished to their squabbled homes or other corners hidden within the fenced walls. A shaking hand reaches out and wraps around the lone strap.

Grrr.

Merchant growls and the boy yips. Shock overcomes balance, and the little vermin falls onto his ass and begins to scoot away. Merchant stands as much as the cage will allow him to.

"Ha, look at the little thief now! You damn near killed him with your voice!" Snake-Eyes laughs and rolls on the ground. "Fuck, man, soon you'll only need to look at them to make them die. Baby killer!"

Neck bent forward, and shoulders rolled until they are pinched, Merchant moves to the bars that separate him from his assailant. The boy's eyes are as wide as saucers and the whites brighter than the snow.

"Looking to take what isn't yours, child?" Merchant asks.

Nothing escapes the boy's rapidly flapping lips as heels kick the snow, and he rolls onto his knees. The other children are screaming and running, leaving their friend behind. Mud and snow lifts into the air, and smoke billows out with the burning of their shoes.

"Maybe you should be some kind of politician there, killer," Snake-Eyes adds. He places a hand on Merchant's shoulder. "I haven't seen someone make a baby cry like that in ages."

Merchant shrugs the ghost away and finds his seat in the back of the cage again. A few men wander within sight and look between the screaming boys and the cage that holds him tight.

He doesn't say a word. There is no need to. All of them turn back the way they had come and leave him where he sits. Another cold chill races across the village.

"Not trying to make any friends, are you?" a woman's voice asks from behind the cage.

Turning, Merchant looks but sees only the boxes they have placed against the back of the bars.

"You are definitely a sight I did not think I'd see again," the woman says. "I took you for dead, and looking at you now, I'd guess you were pretty close to being there not too long ago."

"Death has a firmer grip on me than the blood of a few infected," Merchant answers. "Why don't you come out from behind there."

Snow shifts and a small grunt follows as the woman turns around the corner of the boxes. She moves with a limp, her right leg shaking with weakness, and her arms and neck are bandaged up, but he recognizes her in an instant.

"Don't recognize me, do you?" she asks.

"Well, well. If redhead out there isn't good enough for you to fuck, then you better take advantage of this one," Snake-Eyes says while smoothing out the hair on his head. "She may be a bit banged up, but at least you know she likes it rough. I bet the bitch is kinky as hell."

Merchant moves closer to the bars that hold him for now.

"You were the one out on Interstate 80. Those men took you."

"Yeah, and I thought they cracked that thick skull of yours right in half."

"Takes more than a tree branch to stop me."

The woman cracks a smile and leans against the crates. Her eyes scan for any new gawkers, and a tired look spreads across her face.

"Look, I can't remember if I got your name back there before we were so rudely separated."

"People call me, Merchant."

"Well, Merchant, my name is Elizabeth, and I wanted to say thank you for what you did back there at the interstate. You fought like a fucking demon and, for a moment, I thought we were going to get out of that spot. Guess both our lucks have run out now," Elizabeth says, and then sighs.

She slides down until she is sitting against the corner of the cage and the crates.

"Luck has little to do with what happens in this world anymore, Elizabeth," Merchant says. He slides until he is seated against the same corner as she is. He can see her crinkle her nose at the smell that radiates off his body. "You still looking for the freedom you wanted back before they took you? A life on your own and away from everyone, or have you found yourself a new family here with them?"

Merchant waves his hand in a large sweeping motion toward the village that huddles together around them for warmth and false protection. The first darkening of the sky is taking hold in the east, and several street torches burn to ward off the darkness.

"Fuck them all. I told you once the only way to live was by yourself. You still thinking of committing suicide and going west?"

Merchant nods.

"Then I guess neither one of us is in luck. I'm stuck here to be some infected fuck's bang toy, and if you are lucky, they'll let you man the gate or something."

"If I'm not lucky?"

Elizabeth turns her head towards him, and he sees the fear buried deep beneath the look in her eyes. Dark circles and broken veins bleeding into the whites do a poor job of hiding what she has been through.

"They'll feed you to the infected," she answers before throwing a handful of snow as far as the restricted rotation of her arm will allow.

"Wouldn't be the first time that has happened," Merchant says.

Snake-Eyes chuckles.

She looks at him but does not ask.

"Look, I wanted to say thanks for trying back there, but we are both doomed. Can't say I didn't try to warn you."

Pulling herself up on the bars, Elizabeth gets back to her feet and wipes the snow off her pants.

"Wait, Elizabeth," Merchant says. She hesitates and does not turn away. "Get me out of this cage. I'll take you out of here. There is someone waiting for me to return, and they'll help us both get as far away from here as we want."

"And why would you want to do that?"

Elizabeth takes another nervous look around. Merchant's voice is hardly over a whisper, but she moves closer to the bars anyway.

"We'll call it a debt that needs to be paid," Merchant answers. "Get me out of this cage, Elizabeth. Do that, and I'll make sure both of us get what we want before I am done."

She lets her eyes look deep into his. He can feel her mind searching, wanting to trust his words. He does not move. Still as a stone, he waits for her to answer.

"I'll see what I can do," she says and quickly turns around the crates and is gone.

Merchant smiles.

She is here. He has found her. Now, all he has to do is set her free.

Chapter 19

The streets buzz with whispers and people. A bonfire burns in the center of the village, and people group together by the dozens like school children telling gossip as fast as their lips will move.

Warm, smoky air dances with the cold night, and Elizabeth does everything she can to avoid notice. The way to the medical ward is well known to her, and looking down the path, it is as deserted as it ever is.

The braziers that sit at the bottom of the long concrete steps of the hospital burn bright as the flames reach high into the air. Light shines brightly from the third floor, waiting for her return, but she cannot go back until she has done all that she can.

Alexis would be here to help her, if she could be. Giving her the words she needs to convince the lunatic who thinks himself a god that this man, Merchant, is someone they can trust, but she is nowhere to be found. Probably off *aiding* those infected pukes as she has been instructed to do.

Elizabeth spits on the ground as her mouth fills with bile at the thought. Her hands tremble while the anger rolls through her veins like a raging river. No matter what that girl thinks, she is not going to stay here in this hellhole. It doesn't matter if Elizabeth has to drag her out kicking and screaming, she is getting away from these monsters.

The smell of burning pitch is strong and warm as she hobbles toward the first steps of the hospital. No one has moved within sight since she turned away from Main Street and left the clucking chickens behind.

"It is not safe to be walking at night alone," a voice as deep as thunder says.

Elizabeth's heart jumps, and she spins around. Boots slipping on the snow and ice, she tumbles, and her ass cracks against the steps.

"Ow, fuck!" she says. "Who the fuck said that? Show yourself."

A shadow the size of the abominable snowman disengages itself from the darkness. Elizabeth's throat goes dry, and she tries to push herself up another two steps.

"You are in no shape to be wandering the streets by yourself. Especially now that we have such strange creatures in our midst from the wilds of this ruined world," the Chosen says.

"What is that supposed to mean?"

Eyes searching for help, Elizabeth sees no one but the monster.

"I do not like the look of that man who found our home. He brings nothing but danger to us. People should avoid him until our Father decides what is to be done about him."

"Look, I can take care of myself. I don't need you or any other asshole taking care of me. Besides, that creature you have caged up isn't as bad as he seems."

The Chosen takes a step closer. His face is flat and emotionless, but his eyes are searching. Soft, and for a moment, she can imagine those orbs on the face of a man who cares. A monster who can crush the life out of a man with his fingers and he may, for the first time, show signs of emotions other than anger. Being so large, he looks down at her though she is now seated on the fourth step of the stairs.

"He smells of death and worse. That is bad enough. Things like him don't just wander their way until they find us."

Defiance builds within Elizabeth's chest.

"But what about your father's lost sheep? Aren't the innocent and meek supposed to find their way to him? Stumble their way home?"

The Chosen hesitates.

"The innocent don't smell of guts and emptied bowels."

Elizabeth pushes herself back to her feet.

"Beggars can't be choosers. Maybe he just hasn't had a bath in a long time."

The monster's eyebrow raises as he continues to look at her.

"A very long time. I get it, the man smells and looks horrible, but is that really a reason to just leave him rotting in that cage?"

"He'll be released once he tells us why he is really here," the Chosen says.

"Listen to me closely, shit for brains," Elizabeth says. Anger has completely drowned the fear. "The man is just moving west. I met him before I was taken here. He has something he has to do out west, and no matter how crazy that fucking idea is, it does not make him a bad person.

"So, he is here to see you?" the Chosen asks.

Turning his head, the large beast looks back in the direction of the judging circle.

"Why would you think that?"

Shoulders roll and bones *crack*. A head made of pure stone turns back to her.

"You just said so yourself."

"I never said anything like that, you fucking moron. I told you, I've met him before and told him back then I thought he was as crazy as shit. Now, he's still crazy as fuck, but that doesn't make him dangerous, just stupid. Let him out and I'll bet he'll be gone by the morning. A good night's rest and some food will help him on his way."

"You sound certain for someone who has met this man once."

Elizabeth swallows hard when her mind catches up and she realizes she has already gone too far down the rabbit hole.

"I met him. He tried to help me out of a jam and failed. Gave me the last bit of his food when he didn't have to. Crazy bastard is just trying to be left alone."

She is standing on the fifth step when he moves up one and towers over her.

"Releasing him is not my decision. Our father is the only one who can decide what happens to this man of yours," the Chosen says.

"He is not a man of mine, you bastard. But if you cannot help me, talking with you is a waste of my time. Where is the Father so I can tell him how much of a disappointing bastard you have become?"

The Chosen takes a step back. His eyes narrow, and the meat grinders he calls hands ball up. Elizabeth's heart is racing faster than it has ever before.

"He already waits for you. All you have to do is return to where he has patiently done so much for you without question or request."

Lifting a meaty paw larger than her face, he points to the hospital behind her as if she has forgotten.

"Thanks for nothing, prick. I think I can show myself the way," Elizabeth says.

Turning, she bites back the pain of her leg and ass and moves as fast as she can up the stairs. Putting as much distance between her and this beast will never be enough.

* * *

The monster doesn't follow her. No one does. Her steps echo in the empty stairwell and return to her like the hollow *thuds* of broken bodies and ended dreams.

Sweat clams up the skin of her hands, and her heart pounds. Pain throbs through her shoulders, and she does all she can to hold onto the yellow railing that leads up the stairs to the third level.

To the room where he waits for her to return. She can already see the smile on his face.

Fucking prick.

Elizabeth takes a deep breath, and it stinks of cleaner and old carpet. The wind whips its way around the building and screeches like a whistle blown by a young child with endless abandon.

He is only a man. A fucked-up individual with an even more fucked-up impression of himself.

Looking up the last remaining stairs, she has one more level to go.

Five steps.

They are a lot longer than they used to be. She doesn't know if she can even lift her legs high enough to climb them. Merchant's words return to her.

"Get me out of this cage. I'll take you out of here."

Can he actually do it?

Elizabeth looks back down the passage and knows that the monster waits for her out there. There is no way they are getting out of here without a miracle or an army. Alive or dead, they are both stuck.

She leans against the wall, resting the strain that has tightened in her leg.

If only she didn't have to do this alone.

A small chuckle escapes her lips. Here she is again, worried about being alone.

Fuck that and fuck this place.

She can trust no one but herself. If this Merchant says he can get her out of here, then she'll go along only as far as she needs to. Then the loser can find his way to the west and his death.

A woman's moan of passion breaks the silence of the empty stairwell.

Elizabeth's knees go weak, and she slides down against the wall. She looks up to the door that will lead back to her room.

Silence.

Maybe it was a mistake, a trick of the ear. There is no one in this building besides her and that crazy asshole she now has to convince to let Merchant out of his cage.

Pulling on the railing, Elizabeth makes it back to her feet.

"Uhhhhhhh," the woman's voice cracks and is drawn out for moments of bliss. The sound is pure torture to Elizabeth's ears.

Anger and dread swarm through Elizabeth's body. Breathing heavy, she forces herself up the stairs as fast as her feet can go. The pain of everything that has torn her apart is returning faster than it should.

Muscles feel like they are ripping. Sweat drips down her arms and chest, burning the stitches so bad she knows she is bleeding all over again.

"Please, mooooooore," the woman calls again.

Her voice is young, timid, and even in the thrall of ecstasy, still shy.

Elizabeth shoves the entrance to the third floor open as hard as she can. Candles burn their way all along the hall. Passionate red flowers sit in vases made from drinking glasses and medicine beakers at each waiting table.

A rhythmic thumping is now shaking the walls, and the woman's voice is a whimpering that moves with the beat.

Elizabeth can tell where it is coming from. Her stomach clenches and rolls as she bounces from wall to wall like an earthquake taking the building down with her. The world spins in her eyes as the thunder of the thrusts and the wails of the taken grow with each step.

The smell of sweat and antiseptic is sickening. Metal fastenings scream for mercy as the pounding increases. Elizabeth's heart is so loud it throbs in her ears.

Fuck you, asshole. You can go to Hell!

With her good arm, she throws open the door to the room she has been staying in.

Metal dents and glass cracks. Candles shake with the new wind, and the two nearest the door go out. The smell of vanilla and scented smoke chokes out the stench of sex and sweat as Elizabeth glares at the dark figures copulating on the very bed she sleeps in.

"Ah!" The woman screams in ecstasy.

The man on top continues to pound like a fucking machine, and the moans choke.

"Get off her, you fuck!" Elizabeth orders.

Her throat scratches, and she tastes blood in the back of her mouth.

The dark figures stop.

"Elizabeth, is that you?" the woman asks in a voice as soft as a child's.

"Yes, it's fucking me. Get off her, you asshole."

The man on top of Alexis disengages and slides to the end of the bed, not turning toward her. Even in shadows, Elizabeth can see the smile that stretches across his pretty boy face.

"What are you doing here, Elizabeth? You should be down with the others, staying warm and having something to eat," Alexis says.

The young girl pulls the blanket up over her pale breasts and slides her long legs over the edge of the bed. Bruises and marks line her legs from ankles to groin. She goes to stand, but the man places a hand on her shoulder, and she stops.

"I've lost my fucking appetite. I need to find the Father anyway."

Alexis' face drops down to the floor, and she pulls the sheet tighter around herself. The man, cloaked in nothing but shadow, reaches up and pulls one of the thin strands of hair away from Alexis's face and places it behind her ear.

"You have no reason to search anymore, my child," the Father says.

He slides off the bed and steps into the candlelight. Not a piece of fabric is on the man, and he still carries with him a raging hard-on that would impress her if she didn't want to vomit at the site of him.

"What the fuck are you doing, Alexis?" Elizabeth demands.

She slides her way behind a bed that puts a little distance between her and the man she did not expect to be pounding her one and only friend.

"Our beloved daughter, Alexis, has been chosen to be the first in this world to carry the seed of the father that will bring humanity back from the brink of destruction. She is blessed and soon will bring a child into this life that will change the world."

Elizabeth eyes her friend who still stares at the floor. One delicate hand rests across her belly.

"Alexis, don't tell me you believe this piece of shit?" Elizabeth asks.

Her friend does not answer, but the Father takes a few steps forward, circling the bed.

"Be nice, Elizabeth. Alexis knows the truth because she is a believer. If you took a moment to think and open your mind, you'd see the possibilities right in front of you."

Elizabeth glares at the man whose eyes flicker down

to his pecker, and then back to her face. His smile cannot possibly grow any larger.

"What I see is a lunatic pointing his fucking cock at any pair of legs he can get in between."

Elizabeth shuffles until the bed is between her and the bastard. Alexis has not moved, and Elizabeth finds herself between him and her friend.

"Let's forget the unfortunate circumstances before us then. Why don't you tell Alexis and I why you have come looking for me?"

The smile on the Father's face broadens to impossible lengths, and she is certain his cock throbs with whatever perverted thought runs through the asshole's head.

"The man you have locked up in the judging circle. Let him free. He means no one any harm," Elizabeth says.

"And why would we believe that? The man is covered in gore and reeks of death."

"I know him," she answers.

Alexis gasps, and Elizabeth spares a quick glance at her friend, who now has her hands covering her lips. The sheet that wrapped her has fallen to the bed beside her. Bruises and cuts line her belly and chest as well. Dark purple circles spread over egg white skin.

"What do you know of this man?" the Father demands.

Before Elizabeth can turn, the man is up against her and grips like iron lock down on her wrists. The man's cock pokes her in the stomach.

"I..." Elizabeth starts, and her stomach spasms where he touches her. "I met him before I was brought here. He tried to save me when those infected attacked us.

He's traveling west and, by some luck, found his way here. Let him go. I swear he is of no harm to anyone."

"Elizabeth…" Alexis says but does not finish.

"Well, we have something here, don't we?" the Father says through a smile.

Dread washes over Elizabeth, and she recoils, but the man's grip tightens.

"It looks like you need something from me if you want this friend of yours released. I care for my people and would do anything to protect them. Now, I can see into the heart of men like him, and deep down, I see nothing but darkness. But, I have you telling me otherwise, and yet I'm not sure what you have deep inside of you do I?"

"You know exactly who I am, you bastard. I've told you from the day you met me."

"And yet, I've done everything in my power to help you recover from what this world has taken from you. Don't I get any kind of thanks for the gifts I give my children?"

The Father gives Alexis a small wink.

"Maybe a good swift kick in the balls. Now, let me go!"

Fingers tighten, and the bones in Elizabeth's arms grind together. Pain explodes beneath her skin, and she falls to her knees. The tip of the man's penis is inches from her face. Light reflects off the moisture that glistens across its skin.

"Again with such violent talk, Elizabeth. If only you learned to do something other than swear and hurt people with that mouth of yours."

Alexis gasps but remains on the bed.

"Put that thing near my mouth, and I swear to whatever gods there are that I'll bite the god-damn thing off. We'll see if you're so powerful that you grow it back."

Lightning explodes behind her eyes as the man wrenches her arms to the side, and her head cracks against the metal framing of the hospital bed.

"More threats. I am growing very tired of you, Elizabeth. Day by day, I wonder why I allow you to stay within my community of cherished people. I'm beginning to think I should let you trade places with your friend down in the arena. See if you can prove yourself worthy of staying."

"No!" Alexis shrieks.

Elizabeth growls and snaps her teeth like a dog. Blood trickles from her temple, warm and sticky against her burning skin.

"Don't like the idea of seeing your friend die in the arena? Maybe you should come over here and convince her it would be better to join us than fight us. She can even start tonight, if she wants, my blessed. You might be finished, but I was a long way from being done," the Father says.

He glares at Elizabeth and squeezes again. Pain sears its way down the bones of her arms. A thrust of his hip puts his cock dangerously close to her face again.

Another growl. Animalistic and primal. She can feel fire flaring from her eyes and smoke rolling from her ears.

Soft, naked feet are gently placed on the floor.

"Stay right where you are!" Elizabeth screams. The asshole twists her wrists more, and she bites on her lip to stop herself from screaming. "Don't you get off that fucking bed. There is nothing you can do to make me give myself to you, fucker. You'll either have to force yourself on me and hope I don't tear you apart in the process, or let me go."

"Please, Father," Alexis begs.

"Shut up!" the man demands.

He squats down and meets Elizabeth eye to eye. A moment of silence hangs between them.

"I can tell you are going to be defiant until the end, no matter how much I try to smack that stubborn streak out of you. But I'm forgiving of my children no matter how bad they seem. I'll make you a deal. Join your friend and I willingly, and I'll let your caged friend go. He can leave, and we'll all forget he was even here. It is the best choice for us all, and I promise it'll be the most pleasing decision you have ever made."

His face is so close Elizabeth can taste the bitter stink of his damp breath.

"And if I still refuse?"

"Please. No, Elizabeth," Alexis says.

Neither the Father or Elizabeth turn to look at her.

"Then your friend will find himself in the judging arena at sundown. We'll make him prove how worthy he is. Even if it takes every infected in this world, he'll show us the darkness he has inside of him."

"He hasn't done anything to you!" Elizabeth snaps.

"No? But you have a chance to save him, Elizabeth. Join us. Climb up beside our dear Alexis and your friend can go. We'll forget all of this mess and never speak of it again."

"Just say yes," Alexis whimpers.

Elizabeth looks over at her friend. Tears stain her

skin red and bones poke out of her slender frame as she sobs. The bruises, the cuts, all the damage to her body burns brightly in the candlelight.

"Go fuck yourself, you fake bastard," Elizabeth answers.

The Father rages and throws her to the side. Her ribs crack as she hits the tile and skids across the floor.

"Up, you bitch. Pick another bed to sleep on tonight because it's going to be a long night knowing your caged man down there is going to die because of you."

Elizabeth coughs, and the pain across her chest is so intense she begins to go numb. Arms trembling, she rolls herself over and begins to crawl back to the door.

"Oh, I don't think so, Elizabeth," he says stepping in front of her.

She looks up and his dark eyes burn down at her. The shadow of his cock, raging larger than ever, crosses over her eyes.

"You may not join us tonight, but you sure as well aren't going anywhere. Get your ass up in one of these other beds. Alexis here is going to be blessed with her Father's first child born to this hellhole, and you are going to be her people's witness to the miracle."

Alexis whimpers between gasps. Fear drives the skin of her face pale, and her eyes are swollen with tears.

"Fuck…" Elizabeth starts.

The side of her face rocks to the side as his open hand connects with her cheek.

"Just shut the fuck up and don't make this any harder on yourself than it is. One death is already on your hands. Don't make it any more than it has to be."

Elizabeth looks at her friend, who openly weeps. Fire

sears a hole in Elizabeth's stomach as the man strides to where Alexis cowers. Looking out the windows high upon the wall, all she sees is darkness. What has she done to the only hope she ever had of getting out of this place?

Chapter 20

Five Years Ago

Hell has risen to the Earth. The fiery pits of torment and damnation themselves are broken from the ground and consuming them all.

Automatic gunfire rages into the night, and the fires of three new explosions light the evening sky. The sirens of police cars and fire trucks moan before being silenced with another detonation. Lead slugs tear aluminum and plastic into shrapnel, and men scream for help and cry for their wives and families.

Thunder rolls overhead. Rain chatters on the roof, water runs in rivers down the window frames and drips from shards of broken glass that promise a grueling cut for the first person who touches them.

Inside the sanctuary of their oasis from the hell fire, the room smells of sweat and death. Blood leaks from Merchant's wrists and searing pain lances up his arms as the wires tying him to the chair cut through his skin. The taste of iron pollutes his mouth, leaking between his teeth and drowning his swollen tongue.

Bells ring in his ears, and the lids of his eyes are swollen like a boxer who won't give up.

He can still see.

For the moment.

Paper and other trash lays scattered among broken ceiling tiles and spent shell casings. Opening like a gaping maw, the window at the far corner lets in smoke and the smell of burning fuel where a desk has been pushed out to shatter on the ground below. A mounted fifty caliber rifle, silent for the moment, sits with a box of shells waiting to be fired. The cold and uncaring lid lays open and ready beside the messenger of death's bolted tripod.

Sounding like a mad man, the Dog Breaker hums a children's lullaby as he walks in circles around Merchant.

Humpty Dumpty sat on a wall.

Humpty Dumpty had a great fall.

"You remember how this one goes?" the Dog Breaker whispers.

His lips brush the back of Merchant's ear, and he pats him on the shoulder.

"Fuck you," Merchant answers.

The man slaps him across the back of his head. Merchant can feel the skin of his scalp welt. Blood pools beneath his skull and fire spreads through his brain.

All the king's horses and all the king's men.

"See, this is the part that gets interesting," the Dog Breaker says. He twirls a knife in his hand as he stands at the broken window, the opening reaching from the floor to ceiling. With a smile of pure exhilaration, he looks down at the war below. "None of them could put Humpty back together again."

Merchant spits a wad of bloody phlegm on the floor and stays silent.

His torturer turns and smiles, the lights of fires below glinting off his eyes.

"But here you sit in front of me. Right in front of my very eyes you are all back together again. Bleeding out, but in once piece. How can that be? I left you split in half on top of that hill. I've been sloppy and careless before, but no one survives having their guts spilled on the ground and left for dead."

"My family," Merchant whispers and blood drips from his lips.

"I cut you in half, yet here you are. A fucking ghost in my own fucking house!"

The man punches Merchant across the face, and then backhands him with the pommel of his knife. The tip catches across the cheek and opens skin an inch long and down to the bone. More pain to add to the tally.

"My family," Merchant says again.

"There you go, crying for your fucking family. Tell me how the fuck you show up again, and this time you kill more than half my men. Guns blazing, you walk in like death itself and kill anyone who steps in your way. No one is this fucking good."

Merchant shakes his head, and the pain swims from one side of his skull to the other. He can feel the bleeding that drips from his ears.

"My family."

The words choke from lips that are beginning to stiffen.

"Oh, for Christ's sake, what about your family?"

The Dog Breaker squats down in front of Merchant who doesn't lift his head.

"Why? My family."

A grin marks Breaker's face.

"Had to know if you told them anything. Couldn't let our little secret get out. Oh, don't you worry. That fucking whore of yours put up a fight almost as good as yours. I brought four with me. Told them I was from the VA and wanted to check on their wellbeing. Bitch killed all my men until I trapped her in the basement. Fucking fought like I was her pimp, and she'd finally grown enough balls to try and get free. Damn bitch had claws, too," Breaker says. He scratches at three pink scars that reach from his left ear around the corner of his jaw. You know what did her in? Those fucking brats of hers. Took down her guard to make sure they were okay. Gets them every fucking time. Stupid cunt."

Merchant lifts his head, one eye closed and the other half open.

"She wouldn't let them go, and when I finally got a hold of one, she was mine. Still wouldn't stop until I set fire to the house. I'm beginning to believe this stubborn streak runs in the family."

The Dog Breaker stands up and walks back to the window.

"You should have left them out of it," Merchant mutters between bloody bubbles of saliva.

"Should have? You want to know what I should have done? Made sure you were dead the first time. That is a mistake I plan to rectify right here tonight. No more cutting you until you bleed out. I'm not going to leave you to die here alone. Tiny fucking little unidentifiable pieces. That is what I'm going to do. Starting with your fucking toes, I'm going to cut you inch by inch until there is nothing left. Even if I have to saw at your bones all fucking night long, you will be nothing but a stain on the fucking carpet. Then you know what?"

Breaker turns away from the window and points his knife at Merchant who doesn't say anything.

"You know what I'm going to do? I'm going to burn this whole fucking place to the ground. That way the stain you leave on the damn carpet won't even be around to remember you. Done, Merchant. That is what you are. After tonight, history won't even remember who you are. Unlike us who will forever go down as the ones who saved this country. We'll be remembered, Merchant. And you'll be just a name forgotten long before any of this is finished."

Merchant mutters a couple of words, but they are lost between coughs and pooling blood.

"Oh, no you don't, you bastard. You aren't going to die until I let you," Breaker demands as he stomps his way across the room.

Merchant doesn't move.

Breaker lifts his bloody chin.

"What are you trying to say, you maggot?"

More muttered words.

"Speak, god-damnit!"

Breaker slaps him across the face and kneels until they are face to face.

Merchant opens his eyes. There is strength there. A fire brighter than the pits of hell that have been opened.

"Fuck you!" Merchant screams.

Forehead meets nose and blood spurts across the floor. Dog Breaker tumbles backward, and Merchant drives his heels into the ground. Lifting his chair, he backpedals as fast as he can.

Wooden chair crashes into the wall. White hot fire erupts through lacerations in wrists, but the chair holds. Stepping forward, another rush backward punches holes through the wall, but finally the chair cracks and falls apart.

Merchant tumbles to the ground, his boots slipping in his own blood.

Breaker is back on his feet. Knife held tight in his bloody grip, he screams but the words are lost behind the explosion of thunder and gunfire.

Merchant roars and charges forward.

Breaker tries to sidestep but Merchant jams his shoulder into the man's abdomen.

Knife is driven into his back, but legs do not stop pumping.

Blade is ripped from skin. Blood sprays and the window draws closer.

Breaker stabs again. Weapon cuts flesh and hits bone. Pushes through the side and slices free.

Jagged pieces of glass shred both men deep.

Smoke and ash filled air takes hold of both.

Gravity is not their friend.

Both men plunge from the top floor.

* * *

This tastes a lot like a last meal.

Warm chicken. Stewed winter vegetables. Freshly seasoned with salt to taste and not to preserve.

The food sits like a comforting pillow in Merchant's stomach. A blanket remains folded by his side. Soft wool. Sewn into an attractive pattern of white and off-white with spots of gray. It smells of musty water, but is soft enough to tell him it is at least clean.

Shadows grow long. The sun sets in the west, and no one approaches him. Maybe Elizabeth has been successful.

A rumble of thunder echoes in the distance. Hundreds of voices mix together behind a wall he cannot see over. The movement of a thousand boots walking across boards as fires begin to burn and light up the other side of the barrier.

Snow continues to fall. At first it was a flurry, but another storm is moving in. Merchant begins to grow uneasy. Bad things happen in storms.

"Think the bitch set you up?" Snake-Eyes asks.

The ghost materializes next to Merchant. Lifting his hands behind his head, he sits and relaxes as if the empty cage is as comfortable as a new leather couch.

"She wouldn't," Merchant says.

"That's what you said about Cherry Red and look where that got us."

Merchant eyes the ghost who smiles back. The eyes on his neck continue to blink.

"Not this time. She doesn't want to be here. I'm her only way out."

Snake-Eyes chuckles.

"Pretty confident in yourself, killer. This time might not be so easy. These aren't infected throwing themselves at you to die. I think negotiating may be in order this time, and if history has proven anything, it is that politics is not your strongest suit."

Merchant leans back to get himself as comfortable as he can and sighs.

"I doubt that is what they are looking for," he says.

The ghost picks at his teeth.

"You know, I doubt that as well, but at least they have that big fucker. I've finally found someone I'm willing to put my money on."

"What money?"

"I was a rich man once," Snake-Eyes counters.

"You also flew once," Merchant says. "Not for very long, though."

"Touché, asshole."

A door made of scrapped pieces of plywood and a car hood swings open from the wall that guards all the light. The voices and cheers of hundreds of men and women echo from within.

"Now what do we have here?" Snake-Eyes asks.

Two men with rifles exit the door and approach Merchant's cage. Infection climbs its way up their neck and ends at faces frozen solid in permanent scowls. Scars mark their cheeks below dark eyes, and their heads are shaved where tattoos decorate their scalps. Thick jackets of leather and wool bulge where their bodies have grown too large. Boots crunch in the newly fallen snow.

"Get up," they both order.

Merchant doesn't move.

The closest one kicks the gate. Metal rings and the bar dents an inch. Merchant does not flinch.

"Open that fucking door," the second demands.

The first pulls keys from his pocket and works the lock. The second charges his rifle and steps back for a clean shot.

"Are you letting me free?" Merchant asks.

Both men smile.

"In a way, we are. Time for you to prove yourself."

Merchant stands until his head touches the top of the cage.

"A woman. She was to ask for my release."

"Fuck off. You are to come with us."

Neither man move to pick up Merchant's bag.

"And what about my stuff?"

Merchant steps out of his cage. He is more than a head taller than both men.

"Won't need a bag full of shit where you are going," the first man chuckles. "Now get your ass moving."

No one moves.

"I said move, you monster," the man orders again.

The second flips the safety on his rifle. Merchant doesn't flinch.

"My bag," he says.

"Oh, let the fucker get his shit. There can't be anything in there that will help him anyway," the second says.

"But the Father said—" the first protests.

"Forget what he said. You want to go tell him you had to shoot the bastard because he wanted his bag?"

Both men back up.

"Get your shit and follow us."

Merchant nods. Snake-Eyes laughs from where he sits inside the cage.

"See you on the other side, demon. My money is on the big fucker!"

Bag over his shoulder, Merchant follows both men through the door.

* * *

A gladiatorial arena.

Merchant can feel the semi-frozen sand move beneath his boots. A mix of slush and gritty ice. The heat of a thousand bodies packed around the killing sand is as warm as a spring afternoon.

Snow turns to rain and puddles into mud across the ground. A gruesome bog filled with the souls of the damned. Tufts of brown grass break through the soil and bits of bone from fallen combatants stick out like tombstones.

Boots and shoes pound around the arena. A central podium sits to the west, the sun setting behind two risen chairs which overlook the combatants and audience. Rays of fiery red light gives the man and women who sit in shadow an aura of power that radiates from them like magic and draws attention to them like flies to shit. Merchant shifts his bag on his shoulder and looks away.

Thunder rumbles through the winter clouds, and the wind howls its cries for death. The storm has arrived.

"Ladies and gentlemen! We are blessed to have you here with us this evening," a man's voice bellows out above the crowd. Like trained servants, the audience falls as silent as the swaying ocean, and the man stands upon his risen dais. "Once again, we are called to the sands of judgement to caste our eyes upon the sins of another. Tonight, before you all is a monster, who among you kind and caring citizens will be forced to answer for his crimes against us, against our people, and against humanity itself."

Merchant looks around the crowd. Fires burn

brightly between aisles of people, but the fires are no match to the insatiable lust for blood he can see behind their eyes. Children dart in and out between legs to throw rocks and other debris onto the bloodstained sand.

Hefting his bag higher onto his shoulder, he turns back to the one they must call the Father.

"Here, a man stands before you accused of attempted murder and one of the worst possible offenses, rape!"

The roar of the crowd is a tornado of cries. Sand shifts and the ground shakes as hundreds of angry, bloodthirsty people jump to their feet. Shouts of vengeance and threats of violence echo into the night.

"Quiet, my people!" the Father demands. "Some of you may ask how is this possible. Fear not, my glorious people, for we are a just community and no man or woman would ever face judgement without proper accusation. Last night, in the deepest of darkness, this man was able to slip from his freely offered shelter and make his way through our revered sanctuary. It was then that he stumbled upon none other than our wonderful and respected member, Alexis. Upon seeing the wonderful and youthful beauty that she is, his insatiable animalistic lust drove him to the depths of violence where he forced himself onto her. When he was finished with his grotesque act of sexual depravity, realizing the shame he brought upon himself and our beloved Alexis, he understood the truth of his actions and was lost within a rage. It was then that he took it upon himself to try and destroy the evidence that was the woman herself."

Boos and curses erupt throughout the gathered masses. Rotten food splatters at Merchant's feet and several pieces of frozen cabbage and tomatoes strike him across the back. He does not move. His attention is locked on the woman beside the liar who stands upon his podium.

"Though heinous the crimes are, I want you to be assured he was not able to succeed in such a vial act as homicide. By my love for you all, our sacred Chosen was able to stop this vial beast. In the resulting struggle, Alexis was pulled from the mayhem and is here with us today."

Cheers of joy cry out. Calls for the blessed father and his ever-growing love swoon into the air, and the man who leads them all stands taller with his arms spread wide.

"Before we see what judgement has for such a desperate creature, I am here to announce a tremendous act of love for you, my people. Upon examining Alexis, and treating her gently for the wounds inflicted both on her body and within her soul, I have found the miracle I knew would be given to you all. See, three weeks ago, I began to keep a secret. One that I could not reveal until its fruition was evident even to me."

Hushed whispers roll through the crowd like a wave. Hisses mix in between and more rocks are thrown onto the field. Merchant's eyebrow raises as he watches the lying sack of shit.

"Our great and beautiful Alexis has been blessed with child." Cheers spread across the people. "But this will be no ordinary child. For until this previous evening, our daughter Alexis was an untouched angel of her people. The desperate act of such a monster took that gift she so carefully held to her breast, but the act was not enough to deter the guidance of your one and only God. Alexis, a virgin and devoted believer, is pregnant with God's one true son!"

The cries of the faithful shake the walls of the arena. Chants of freedom and praise roar and the storm in the sky struggles to keep up.

Merchant puts his bag down at his feet. He won't be needing it for the time being.

"Death to the monster!" the people chant.

Smiling like a man crowned king, the Father extends a hand and the slender woman who sits next to him stands and makes her way by his side.

"My people! Who better to cast judgement on this man than the very person who he violated and let her words go down in history for the power I bring you all shall be her words themselves."

She is a petite woman. Starved of food and soul itself, Merchant can see her narrow shoulders hunched beneath the weight of the people who stand on her every word. Deep down, he may have once pitied her. He can feel the fire boil within his blood.

The person Merchant once was died a long time ago. Now, he awaits what he knows comes.

"Tell the great people of our community what you decree should be done to your attacker, Alexis. Show your faithful what happens when a man determines he is greater than the world as a whole. Make him understand that the people of this community will no longer stand for this kind of vile behavior," the Father coaxes.

Stepping forward, the young woman inches to the end of the podium. Her head looks all around, and then to the ground dozens of feet below where she stands.

Shoulders lift and drop with a deep breath.

"I sentence him to death by judgement in the arena," she says.

Her command is barely louder than a child, but the words bring the crowd to a raging frenzy.

The Father wraps his arm around her shoulder and begins to speak. "Let us all be witness today to the glory which is ours! Unleash the first trial!"

Doors across the sand scream as gears grind and cages open. Merchant eyes the darkness. He can feel their hunger. The thirst for his blood is insatiable, and he knows what comes.

There is no reason to move. He cannot escape this pit without the death of hundreds on his hands.

He braces for the fight. His hands sweat. The heart in his chest slows as his lungs expand. If this is what it will take to make it out of here alive, so be it.

Let them come for him.

Chapter 21

Darkness decorates the entirety of her room except for the light that shines from the hallway in square boxes on the floor. Imaginary hopscotch drawn across a hospital floor for children with one leg and little else to entertain them. Even the little green lights of the heart monitors have been darkened.

The roar of the crowd is thunder that rolls with the storm that rages across the world above their heads. Snow collects on the edges of the windows near the roof, and she can see a new layer of ice cracking its way across the glass. The sky above is gray and holds tiny shadings of light as fires burn outside.

Why can't the whole place burn?

She smiles at the thought of their screams as the fences fall apart, and the whole area is awash in the flames of damnation. Dark silhouettes fleeing in terror as their little home of protection and false freedom crumbles beneath the weight of reality and the cold hard ice of winter.

None of it will happen now.

Not after what she has done.

Elizabeth kicks at the nearest bed and tiny rubber tires grind as the gurney rolls away.

She can still smell them. The stench of sex and sweat. Ejaculate and blood hang heavy in the air. Thirst burns at her throat, but there is nothing to drink. The taste of them is on her tongue, and her stomach rolls.

The bloodthirsty call of the arena sickens her more. He is there fighting, surviving as long as he can.

How many infected will they unleash on him?

The memory of this man, Merchant, killing without hesitation to save them both flashes in her mind. He was a machine, but he is only a single man.

Anger swells her chest, and it begins to hurt. She eyes the door. Fucking bolt locks keep her tied up like a new puppy trapped within its own crate. Frustration and self-pity takes over.

Running as fast as she can, she rams the double aluminum doors that hold her in. Pain lances through her body, and she falls backward.

Her back cracks. The skin of her shoulder is raw, and the taste of blood stains her teeth and taints the spit in her mouth.

"Fuck you, you asshole, cock sucking motherfucking tits, ass licker!"

The words roll from her mouth. Unencumbered, she continues though no one can hear her. Deep inside, it soothes the pity she bathes herself in. She would rather die out there. Not him. Not for her.

He asked her to get him out, open his cage and let him go. In return, he'd set her free. What did she do? Kill him.

Back on her feet, she screams and sends a tray of medical swabs and bandages flying into the doors. The tray vibrates and clatters to the floor.

This is useless.

There is nothing she can do.

Slumping to the floor, Elizabeth slides against the barrier that holds her in. Tears flow down her cheeks, and the cold frame of the door soothes the burning skin on her back.

What is she going to do?

Crack!

Her mind swims as the back of her skull slaps the door. Fuck it. If Merchant is going to die for her sins, she may as well go with him.

Rolling her head forward, she snaps her neck back, and her head dents the door. Stars flash in her eyes, and she becomes disoriented.

God-damnit, it hurts.

Warm blood trickles down her neck. Trembling fingers poke at the broken skin. Blood coats her fingers, and she sighs. A big, belly emptying release of emotion.

Another roar of the crowd disturbs the night. The voices of hundreds of guilty murderers ignite the fuel that boils in her belly. Grabbing wildly with her hands, she finds purchase around the handle of an unidentified object. It could be a knife, it could be a fucking spoon.

Elizabeth rears back and throws the projectile. Metal clangs as it strikes one of the gurneys.

"Fuck!" she screams.

The small scratching of rubber and metal answers her as one of the bed shifts where it was hit. She looks up with another roar of the crowd.

Gently, she taps her head back into the doors. Pain races through her skin but the doors vibrate. They don't move. No matter how hard she hits them with her head, they will not open, but maybe?

Scrambling to her hands and knees, Elizabeth slips on her own blood. Soft shoes squeak on tile floor as she makes it back to her feet. Bloody fingers grip cotton sheets, and she pulls the nearest bed against her body.

Too close, not enough distance.

Elizabeth heads for the farthest wall.

One of the beds rests a dozen feet below the windows on the wall. Turning the gurney, she positions herself until her back and feet can be pressed flat against the stone that is cool against her skin.

Biting down on her lip, she lets the blood and anger fill her mouth. She won't have many chances at this. Fury sends waves of heat and exhilaration through her legs. She pushes with everything that she has.

Her legs pump. Her shoes slip but she doesn't go down. Two inch tires stick and wobble as the bed barrels across the room.

She aims for the center of the doors. Rolling her shoulders forward, she gives it everything she has.

Aluminum crashes into aluminum. Bars buckle and facial bones crack against railing. Door frames bend and Plexiglas pops out.

Elizabeth falls to the ground.

She is dizzy.

Her nose is bleeding and a ringing tortures the inside of her ears. She rolls onto her belly and struggles to open her eyes. Through a broken nose, she can smell the dust that has collected against the corner of the wall. It is salty and stale. Cleaner burns her throat, and she wants to vomit.

A thin stream of light infiltrates the room.

"Fuck!" she screams, beginning to cry and let herself go.

Her battering ram has buckled in half. An opening calls to her, but it is no wider than a thin, malnourished child.

Elizabeth curls up on the ground. Blood pools beneath her cheek, warms her neck, and itches her ears that scream with the cry of bent metal.

She has to find a way out. Somehow, there has to be a way to leave this room.

A roar shakes the ground, and the clouds above answer with an explosion of thunder.

Elizabeth loses her minds. In a rage, she climbs back to her feet, grabs the destroyed bed and crashes it back into the door. Metal shakes and begins to dent even more. A second piece of Plexiglas falls and bounces across the floor.

Uncontrolled rage is unleased against a hospital bed that is streaked with fingers of blood and tears.

Bang!

The accordion crumples against the barrier that holds her in. She retreats and throws herself again. Pain is washed away in the fury of pent-up rage and self-pity.

Bars crack and snap fastenings. Bolts break and hexagonal nuts roll across the blood-streaked tile. The opening to her freedom is wider, but still not enough.

Elizabeth grabs a leg from the bed's frame. Thrusting with everything she has she jams it between the locked door. Jagged edges cut her skin, and her grip is slippery with the salty life that drains from her body.

She cannot give up.

She will not fail.

Pulling with everything she has, the light from the hall grows wider. Aluminum tubing bends and begins to buckle. She continues to pull. Fire sears the muscles of her arms and shoulders.

A howling rages into the night as the doors open wider.

Blood slick bar snaps and throws Elizabeth across the floor. She skids on her shoulder, and the light coming from the hall spins before her eyes. Turning on her side, she vomits, and her mouth is full of iron and bile.

Shuddering coughs rack her body, but she fights everything to push herself back to her feet. Her legs are weak. The joint to her left shoulder is destroyed. Moving it at all brings darkness to her eyes, and she stumbles.

Taking a deep breath, she tries to squeeze between the junction of the two doors. Broken edges catch on the cloth of her shirt and tear at the skin of her back and chest.

Searing pain takes over her body as she pushes herself as far as she will fit through.

There isn't enough room. She is stuck. Breaths come harder as the doors tighten against her chest.

She will die here. Bleeding out between two doors, leaving herself a fucking mess on the floor. Her eyes fall shut, and she chuckles. Muscles relax and tears burn their way down her cheeks.

What can she do?

Thunder roars through the building, deep and wild as the wind shakes. A roar of the arena quickly follows.

Metal shards from the door dig deeper into her skin, and the searing pain races through her neck and into her brain.

All she can see is red. Screaming, crying, begging, and dying she pushes through the door.

Light floods over her as she collapses against the hallway floor. Hard carpet burns at the thousand cuts on her body as she looks at the ceiling that looks down at her. The burning candles along the wall flicker and sizzle.

Heavy breaths fill with blood.

She has made it.

Elizabeth rolls to her knees.

The unmistakable sound of boos begins to mix with the roars of the crowd.

He is still fighting. They won't kill him so easily.

Elizabeth stumbles from wall to wall as she makes her way toward the stairs that will lead her out.

He needs her. Somehow, she will find a way to save him.

* * *

Two dozen bodies lay sprawled in death and guts. Women, men, all of them in various degrees of infection have died on these sands. A man, his eyes glassed-over, holds his guts in his palms as he slumps against the wooden walls that cage Merchant in.

Vomit streaks its way across the barrier where a man in the audience lost his last meal when the combatants stomach was ripped open and blood fountained in a wide arc that covered the front row.

Merchant can feel the layer of filth that covers him. It drips down his face. Infiltrates his mouth, and he can taste the salty flavor that tickles his tongue. Scratches across his skin, but his muscles beg for more. Fingers twitch.

The audience is growing wild, and the man who watches from his podium continues to fidget. He cannot sit still. One leg taps the wooden base and angrily points at the guards who let the next wave of monsters in through gated doors.

Six come charging in. All of them are men, and each is young. Muscles are still taut, their movements quick, but the eyes are different. They are not glossed over. Fire burns behind them. Anger and pride drives these men.

Newly infected.

Just like the ones who started this whole fucking mess back along the interstate.

Merchant does not hesitate.

One reaches him and is dead before he touches the ground. Neck snapped in three places, Merchant turns and is quickly barreled over by the next two.

They roll on the ground. Teeth snap and fingers scratch.

Merchant finds his way on top and presses fingers into eyes sockets that pops gushy balls of flesh and does not stop until nails dig into gray matter.

Boots meet ribs, and the air is knocked from his lungs. He tumbles and takes out the legs of another. Two are dead and four begin to circle.

Merchant stays in a crouch.

One jumps for his back. Merchant catches him with an elbow to the jaw. Head snaps back and throat is exposed. Grabbing with everything he can, nails dig into flesh, and the trachea rips out like fatty tissue on a warm chicken leg.

Gore sprays and Merchant throws his trophy at the nearest while the dying falls to his knees, blood pooling in hands and last growls lost in the bubbling gurgles of death.

Three remain.

They hesitate.

Merchant keeps his distance.

Boom! Boom! Boom!

Automatic gunfire explodes into the night.

The crowd begins to scream in fear, but are quieted as the Father steps to the end of his podium. A guard with a rifle stands by his side. The end of the rifle smokes into the cold air. Merchant begins to back away from the infected. Blood pools around his boots. The smell of death mixes with spilled bowels and blood.

All three infected turn from him to the man with the rifle, and then back.

"We have seen enough!" the Father screams.

Merchant's shoulders slump. He lets the fire in his muscles fade.

One of the men jump for him. The infected makes it two steps. Skull and brain tissue erupts as the bullet exits through his temple. The sand makes a sloshing sound as the body crumples into a heap. The two remaining back away.

"I think our community has seen enough. Obviously, the security and purity of our community cannot be trusted to the hands of the infected," the Father orates, and the crowd quickly fills in with the faithful bleating of sheep. "It is obvious that this monster here is capable in the arts of death. The blood of the fallen covers him, and he wears it as a king would the crown that sits on his head!"

The people of the isolated community cheer every word.

"But enough is enough. Vengeance will be had for our dear, Alexis!"

Merchant looks at the young women who is now so white she is a ghost shining through the darkened shadows.

"This monster will pay the punishment he so duly deserves. For this, I am going to bless his tainted soul with the opportunity that has not been seen in this arena in years. Our first blessed, the seeker of truth, the deliverer of our vengeance, the man you all call our Chosen Son will be the instrument of our faith!"

Jubilation and cries of vengeance mix with trepidation that rattles the walls that hold Merchant in. The two infected back away as Merchant turns back toward the doors that have opened six times now to bring men to their death.

A chant begins to move through the gathered masses.

Chosen.

Chosen.

Ccchhooosssseeenn.

The word begins to slur into the wind. One door slowly begins to creep open. Metal hinges grind as the darkness begins to leak out into the arena.

A shadow stands waiting. Shoulders as wide as the door rub the frame.

The man who stopped him when he arrived steps

through. He is big, bare-chested, and rippled with more muscle than Merchant has ever seen on a single person. Arms flex as fists are pounded together. Skin stretches as veins pop, and the man's steps rumble across the frozen dirt.

Merchant *cracks* the knuckles of his hands and *pops* the bones in his neck. Muscles loosen, and he watches as his opponent approaches slowly. This *Chosen* is inches taller than he is.

Hard eyes stare at him. Dark, judging, and dead of any emotion.

Merchant knows that feeling.

The Father yells out to the crowd. Light dances as the bleachers shake with the beating of a million feet. Merchant cares for none of it. His only care is this fight.

Only one of them will walk out of this arena. This world is not big enough for two harbingers of death. There are no more reasons to wait.

Balling his fists, Merchant charges forward.

Chapter 22

Five Years Ago

Gravel is rough and sharp. Pieces as large as quarters puncture skin, and Merchant rolls onto his back. Tall pillars of dark smoke roll into the sky. Rain bubbles on his face and splashes in his eyes.

Lightning arcs across the sky and bullets slap the building, popping like firecrackers dozens of feet below. Sirens wail and men scream. The lights of cars and trucks rush down the road that leads them into the teeth filled maw of automatic weapon fire.

Lead punching through aluminum, the sounds of war rattle into the night and taste of burned ozone.

Merchant coughs.

A man groans off to his left.

Looking to the side, Merchant sees Breaker moving. The window they plunged out of is over ten feet above their heads. They did not fall to the ground. They hit the roof of the next building.

Rolling onto his side, Merchant can feel all the broken bones in his body grind and cut him internally. Blood fills his mouth, and he coughs a wad that splashes onto his hands.

He fights the pain.

There is still too much to do.

Knees scream as tiny rocks cut into exposed skin. His pants are heavy, soaked with blood and guts.

He is off the ground, torturing himself on knees and the balls of his feet. Breaker is no better.

The man is soaked red, his skin yellow and stricken.

"You fucker, why can't you fucken die," Breaker says as he rolls over.

He is successful at getting to his hands and knees as well. Blood drips from his lips, and a cut that has torn his flesh to the bone slices through his forehead down across his face. His left eye is gone, and a dark, wet, empty hole is all that remains.

"Where is the general?" Merchant asks, his voice gritty and harsh.

Bones and joints crack as Merchant rolls backward until he is on his feet. The world spins before his eyes. Balance is lost, and he stumbles until his hand catches on an exhaust pipe, and he holds himself up.

Breaker tries the same, but gets one knee stable before stumbling forward. Mud splashes around, and the man claws at the gravel until he is back on his knees.

"What does it matter anyway?" Breaker responds.

His lips are going blue and blood trails its way from both corners of his face.

Merchant squeezes his eyes to force the pain away and finds the balance to stay on his feet. His fingers wrap around a wooden stake that fell as they plummeted from the open window. Rusted wire hangs bloody from a nail at the head of the weapon.

"Tell me where he is. When I'm done…" Merchant says.

Breaker lets out a belly laugh that is cut off with blood filled coughing.

"When you are done here? It's too late, Merchant. You can't reach him in time. The mission is complete, you fucker. All this fucking shit you started is over nothing. You accomplished nothing!"

Rage erupts through Merchant. Diving forward, he raises the wooden stake and goes to fall on the man who tortured him until he died on a hill by himself. The man who cut wire into his skin until enough blood to fill a river flowed from his veins. The man who showed no mercy in killing the only people he ever loved in this entire world.

Merchant falls at the man he hates more than words can describe. Breaker smiles as he slumps to the side. Sharpened steel shines in the night as the man arcs the knife at Merchant's heart, ready to impale the only person he has ever failed to kill.

Metal tip cuts into flesh. Bone turns weapon and blood covered handle slips between puckered fingers. Knife drives into chest. Air is driven from lungs. Heart is missed.

Balled fist catches the corner of a jaw. Head snaps sideways, and two men fall to the ground. Groaning, Merchant tries to lift himself. His left arm useless. Blade cuts into muscle with every movement. He tries to breathe but his lungs are filling with blood.

Breaker stirs. Merchant cannot let him go. Reaching out with his right arm, he wraps his fingers around the man's shirt. Hit squeezes until the material is pulled tight.

He slides over, his body inching on top of the other. Chest rises and falls below him. Breath is shallow. Blood pools around Breaker's mouth.

Excruciating pain explodes through Merchant, but he forces himself back onto his knees through pure determination. His body is broken. He can take breaths in small coughs, his vision darkening.

The wooden spike is back in his hand.

Breaker smiles up at him.

Pink teeth show as the man smiles.

"It's over, Merchant. You are done."

Screaming, letting every last bit of rage out that remains in his dying body, Merchant drives the stake down. Splintered wood pierces eye and flesh explodes. Bones crack. Skull ruptures and brain matter spills across the roof.

Merchant rolls off Breaker.

He looks up at the sky. Dark clouds roll as hell spreads around. The gunfire is slowing. Another explosion rocks the building's foundation, but the symphony of sirens and emergency lights is an army in itself.

For the men below, the fight is ending. There are more police than there are soldiers. Merchant feels his body going cold.

His fingers twitch. He wants to pull the knife out, open the wound more and bleed out faster. He cannot do it. There is no strength left in him. His eyes fill with tears.

No breath will fill his lungs.

He is not done yet.

He tries to speak.

Blood floods his mouth.

Eyes go dark.

* * *

The crowd is as quiet as death. Cheering is the last thing on their minds. Groans and shrieks of shock are intertwined with gasps and words lost to confusion.

Lightning burns through winter clouds. A storm of apocalyptic proportion brings a blinding snow that reduces visibility to close to an arm's length.

But not here.

The heat of the arena. Muddy puddles filled with blood splash and rain soaks everything down to the bone. Clothes sit heavy with saturation and tears mix with cold water that bites down to the soul.

In the sands, boots clogged with gore and gritty sand, two combatants tear at one another like gods who do not fear death. Blood runs down Merchant's face. Sweat stings a slash that opens his forehead from eye to eye. His heart pumps faster with every passing moment. The heat of the fury in his soul burns to a bright ember. Raking his fingers like claws, his hand catches the shirt of the man he fights. Skin rips, but his opponent shows no sign of slowing down.

They call him the Chosen. He's taller than even Merchant, and his muscles are the living embodiment of iron. One fist into Merchant's ribs and it's like he is hit by a truck.

Stumbling, Merchant feels his legs go weak. He backs away to create distance. His legs are heavy and the thick muddy gore of the dirt pulls at his boots like greedy hands. He spits a wad of blood at the behemoth that tracks him. The monster smiles.

Merchant feigns a dive forward.

Arms wide, he looks to wrap the Chosen into a bear hug. All muscle, even more speed, the Chosen takes the bait and braces for the impact with his arms brought up.

Tucking his arms in, Merchant goes low and kicks out. The steel tip of his foot catches the edge of a knee. He can feel something give. The big man does not scream. He does not shout.

A grunt escapes his lips, and he topples to one knee.

Merchant is on top of him now. Delivering blow after blow. The crowd is a frenzy. The screams are of hate and shock.

Welts open across the back of the creature's shaved head. Dark blood pours out and sprays with Merchant's next blow.

Hands the size of a grizzly's paw clutch at Merchant's arms. Nails dig into flesh. Arms flexed, Merchant tries to pull away.

He can't.

The Chosen rolls forward and Merchant is pitched over his back.

The crowd is on its feet.

Mud and black bile fills Merchant's mouth. He coughs, and his breath will not return. A thousand-pound boulder crashes into his spine. Pain rips from his lips.

Fingers swallow the back of his head. He catches the sight of the fire burning on torches as the shadows of the audience riot for his death. Bones *crack*, and he tries to keep his face above the mud.

Darkness swallows him whole. His nose *crunches* as his face is ground into the earth.

Lungs burn.

Arms going numb.

He bites down and forces his arms up. Bent, he begins to push.

A gap opens between mouth and ground. Cold, dirty oxygen fills his lungs. The flames are subdued. Pain ruptures through his spine. Hard, frozen dirt cracks his skull, and all the air in his body is forced out.

Fury rages within him. Pain and destiny begins to fade. Darkness approaches.

The sound of the arena weakens, drowned behind the pounding of his blood in his ears. Nails dig into the earth. Muscles cramp.

Merchant has nothing left. His shoulders throb. His legs are frozen. More pressure cracks his spine.

This is it.

Death has finally arrived.

* * *

The roar of the crowd cracks the ice at her feet. Snow is pilling across the village. Giant, heaping mounds of white powder that go untouched. Cold, bitter air stings every cut and scratch on her body.

Shoulders throb, and she has the largest, mind-splitting headache she has ever felt. Teeth chatter but she can see the steam that rises into the night sky. Giant plumes of white smoke lit by torchlight as the moan of the crowd ebbs and flows.

Elizabeth stays to the shadows. She has to get inside and save Merchant.

What can she do?

She holds the blanket she found in an empty room

tight against her body. It smells of dust and scratches at the open wounds on her arms, but at least she hasn't dropped of hypothermia yet.

The arena looms ahead of her. Tall walls of miss-matched plywood and scavenged pieces of roadside advertisements block her path.

She slows her pace as she approaches the barricade. There are openings from Main Street and the holding cages where Merchant was held. She heads toward the cages. Guards will be holding each entrance, but they won't be as steadfast there.

Thunder explodes within the clouds. Frenzy breaks across the arena, and snow falls from the wall. Small bits of paint and a screw work free as she walks casually along.

She can't run.

If they see her, they will know something is wrong.

Pulling the blanket closer, she can feel her time passing by. Merchant needs her. She must not fail.

Turning the next corner, she sees the open gate that leads into the arena. A single man waits by the entry, but he is not watching. His eyes and attention are lost by what is happening within the killing grounds.

Elizabeth hunches her shoulders and closes her covers over her body as much as she can. If she can just get close enough.

The man is older. A head taller than she is, his gray hair reaches between his shoulder blades where it isn't balding across the middle of his scalp. Thick, flaky scales crack across his skin and liver spots mark where age has set in.

Quietly.

Slowly.

She approaches. Her feet softly crunch the snow, but he makes no move to see her arrival.

What can she do?

"Excuse me, sir," Elizabeth says.

Stooping shorter, she feels all the part of little old lady asking for help from a stranger.

The guard does not turn. He shifts his weight from his left side to his other. A rifle swings around and stops where it taps against his leg. He reaches for a cup that sits on a box next to him. The contents inside steaming into the cold air.

"Excuse me, sir," Elizabeth tires again, this time with more emphasis.

Shifting his shoulders to the side, the man stirs but gives only a quick non-committed look over his shoulder and misses where Elizabeth stands directly beside him.

Anger stirs deep within her. She does not have time for this.

"Hey, asshole!" she shouts.

Dropping her blanket, she taps the man on the back.

"Oh God, what the fuck now, Julio. I told you if you left your post again I wasn't going to let you back in. We are in the same…"

Elizabeth smiles as the man turns. His words lost as she is not Julio, whoever the fuck he is.

He looks over her shoulder. Probably looking for anyone else, but she gives him no time to regret his choice.

Throwing a punch as fast as her broken body will allow, she does not aim for his gut or his face. She does not have the strength to hurt him there.

Knuckles crunch throat and the man drops back, coughing and grabbing at his closed wind pipe. Rearing back with her leg, pain shoots through her muscles, but she ignores it as much as she can. Boots rupture groin and the man drops to the ground.

Weak fingers reach for rifle. She stomps his hands flat. A scream is scratched through his closed throat, his face is red.

Grabbing the rifle, she checks to see if it is loaded. One full magazine and the safety is off.

Good enough.

A dirty hand grabs her ankle. The fingers are weak. The arm shakes, and the man still claws at his throat. Driving her heel into the side of the man's face ends the argument and the pain.

Elizabeth moves on. Rifle in hand, she makes her way into the arena.

Feet thunder above her head as she enters the small tunnel that will lead to the killing ground. Dust and flakes of paint fall all around her. Nails and joints creak as the crowd is going into a frenzy. They are losing control. With this much enthusiasm, she can't imagine they'll remain on the bleachers for much longer.

The end of the tunnel begins to lighten. A gate sits locked to the field where she knows Merchant fights for his life. She readies the rifle. The crowd is on its feet now, and the roof above her head begins to sag.

Her time is short.

She could blast her way through the door and kill whomever he is fighting. There are enough bullets in the rifle for that.

They'd both be dead long before they ever got free.

She needs to stop the fight. She needs to end the madness.

The answer to her problems clears her mind.

So simple.

But only if she can reach him in time.

Turning away from the gate that leads into the arena and to Merchant's side, Elizabeth back tracks down the path and turns up a set of stairs that leads her farther into the darkness.

Chapter 23

Five Years Ago

"You really are a specimen to behold, if I say so myself," the disembodied voice says.

Merchant can't feel a thing. He is dead, or at least he should be. The pain is gone. The sounds of war are a distant memory, and he is weightless. He sees nothing and hears less unless she speaks.

Her words are like warm honey to his ears. He needs more. The pleas come to his lips but the sounds do not come alive.

"Seeing what you have done, what you have accomplished. I had my doubts, but now I know. You are the perfect choice, Merchant. I could not have chosen better," she whispers.

Merchant feels the electricity of ecstasy course through his veins. If he could feel anything, he'd have an orgasm right where he is. Maybe he has, he can't tell.

"See, the problem with what you wanted, Merchant, is it has cost you so much. Nothing is received without something being given in return. For that, I have done what I can."

Hot fire, carried from the pits of Hell itself sears

its way through Merchant's blood. Organs burst and muscle melts. He can feel his soul char and become ash.

Screams evaporate into the air before the words can reach the air. His back arches, and the sounds of the world slam into him like a truck rolling downhill. Sirens roar in the distance and cold air slices through him like a brand of iron tearing away his insides.

He sits on the rooftop where he fell. Legs spread before him, he rests against the side of an air conditioner that hums gently into the night air. Fires rage across the yards that surround him. Lights of red, blue, and yellow dance into the night.

Dark blood pools around his legs. A body lays stiff at his feet.

Breaker.

The stake he impaled in the man's head drips dark and red. The hole through the man's skull yawns wide, and the skin of his face pulls tight against narrow cheekbones.

Merchant tries to feel something.

Happiness.

Vengeance.

Anger.

He is dead inside.

This man killed his family. Burning them as they were trapped in the basement of his home for secrets only he knew.

Anger takes hold and fills him.

Fuck him. Let him rot in Hell.

"Looks like you are beginning to come around," the voice says from behind him.

Merchant tries to turn but finds he doesn't have the strength.

A pair of perfect legs slip down beside his shoulder. Deep brown flesh, smooth and firm rubs against the tortured skin of his shoulder. Warmth and sexual desire runs down his arm.

The feeling begins to fill in the gaps where the anger does not have its hold. Bare feet sway next to him. Tilting his head back, he looks, and his heart skips a beat.

She has returned. Perfect curves and the smile that could light up the world watch him as he sits motionless beside her. Dark hair lays delicately across her shoulders, and her eyes are bright and playful.

He smiles.

She smiles back.

"What have you done?" he croaks.

The taste of blood is in the back of his mouth. He feels like he has been screaming for a thousand years.

"I gave you what you wanted. A chance to strike back at those who took everything from you."

Merchant turns back to Breaker. The body will never move again.

"How? How did you?" he asks.

She runs the inner edge of one foot over the muscles of his shoulder and arm, the dark blood smeared across his body not touching her at all.

"Those secrets I must keep if you are to complete what you were made for, Merchant. You can't comprehend what I have had to do to get you here. Set you on a path that will let you finally realize your true destiny."

"Destiny? My family is dead. One of the two men

who are responsible for their deaths lays cold at my feet. The other is hundreds of miles away probably doing what I failed to stop. Just be straight with me. The cops will be storming this place any minute now, and I doubt I'll be good for anything other than a needle full of drugs."

Merchant lays his head back against the air conditioner. The cold metal feels terrific against his burning skin, and the vibration soothes the pain that builds in his skull.

She sighs and looks toward the horizon. Golden light reflects off her spotless brown skin and dances on the ruby red lips that draw him so close he can feel himself move though he's pinned to the ground by an invisible weight.

"Shortsighted. That is what has always been the problem with your kind," she says.

Sliding from her perch, she lands delicately on the stone beside him and shows no sign of pain at the sharp stones that cut at the delicate skin of her heels. Merchant's heart throbs in his chest as he watches her walk toward the edge of the roof overlooking the field where the battle took place. Her hips sway back and forth and the white dress that clings to her rides dangerously close to the bottom curve of her ass.

His mouth is dry and nervous itching runs throughout his body.

She looks back at him, her lips curled in a mischievous smile.

"You really think only two men were responsible for your family's death?" she asks.

"Who else was there? The general and this piece of

shit ran the whole show," he barks.

The anger ignites within him, refusing to drain the strength it continues to give him. Slowly, and wobbling, he lifts his arms but it takes everything he has.

"Good, let it fill you up," she answers and turns back to the fires below. "I cannot answer that for you, Merchant. One day, you'll be able to look back and find the answer you seek. May God forgive me the day you do, but one day my pet. You'll find your answer."

Merchant's insides are molten lead. His eyes are closed, and he can feel the bones of his legs melting and pooling where his skin threatens to burst in a bubbling mess.

He bites his teeth against the pain.

He will not scream.

The pain passes.

He gasps for breath but needs more answers.

"Then what good are you? I need answers, and if you aren't willing to give them to me, I'll find someone who will."

She does not reply.

Her hands come together before her, and she takes a deep breath.

"Exactly, Merchant. Now you are starting to understand."

Merchant can roll now. Squeezing his muscles to the point of cramping, he falls and rises until he is on his knees. She does not try to help. He bites down so hard on his teeth that his mouth tastes of fresh blood again.

"Understand what?" he chokes out.

The woman tilts her head and takes a deep breath. Her hair falls back and ripples a darkness deeper than the furthest reaches of the universe.

Beautiful.

Mesmerizing.

Deadly.

"Do you smell that in the air, Merchant? Change. It is coming to this world. Something no one could have ever imagined. And here we both are to witness the beginning."

Knuckle-sized stones dig into Merchant's skin as he crawls across the roof. His back spasms, but he keeps his gaze locked on her. He watches the muscles in her legs and shoulders tense and relax. The way her hips move and her ass rounds seduces him, but the anger will not dissipate. His nails dig into the roof, and he continues to draw closer.

"The time is upon us, Merchant. I have given you what I promised. A second chance at finding what was taken from you."

A bloody hand finds hold on the stone ledge that holds them back from plummeting to the ground below. Rough brick scratches skin, and Merchant pulls himself up until he is kneeling.

"I have only found half of that."

She looks down at him, her eyes sparkling. Her smile falls flat. She turns back to the horizon.

"The rest will be revealed in time. If you complete the tasks I have set for you. And then, only if you complete them will you find the final answers you seek."

"That was not part of the deal," Merchant says. Searing agony moves through his body, and in his vision, all but her is ablaze with the fires of Hell. "You promised I'd have what I wanted, then you'd have your request.

Not before, but after."

"Semantics, Merchant. Your answer waits for you out there. All you have to do is make your way to it. One step at a time will bring you closer to what you want."

"That brings us back to why you are here."

The smile returns.

"That's it, Merchant. I want you to find your answers, but along the way there will be people."

"People? The world is full of people."

"For now. But nonetheless, these individuals will be special. They will request things of you."

Merchant tries to push himself to a standing position but only reaches one knee. The leg shakes as the muscles cramp.

"What kind of requests?" he asks.

"Special circumstances born of desperate need that you'll be able to offer a unique resolution to."

"And how am I supposed to do that?"

A chuckle like the muffled laughter of a thousand happy children escapes her beautiful lips. The glorious light it brings to her face fights the unanswered rage that builds within him but is quickly extinguished.

"You have special skills, Merchant. Something only you bring to the table, which makes you the perfect person to solve their problems."

"And if I don't?"

Lightning arcs through the sky, and thunder, like a canon, explodes above them.

"Once you start on this path, Merchant, there will be no ending. Your trail does not stop until you reach the city that touches the sky. Do not deter. Do not waver. You'll see why in the end."

"The city that touches the sky? Do you mean?"

The woman puts a single finger to his lips, letting the delicate taste of salt touch the edge of his tongue. Electricity ignites within him, and he finds the strength to keep himself from tumbling back to the ground.

"Quiet for now, Merchant. It is time to enjoy the show."

With the hand that touches his lips, she places it gently against the hard skin of his face and turns him toward the south.

A darkness holds everything behind the fires and lights that swirl below him. He can see nothing. The edge of the world is empty.

Then, in the distance, a bright light flashes. At first, it is only a tiny, single bulb that is burned out in an instance. Within half a heartbeat, the flash grows. The horizon starts to bleed red. Clouds, burning in fire, rise into the air.

Rumbles carry with the wind as the clouds continue to climb higher and higher. Thunder steamrolls along the ground, followed by the wind that grows until it is steady and struggles to push Merchant off his feet.

The cloud is high into the atmosphere now. Its head is bulbous and a funnel like cloud reaches the ground. Horror screams through the night as the burning light grows and the deathly cloud reaches higher and higher.

Merchant balls his fist.

His enemy has succeeded. The general has finished his plans.

Washington is no more.

The war has started.

* * *

A grunt breaks the darkness.

Pressure is released. The thunder of a thousand feet rolls through like a locomotive. The ground trembles. There is screaming, and people go crazy.

Two explosions rock the frenzied air, and chaos ensues.

Weight falls off Merchant's back. He lifts himself out of the mud. Cool air, tainted with the stench of death and blood, fills his mouth and lungs. It has never tasted sweeter.

A ton of bricks hits the mud beside him. Dark water splashes.

He rolls to his side, and then flops onto his back. Rain splashes against this face. Melted snow. The droplets cool his burning skin. A man moans. A body shifts. It is the Chosen. He spits words from his mouth Merchant cannot understand.

Ears ring. Lights burn bright and sear pained eyes.

The world spins but begins to slow. Merchant squeezes his eyes shut and lets the world set its own pace. The Chosen is moving. Mud drains away where the big man digs holes into the ground with his legs and boots.

Merchant opens his eyes.

The monster is not looking at him. His attention is drawn to the audience. No, not the audience, the podium where the Father had sold his lies and played his magic. All around, citizens run for their lives. Blood drains from the man's arm and right shoulder. Holes ripped through his flesh.

Bullet holes.

Above the frenzy, a woman's voice shouts. Merchant turns.

Elizabeth barks orders. Rifle in hand, she points it at the Father. Her body shakes. Her strength fails. From the arena, Merchant can see the anger that burns within her.

People flee for their lives. Climbing over one another, they struggle to reach the exits and the horror that has awakened around them.

Women scream.

Children cry.

Merchant rolls until he is on his knees and hands. The Chosen kicks him in the ribs. Pain explodes in his side, and he coughs up blood.

Two shots ring out. Mud explodes beside the monster. He stops. She begins to bark orders again. Merchant cradles his stomach and rocks back onto the balls of his feet. His vision is blurry. Torch fires are dancing fireflies in the summer breeze. The Father is giving orders now. His voice carried around the arena.

Elizabeth answers back.

Merchant spits out the taste of blood and the mud that grinds between his teeth.

He turns toward the podium. The Chosen is closer now. She does not watch, and he moves silently within the confusion.

The end of the rifle shakes. Her face is red with anger and exhaustion. Men move in the shadows. No longer citizens, these creatures move to intercept.

Guards.

She does not see them coming. Her attention

is drawn solely to the man she must hate the most. Merchant begins to claw his way to his feet.

One wobbly leg finds purchase in the ground. His muscles cramp. His fingers ache and *pop* as he pivots himself on his strained muscles.

The screaming reaches a higher pitch. Alexis is moving forward now. Not to Elizabeth, but to the Father. The rifle sweeps between both. Anger blinds her. Guards are arriving, their presence still hidden by shadow.

Merchant tries to scream a warning. His words are lost in a mess of dark liquid and swollen throat tissue.

Three shots ring out. Red explosions erupt from Elizabeth's chest. The sound sick and hollow. Wet dough slapping against a wall.

She falls backward, and the rifle goes off. The bullet hits the Father, and he spins. Guards charge toward their target. The Chosen roars, and his feet shake the ground.

Merchant lets the anger build within him. His muscles react, and he pushes himself to his feet.

He is dozens of feet behind the monster. His muscles ache. The other's pump with ungodly strength.

The man jumps and meaty hands take grip on the podium. Blood spits from open wounds, but the monster pulls itself up.

Merchant slows to watch.

The guards circle Elizabeth's fallen body. Alexis is screaming. The Father barks orders as he tries to stem the flow of blood from his wound.

One man steps up to finish the job. Merchant is too far away to help. He could jump up and climb like the other, but it would be too late.

A voice, high-pitched and wild, breaks over the background chaos of the fleeing citizens. Arms flapping like a flightless bird, the guard launches from the elevated ground. He lands head first. Bones snap, and his body flops like a limp sack.

The other two turn on the Chosen. Merchant begins to climb.

They are distracted. His chances will get no better. Muscles scream and tear as he pulls himself further from the ground.

Men roar in defiance. The sound of bones snapping fills the air, and a body hits the ground.

A shot is fired.

Large bootsteps shake the wooden floor. Bits of dirt and water fall from the edge. Merchant pulls his head over the end of the podium.

The Chosen has his hands over the guard's face. Fingers like Polish sausages squeeze the man's eyes. Primal screams of terror and pain pierce the air followed by the sound of popping. Blood explodes from the man's eye sockets. The back of his head ruptures, and his body convulses where his feet do not hit the ground.

The Chosen drops him.

Merchant finishes his climb.

He waits at the edge.

Alexis screams. The Father holds her back, his dark blood runs across her pale shoulders and smears across her neck and arms. The Chosen eyes him with disdain but makes no move to attack. The monster bends to the ground and picks Elizabeth up.

Moans and slurred words escape the woman's lips.

She is still alive. Blood pools across her chest and

drips from her ears and mouth. She does not have much time remaining.

Merchant goes to step forward.

Wood chips erupt into the air with the sound of gunfire. The Father aims a pistol at him. His hand soaked with his own blood, the weapon shakes, and he holds the bawling young woman in front of him like a shield.

"Get out of here. You are free," the Father demands.

He waves toward the exit where hundreds of his people flee for their lives.

Merchant does not turn. The Father, with Alexis, backs away from the podium. The Chosen, carrying Elizabeth, follows beside them.

Thunder rolls through the night sky. Merchant watches them go. They back their way through a door that leads deeper into the arena. He will follow them. They cannot escape.

Tonight, Elizabeth will be free.

* * *

The world sways like a ship lost on the ocean. The air is salty, tastes of blood and iron. Elizabeth tries to breathe and liquid chokes in her throat. Her vision narrows. Torch light goes past, swaying with the movements of steps. She can hear Alexis crying to the point of hysteria. The Father screams at her. Elizabeth does not understand.

Her tongue is fat. There is too much ringing in her ears.

The Chosen carries her. How can this be? She shot him when he stood atop of Merchant. She watched him fall. There was no time to see if Merchant still lives.

Fire burns deep in her chest, but she feels a cooling that spreads through her body. Her limbs are heavy. She wants to slap the monster who carries her across the face, but she can't find the strength. If she had a knife, she would try and drive it into his neck, but her hands are useless. She can't even feel them.

They race through the hall. Boots pound on floorboards, and the Father barks frantic orders as strangers shrouded in darkness pass by. The Chosen does not answer or speak. Part of her likes him for that.

She coughs and blood pours from her mouth.

Fuck him.

If it wasn't for him and his kind, she wouldn't be in this mess.

They turn a corner. The world swims, and darkness closes over Elizabeth's vision. She bites down, forces back the sleep.

It feels like they are running again. Away from some kind of pursuit. Her mind is fuzzy. Memories are hard to recall. Only the deep-seated anger remains.

The footsteps stop.

Her legs are cold. She can feel the pain, but they are going numb.

"Let's get in here," the Father demands.

His words are frantic and short.

A door slams open. The Chosen carries her through.

Alexis screams words but they are too fast to hear over the ringing. A slap slices the air. The Chosen goes stiff. Alexis' voice turns into a soft whimper.

The only light in the room is a set of candles in the corner. Dark shadows fade the edges of boxes and canisters that sit along the wall made of dull metal. Everything is cold. Even the air has a bite to it. Elizabeth shivers. It hurts her body.

"Put the bitch down over here if you must," the Father says.

The Chosen moves slowly and gently. Visions of demons attack from the shadows and tear at her chest. She coughs more blood that splatters onto the giant asshole's chest. He does not seem to mind.

"I still don't fucking know why you bother with her. Look what she did to me!" the Father barks. The Chosen stands tall after placing her onto the ground with her head propped and places his body between hers and the fucker who won't shut the fuck up. "We should just finish her off and find our way out of here."

The Chosen takes a step closer to the man. Shoulders widen and bones crack. The Father's eyes narrow, and he takes a step back.

"All right, suit your fucking self. She'll be dead any moment anyway," the Father responds.

Alexis drops onto her knees beside her. Tears have washed the young woman's face a sticky color. Her hair is plastered to her face, and blood is smeared all over.

Elizabeth tries to speak, but the words are drowned in blood. Her friend looks like shit. Elizabeth's mind begins to swirl. She probably doesn't look any better herself.

"Help me with this, why don't you?" the Father asks.

He's wrapping a white bandage around his shoulder. The cloth goes red instantly and more blood leaks down his hand to drip onto his shirt and the floor at his feet. The Chosen doesn't move. His feet are rooted into the ground, his boots bolted to the floor.

"Did you fucking hear me or not? Don't just stand there!"

The Father's first creation remains still. His hands flex, and the veins in his arms bulge. Blood stains the skin of his right arm red, and the slow drop of a red river drips from his knuckles.

Elizabeth smiles. The massive bastard finally grew some balls.

"Oh, for Christ's sake. At least take this and go out there to finish the fucking job you failed to do," the Father says.

Turning to the pile of boxes along the wall, Elizabeth sees him removing small vials and syringes packed in soft rags and cotton-laced plastic. A green liquid swirls in the tiny glass containers. Medication from the old world.

"This will make you what you should have been from the start. Now be a good servant and go get rid of our problem, will you?"

Liquid squirts from the end of the needle.

The Chosen doesn't move.

Drug in hand, the Father sticks the working end deep into the injured man's right shoulder, tiny shaft piercing torn flesh.

A grunt forces its way through the silent killer's lips. The muscles of his back flex and tighten. Every vein in his arms bulge, and the skin pulls tight. New stretch marks, angry red and jagged rip across the skin.

Elizabeth tries to gasp but chokes on blood. Alexis does enough for the both of them. The blood flowing from the Chosen's arms stops. He rolls his shoulders, and the bones beneath *crack*, and he stands up straighter.

His head skims the ceiling above. The legs of his pants stretch, and new scales flake away from the back of his neck.

The infection is spreading, and quickly.

The Father smiles. His eyes bent on murder.

"Now go. Finish the job. Come back and whatever you want is yours. Just get rid of him before he finds us," he commands.

The Chosen turns and eyes Elizabeth and Alexis. The calm and controlled violence that laid dormant behind his eyes is gone. A wild rage burns bright and pulses with the blood that pumps through the veins that beg to burst beneath his skin. Ripples of muscle stretch across his body as he moves.

Alexis cowers beside Elizabeth, holding her close.

Elizabeth can't feel anything but the warm burning in her chest. She tries to glare her hatred for the man, but his expression doesn't change. She doubts she is successful.

Without a word, the Chosen leaves. The door slams behind him. Dust and chips of rust fall in his wake.

"You are going to be okay, Elizabeth," Alexis whimpers.

A gentle hand is placed on Elizabeth's chest. The skin is a mix of milky white and dark putrid red.

"The bitch is going to die, and you know it. Leave her in the fucking corner and get over here and help me," the Father says.

He's sitting on one of the boxes in the corner. His skin is white like Alexis', and his hands shake as he tries to hold the bandages to his shoulder.

"Don't listen to him. He doesn't know how strong you are," Alexis says.

Elizabeth smiles.

The cold has moved through her body. She knows what is coming. There is no returning from where she is going.

A calm washes through her and takes the pain away.

Her vision clears, and the strength she once had returns to her body.

She smiles and lifts a sturdy hand to her friend's face. Her blood smears across Alexis' soft cheek. She wants to apologize but doesn't want to waste the time she has.

"I'm going to be all right, my friend," Elizabeth says. Alexis coughs and tears drip from her blood red cheeks. "I want to thank you."

"For…for what?" Alexis asks, her voice shaking.

"Everything you did for me," Elizabeth says. The pain in her chest erupts into a bolt of electricity that runs courses through her body. The muscles in her arms and legs cramp, and she bites down hard to hold back the scream that threatens to steal away her breath. "For being my friend."

Alexis begins to ball. Her bloodshot eyes squeeze shut and tears flow like a waterfall from her beautiful lashes. Elizabeth uses what strength she has left to touch the edges of those young eyes, so full of life and love.

"Please, don't leave me," Alexis whispers.

Coughing shakes Elizabeth's body. Blood fills her throat, but she spits it out to say what she needs to say.

"I'll never leave you, my love. Like you never left me," Elizabeth chokes out. Blood drowns her tongue, but she must get the words out. "Thank you, Alexis. For teaching me I wasn't meant to be alone."

Darkness closes in quickly. Alexis is hysterical and screaming. The Father joins in, his words full of anger and malice, but Elizabeth hears none of it.

She refuses to turn away. Her eyes watch the tears fall from her one true friend's face. Only when the shadows close in, holding her close and stealing away the pain, does she finally let go.

Chapter 24

Men, women, and children run. Hundreds of feet pound on floorboards and trample each other to get away. Sweat and fear fills the air. The tunnel where they took Elizabeth sits empty like an open maw with teeth of shadows and broken nails.

Torches burn along the empty path. The smoke carries the stench of oil and death. Merchant does not wait before entering. Men with rifles and panic stricken across their faces run by. The entire community is in chaos, and no one has the strength to pull it together.

Somewhere above, voices scream fire. More hysteria breaks out as a man's death screams pierce the chaos, and he falls to his death in the arena below. Merchant growls and flexes the muscles of his battered body. Just what he needs. The arena is burning down around him, and Elizabeth is lost somewhere within its inner guts.

Lightning flashes across the sky. Shadows dance across the wall, and he moves down the darkened path. Blood trails are easy to follow. Dark stains drip across the floor and smear across the walls.

Doors sit open or locked shut as he passes. Handles refuse to turn or are nothing more than empty closets filled with dust and cobwebs. The red crimson brick road leads him on. He begins to slow. The pools of dark liquid grow.

They have slowed down.

He is getting closer.

Footsteps follow behind him. Tiny echoes that do not draw closer.

He stops.

They stop.

He turns quick, but there is no one there. A hazy smoke fills the air and reduces his visibility.

He puts what is behind him away and concentrates on what is ahead. The blood trail drags across the dirty floorboards. Sticky pools puddling between boards and darkened boot prints.

Three doors remain before the hall ends and turns to the left.

They did not make it that far.

Merchant looks into the bright light that shines where a torch burns at the corner. Thunder shakes the floor. Tiny stones and bits of sand rattle between the boards at his feet.

Something is coming.

Merchant braces himself in a crouch. The sounds echo. He can't distinguish where they are coming from.

Beside him, to his left, the door explodes and wooden splinters fly through the air. Arms like steel wrap him tight, and they crash together through the wall.

Pain lances through his head, and the breath in his lungs is driven out. Bones *crack*, and his right shoulder goes numb.

The Chosen squeezes him tight as they roll along the ground. Wood and nails cut skin as the two wrestle in a mass of arms, legs, and human flesh. Teeth snap and blood smears together. Sweat makes skin slippery, but the grip that tightens begins to strain muscles that resist and bones that do not crush easily.

Merchant's forehead crushes into the monster's nose. Blood spirts out. Vision blurs. The man does not loosen his grip.

Pain lances through Merchant's back.

His bones scream in agony.

He closes his eyes and drives his forehead down again. Bone snaps and sinks in. Blood clings to his face.

Another crack, the arms tighten. Sticky liquid runs down between his eyes. His brain swirls, and he wants to vomit.

Stiffening his jaw, he drives his head down again.

Blood gushes warm against his face, and the arms release.

Merchant rolls to his side and opens his eyes. The Chosen lifts himself to his knees. The middle of his face is crushed, and his eyes are lost to a chaotic rage. Flakes of infection have moved up the side of his face. He is bigger than he was in the arena.

Merchant stands, and so does the monster.

The Chosen roars like a rabid beast. Boxes rattle and tools fall from the wall.

Arms wide, the crazed monster charges again.

Merchant tries to avoid him, but the man is too big. Meaty hands and arms as thick as trees grab hold, and they crash into the wall. Heads smash into wooden beams, and the world begins to swim.

Blood spirts from Merchant's mouth. His insides feel like mush. The Chosen's teeth snap and miss Merchant's throat by a hair length.

Arms free, Merchant drives his elbow into the big man's neck.

The man growls and hurls Merchant like a doll across the room. Wooden crates explode and long-armed tools fall from the wall.

Merchant struggles to get to his feet. The infected man is growing before his eyes. His skin is red, and the disease spreads as skin *pops* and cracks. Puss and blood runs down his face and arms. Veins explode, and the man's breathing is shallow and angry.

Rage smokes from his ears.

Merchant eyes the door. He can't fight this man in such a tiny room.

He grabs the nearest tool and throws it at the monster.

A rake.

The Chosen swats the projectile away like a fly. The wooden handle shatters against the wall. Footsteps rattle the floor.

Merchant pushes himself against the wall. Using the strength in his legs, he begins to stand. His knees ache. His back is stiff.

The Chosen closes the distance. His head presses against the roof. Light shines from the hallway, shadows darkening the side of his face, the fire of hatred lighting his eyes.

Merchant grabs hold of another weapon.

He does not have time to bring it around.

A fist the size of his head swings. Merchant drops to the ground. Knuckles and bones crush the wall, leaving a hole through studs and into the room beyond.

Merchant kicks out. Boot hits knee.

Leg twists, but the monster does not fall. Merchant scoots backward over broken plaster and shattered wood.

The Chosen turns. He lifts his leg to crush Merchant where he sits. The fabric of his pants rip. Muscles ripple.

An explosion from the door shatters the chaos of the room.

Blood erupts from the Chosen's shoulder. A second shot tears flesh and muscle from his ribcage.

Howling in anger, the monster stumbles backward.

Merchant spins and swings out the weapon gripped between the bloody fingers of his hand.

An ax.

Sharpened head slices deep into the muscle and flesh of a giant's leg.

Merchant pulls himself up and yanks as hard as he can. Sharpened steel rips from leg and sprays blood across the wall.

The Chosen falls to his knees. Blood pools around him.

A primal rage erupts from his throat. Tendons and muscles stretch along his shoulders and neck. Eyes bulge as he tries to get back to his feet. Blood gushes as destroyed muscle rolls into a ball.

Merchant turns and swings again.

Ax splits skull in half. The killing end buries itself deep and both of the Chosen's eyes split apart.

Weapon is pulled out again.

The Chosen is a bloody mess. His body does not fall.

Merchant rears back and swings again. Like chopping wood, the blade cuts clean down to breast bone. Blood soaks victim and murderer.

Merchant does not pull it back out. Three hundred pounds of dead weight hits the floor.

"My fucking God," Cherry Red mutters in horror.

Merchant turns, and she is standing in the doorway. Her pistol hangs loose in her hand.

"Why are you here?" Merchant demands.

Red looks at him, his body covered in gore from head to toe and the body that lays split in half on the floor.

"I-I decided to check on you when you didn't return," she says. "There was so much chaos the guards left the gate wide open. I kind of walked myself in."

"You were supposed to wait until I brought Elizabeth. Get us all the hell out of here."

Red takes a look at the body, puts her hand to her mouth to hold back the vomit, and then turns back to the hallway.

"Well, we don't have as much time as we thought," she says.

"What do you mean we don't have time?"

Merchant steps up to her, and the woman backs away. Her skin is ghostly pale except for the green of her face, her red hair dulled.

"He's coming. We might have a couple of days at best."

A bloody hand falls on her shoulder, and she struggles to stand on her feet.

"Who is this *he*?"

"The…" Cherry Red stammers. "The one who demanded I bring you down into the ravine. He's looking for us."

"She's right," Snake-Eyes says. The ghost materializes and sits down on the Chosen's warm body. He picks at the dirt beneath his nails. "I can feel him drawing closer. Whoever it is, is not happy. For once, I'd say we do what the bitch says and get the fuck out of here. Even dead, I don't want to be here."

"Not until we find Elizabeth," Merchant says.

"Ah!" A woman's voice shouts from the last remaining door in the hall.

The voice is primal and hoarse. Like a banshee going berserk.

Merchant shoves Red out of the way and throws himself into the door. The door cracks and the frame bends. Ignoring the pain, Merchant throws himself against the barrier, and the wood splits into a dozen pieces.

He falls into the room and catches himself before he steps into a mess as bad as the one he created himself.

Blood is everywhere. On the walls. On the ceiling. A woman kneels over a man, a piece of broken wood soaked with blood and gore stabs down over and over.

"What the fuck?" Cherry Red asks.

Merchant ignores her.

He walks over to the woman who does not notice him. The stake is dull but she continues to stab. He grabs her hand, and the weapon falls from slender fingers.

The Father lays beneath her. His chest is nothing but a soft pulp where small bits of the ground can be seen through his back. A look of shock and fear stretches across his face, and his eyes are dead and dull as they stare at Merchant.

All the strength and fury that fueled the violence drains from the woman. She slumps, and Merchant wraps an arm around her.

She weighs nothing in his arms. Tears streak across the blood that covers her body like mud. Her hair is heavy and wet with gore. Her sobs are deep and shake her entire body.

"Is that Elizabeth?" Cherry Red asks.

The woman in Merchant's arms convulses and screams in agony.

Merchant looks up and notices the body lying on the floor in the corner.

Elizabeth, blood pooling beneath her, lays silent in the shadows, alone. Her shirt and jacket is stained red, but her face is peaceful. From what he can tell, it may be the only smile he has ever seen on her face.

The woman in his arms curls into his shoulder and holds him tight.

Merchant nods to the corpse. Red looks and shakes her head. She does not say a word.

"Ah, fuck. I liked that one," Snake-Eyes adds.

The ghost never fucking stays quiet.

A moment passes. The chaos of the village outside fades into the distance. A silence settles over the living and the dead. Smoke, thick and acidic, burns their lungs.

"We need to get out of here. It may not matter to them, but I sure as well don't want to burn down here," Cherry Red says.

Merchant looks to the door. Dark clouds, thin and high against the ceiling, roll through the hall. He turns to the girl in his arms.

"Can you walk?" he asks.

She does not open her eyes. Her arms pull her tighter. Death's dirty touch reeks from her body.

Red steps over and places a gentle hand behind the

young woman's head.

"Here, you come with me. Our big man here has some unfinished business he has to take care of," she says.

Alexis slips from Merchant's arms, and with wobbly knees, leans heavily against Red. Merchant wipes his hands as clean as he can before he gently removes Elizabeth's body from where it lays in the dusty corner of the room.

Together, they head to the hall, following the path out and leaving the horrors of this village behind them.

Chapter 25

Thin streams of gray smoke lift slowly into the morning air. Tiny wisps, nothing more. The village was saved, only the arena of death was destroyed. Men stand guard, pacing and making their rounds along the gates that have shut. Watchful eyes search the horizon for danger, and the people inside continue with their lives under new leadership and with a renewed faith.

Cherry Red watches them like ants from atop the hill. A cold breeze carries the brisk ice of new fallen snow, and she pulls her jacket tighter against her skin. Part of her wishes all of them would have died in that fire. Her brother would have liked to have known they died miserably. But he also died miserably, yet she still lives. Shivering, she turns around and stares at the big man who has not moved in over an hour.

"So, what are we going to do now?" Red asks.

Merchant looks at the dirt mound, the soil dark and as broken up as he could make it. Callouses burn on his hands, and the shovel he carried from the arena sits dented by his feet. His shadow sits heavy over the shallow grave, dark and menacing.

"I head west. You go wherever you want to," he answers.

A bird cries as it circles in the sky above. Winter robins looking for food in a world of white, a single patch of fresh earth the only blemish for miles.

"Hey, you aren't leaving me out here by myself. Not after what you did," Red says.

Merchant looks back at the grave. She's finally alone. No one will bother her here. He tells himself this is what she wanted, but for the first time, he isn't sure.

His hand is unsteady as he reaches into his pocket. The cards, bent and crumpled beneath miles of torture and abuse, wait deep within the fabric of his pants. Pulling them out, he takes a look at them. The Queen of Swords and Death.

How fitting.

Opening his bag, Merchant drops them in.

His burden will be heavier now. A million more steps to go and so many more lives resting on his shoulders.

"Do what you want," he finally says. "I go west until I find the city that touches the sky. A lot of people are going to die before I get there. One of them could be you."

Cherry Red looks back at the village, and then to the bright snow in the north. The sun is a murderous glare across the wastelands, and the plains are empty and flat.

"Look, I know we've had our differences, but we make a good team," she says.

He turns to her. Flakes of infection cover her neck and the left side of her face. The skin is red and angry where it isn't pale, and her hair is a bright carrot in the afternoon light. Shrugging his shoulders, he turns away.

"Plus, I have a better chance with you than I do on my own out here. With him chasing us, two sets of eyes are better than one, right?"

Merchant hefts his bag across his back and treks toward the Interstate. Cherry Red does not move, at first. She hesitates, but he does not stop. He doesn't speed up either. Slow and steady.

"Hey, come on. You're all I've got left. I'm a dead woman if I don't come. Even if it gets me killed, I have a better chance with you than I do with them," she says.

She hikes a thumb back at the village, which already fades into the distance.

"Their fate is what they make of it. I didn't come here for them," Merchant says.

Red looks at him. Then back to the world ahead.

"Part of me wonders what would have happened had you come looking for them instead of Elizabeth."

He looks down at her. Bundled up, walking by his side, it reminds him how young she really is.

"And the other part?" he asks as they continue to walk.

"Too afraid to know," she answers.

Merchant smiles and continues on. For the first time in years, he isn't alone. And thinking about it, part of him remembers what it feels like to have someone there, walking beside you, sharing life through its ups and downs.

Two sets of boot prints make their way through the snow, going west toward the setting sun.

In the distance beyond the recovering village and its new pregnant leader, a rumbling follows.

A legion of hunger, an army of hate. To the west, they will go. They will not stop until he is found. Nothing will end until he is stopped.

* * *

Four Years Ago

Interstate 80 is deserted. Dark clouds, a mix of risen moisture and the lingering remains of bombs pollute the air. The east coast of America burns with the devastation of war from Canada to what remains of Florida. No one knows what has happened in the west. All communication was lost within days of the first attack. Rumors say the Midwest is a wasteland lost to the souls of the damned.

Families fight each other. Brother against brother. Father against son. The civil war of two centuries ago is nothing compared to what has been ignited. Bombs and weapons used to threaten other countries into thoughts of peace fly through the air and detonate over friendly ground.

People die by the millions. The government is dissolved in the unregulated belief military order is the best option. Time will tell if that was the correct decision but, for the moment, it has also fallen.

City states are destroyed and others rise.

Disease spreads through the world. A sickness that drives the victims mad. Bodies deteriorate, hunger increases. People; men, women, and children, become animals. They search and tear at everything for their next meal. Animalistic functions increase as their ability to reason is eaten away by the invisible parasite.

They are monsters. Driven to feed until death.

What remains of the media calls them the infected.

Still human.

Still alive.

They are better off dead.

Merchant stands with his boots on the road, facing west into the fading light that ignites the horizon in a bloody red shroud. His Army bag sits strapped over his shoulder, empty and light. The bodies of two infected lay crumpled in the ditch. Steam escapes from their corpses as warm blood cools and muscles harden.

Cars and scattered parts litter the road. Technology is failing faster than it was built. Electricity is scarce and hoarded by the masses that survive within the cities.

The asphalt, like the world itself, is broken into deep cracks and fissures that will never be fixed. Gravel scatters through the waist high grass the grows unattended along the side of the road, and the smell of poison and death is in the air. Civilization is a wasteland. The Dark Ages have returned. Diseases beyond infection have returned with a deep-seated vengeance. People die of measles and tuberculosis. Cancer is all but forgotten behind constant hunger and the threat of violence.

Merchant shrugs his shoulders. His muscles are tight, but his wounds are healed.

"There is a long road ahead of you, Merchant," the woman says.

She appears beside him. The top of her head reaches his shoulders. Her skin is flawless, and she stands barefoot like a child on a warm summer afternoon. Even at night, her skin radiates a light that burns away the darkness and ignites a fire in his blood.

"More than two thousand miles," he answers.

She smiles and nods.

"Even more lives than that will be touched before you get there. They wait for your arrival, though almost all of them won't know it until you are there."

He looks at her. A warmth spreads through his body, but he pushes it away. The anger that feeds the strength in his body kindles, and he stokes the fire.

"What will these people give me in return for my help? How will they know who I am?"

She turns to him. Her smile is childish and filled with secrets.

"Your services are special, Merchant. People must give what is most precious to them, for what they ask demands an even greater price."

He frowns. She is playing her games again.

"Money means little now that the world has fallen apart."

The woman turns back to the road ahead.

"There will still be some use for coins and other forms along the way, but you are correct. You always were a quick study. Their payment will not be in money, and anyone who believes that money is their most precious belonging, your services will not be adequate."

"Then what will I be asking for?"

"What is most precious to you, Merchant?" she asks. "Is there a possession you still have in what little remains of your life that you would never give up unless it was for the greatest of rewards?"

Merchant looks to the west. The sun is below the

horizon, and the red blood of the retreating day is only a fingernail above the darkness. He reaches into his pocket. The cold metal of a broken necklace burns the skin of his hand. Gritting his teeth, he takes hold and pulls it out.

"They were all I ever had and all I ever cared about."

The silver horse dangles on the delicate chain that hangs from between his fingers.

She smiles and places a gentle touch of her hand on his wrist.

"You now understand what those who seek your help will be willing to give. Now, carry this with you always for your desire has not yet been met," she says.

Merchant goes to place the necklace back into his pocket, but she wraps her fingers around his forearm. The grip is strong and holds his arm still. She shakes her head no and points to the bag that hangs from his shoulder.

He growls and pulls the Army strap away, and the canvas hits the pavement. The smell of smoke and dried blood radiates from the old material.

Opening the top, unlatching its single plastic button, he looks into the sack. Empty and dark, the opening is the great maw of a shark ready to swallow everything whole.

The silver of the pale horse reflects into his eyes. He doesn't want to let it go. Images of his family flash through his mind. Their smiles. Their laughter. A white hot furry explodes within him.

With a glare, he turns back to the woman. She smiles at him and looks down at the waiting bag.

She gives him a quick nod of her chin.

Merchant drops the necklace.

"Good, now never let it out of your sight," she says and turns back to the road ahead.

Wrapping the strap on his arm, Merchant pulls up on his sack to steady himself for the first steps of his trek.

A thousand pounds threatens to pull him over as the bag falls back to the ground.

"What the…" he mutters.

She chuckles.

"The hopes and dreams of all those who survive these times will not be an easy burden, Merchant. Did you think they would be light upon your shoulders?" she asks, her words light and inquisitive.

"But how?"

"Don't ask so many fucking questions, asshole," the Dog Breaker says.

His ghostly form waits near the edges of the shadows. Half his head is caved in, and his eyes are removed, but his bastard mouth still works.

Merchant grits his teeth, but doesn't turn around. The pressure of the strap across his shoulder burns his skin.

"They'll follow me, won't they?" he asks but does not look at her.

"Until the end of times, Merchant. You will be their keeper as they will be your burden. When the road ends, and you find what you are looking for, they will finally find their peace. Not until that time will you be allowed to forget."

He shifts the bag across his back and realizes how much lighter it has become.

"Forget what?" he asks.

The woman disappears as fast as she appeared.

He stands alone on the road. The darkness of the night complete, and the sounds of nighttime insects and the scurrying of animals lost to the hunt fill the air.

"What you are, Merchant. Soon the world will know what you are," the woman's voice says.

Merchant begins his trek. Boots crunch gravel and grit, the sounds lonely and hollow in the night. He takes his first steps along Interstate 80. In search of the city that reaches the sky, Merchant travels west. Ghosts and the burden of a thousand lives sit heavy across his back and follow his every movement.

Cold hard determination sustains him. Hatred and anger drives him.

He will not stop.

He cannot be deterred.

The road is his market, and across a world lost to the depths of Hell, death is always open for business.

THE END

About The Author

William J. Seymour is the author of Dark Fantasy which includes the titles Dark Choices, Trail of Darkness and numerous other titles. He lives with his family in southern Pennsylvania where he writes into the darkness of the night.

Other Works By William J. Seymour

Dark Choices
Trail of Darkness